D0959321

Zombie Theorem

The Culling

Book One

James Wallace

Copyright © 2016 James Wallace

All rights reserved.

ISBN:1533486786
ISBN-13: 978-1533486783

TO
Chris &
Christina
enjoy the
ADVENTURE!

Dedicated to My wife Julie, and our awesome kids. Thanks for
always pushing me to follow my passion. Love you guys!

CONTENTS

Acknowledgments i

Zombie Theorem

ACKNOWLEDGMENTS

Thank you to the following, whom without I would still be on page one. Tanay Williams, my best friend, I can't live without her. The Allen brothers, Will and M.C., Mike Evans, Ian Smith, Stephen Knight, Kim Leeder, Laura Jarvis, Josh Jarvis and all the people on Facebook group Committed Authors and Readers only. The people here are life savers and a great source for a new and existing author. To my Beta Reader Leslie Bryant, thank you for all your help, support, and kind words.

Chapter 1

"If you could state your name and occupation for the record please?" asked Detective Reynolds, a forty-something-year-old black man with a fair amount of salt and pepper peach fuzz on his balding head. He wore small wire-framed glasses and a charcoal colored, big box store suit with an orange tie resting on the chest of his white starched shirt.

The room was bland; cold grey concrete, two-way mirror and six very uncomfortable folding chairs surrounding a sturdy metal table. It was an interrogation room at the Eddy Street SFPD station, even though it felt more like a meat locker, complete with a drain in the floor. I was surrounded by two detectives and two others who had to be lawyers, dressed in grey pinstripe suits and looking like they had no personalities. I fought hard to listen to them even though I was shivering, tired, hungry, and a little out of my mind. I needed to get what was in my head out before it could drive me insane.

"Dan Welko, Process Manager for Next Level Analytics." My voice came out whispery, but I spoke directly into the microphone they had put in front of me.

"Great. Thank you. Where are your offices located?" I could see Reynolds was writing everything down on the yellow legal notepad he kept on his lap, even though he was recording our entire conversation.

"Transamerica Pyramid Building, 600 Montgomery Street, San Fran 42nd floor." I waited a beat and then asked, "Hey I'm really cold and hungry. Can I please have something hot to drink and maybe something to eat?" I was sitting on this cold chair bare footed, dressed in blood-encrusted chinos and what had once been a blue polo shirt.

Detective Reynolds looked up at the other detective and pointed at the door. "Faulks, can you handle that?" Faulks, a typical detective straight out of a TV cop show, square jawed, blonde flat top and a sour look, unfolded himself from his chair and left the room. He didn't seem happy being the gopher boy. "So, Mr. Welko?"

"Just call me Dan please. I'm too tired for formalities," I whispered. My head was pounding, my vision was slightly blurred and it tasted like a rat had taken up residence in my mouth. I just wanted water, food, a hot shower and to brush my teeth, then maybe a nap for like three days.

"Dan, then. So tell me what happened. Let's start from the beginning if you don't mind. Cause we are really confused with what we found." He tapped his pen on his notepad.

I cleared my throat and swallowed hard. This was going to be a bitch, but it really had to be done. A record had to be made of what we'd gone through. I locked eyes with Reynolds and began my story.

Chapter 2

Tuesday morning, I rode the bus into work. Every weekday morning, I would sit in that bus as it crawled through the grid-locked traffic concrete jungle, and wonder why I'd moved here. I refused to listen to news before work, I preferred to start my day with a clear head, opposed to having the light of my soul sucked out and replaced with despair. Instead of turning on that torture device called TV, I would download the previous night's reports and data from work's servers to my tablet, and go over the data on my way to work. Too many times, I had been ambushed with corrupt reports and data first thing in the morning, I refused to ever be blindsided again. That morning, the bus wasn't crowded and I thought 'wow it must be my lucky day' – I scored a seat all to myself, which rarely ever happened unless it's a holiday and five a.m. in the morning, and even then it's luck. With that small moment bringing a smile to my face, I pulled my tablet out and started analyzing the data from the night before. My smile faded, none of what I was reading made sense, but I didn't have time to ponder it long because the bus got me to work in record time for a prime commuting hour. Usually the sidewalk was packed with people hurrying to their jobs, but now I was primarily alone on the sidewalk.

Weird.

I walked into the lobby and up to the security checkpoint. The building's security guards were clustered behind the counter, talking amongst themselves. I caught the eye of the head guard, Ryan. He recognized me and pushed the button behind the counter that allowed me to push through the small gates blocking passage to the elevators. He said what I took to be a good morning, but my mind was a million miles away still pondering the reports I'd skimmed over on the bus. I waved over my shoulder at him and jumped onto an elevator before its doors could close. I rode it up to my floor and got off. I cannot remember if I shared that ride with anyone. I really was in my own little world of data and numbers.

I said hello to Stacey, my receptionist, a young lady who copies her looks and style from Emma Watson, but she was preoccupied with something on her phone. I walked down the hall of cubes, heading towards my office. Checking out the floor, as I do every morning, I was flabbergasted at the emptiness of the cubes; it was as if half the floor had decided not to show up today. That pissed me off. We had a critical check on a procedural milestone within our latest project, and without key staff being here, we were going to be fucked. I needed to get to the bottom of this and fast.

I threw open my office door, tossed my bag onto the corner of my desk, and sat down heavily in my chair. On the window ledge behind my chair was my only religious idol, my personal coffee maker. Everyone on the floor knew I had my own machine. I'd always told them that it was because I was a slave to my desk, but the real reason was that I am a coffee snob. I even have a special grind I get from a little farm in Colombia. I got my brew going and turned on my desktop workstation. I typed in my password at the prompt, and was greeted with my email box showing two hundred and fifty-two new messages. I cracked my neck and back and tilted back in my chair. *Oh crap—what happened last night?*

"Sarah, get in here!" I yelled from my office. Sarah was a short elfish-looking woman, and was my right hand woman. She ran the early morning team and never left until after our morning meeting at ten a.m. I sat there for a minute, but no Sarah. I got up, poured my mug of life saving coffee, and headed to her cube. It was empty and her workstation was a mess. Which was weird cause she was an OCD kind of person. Everything was usually in its place and tidy all the time. Her workstation monitor was still on, so she couldn't have left more than ten minutes ago. The screen saver pops up and the system locks itself after ten minutes of inactivity.

I looked around for Matt, Sarah's second in charge. At least, he was at his desk. He was reading something on his phone, something that had him looking very unsettled. He jumped when I put my hand on his shoulder, and I took a step back, surprised by his reaction.

"Whoa, take it easy, buddy. Where the hell is Sarah?"

Matt looked up at me with hollowed eyes. I looked him over, a little surprised to find him dressed in wrinkled tan jeans, a blue company polo shirt and a zip-up hoodie. His long hair was hanging down, unbrushed and stringy. Matt was usually put together much better than he looked today.

"Oh ... hey, Dan. Sorry, you scared me. Yeah, Sarah, she went home. Said she had an emergency..." His voice trailed off as he went back to looking at his phone.

I shook his shoulder, amazed he would go back to his phone and just ignore me. "Matt, what's going on? What kind of emergency? What's so important on your phone?" I was starting to become a little frustrated.

Matt looked up from his phone. "Sorry, Dan. Uhm, her wife called, saying she and their daughter were sick. Hey wait, you haven't heard the news, have you?" He dropped his phone and finally looked at me, cocking his head to the side like a dog hearing a far off sound.

12

"Heard what, Matt? All I know is I have a shit ton of emails and it looks like none of last night's projects were run or the reports updated."

Chapter 3

My story was interrupted when Faulks came in carrying a large coffee and a bag of food. He put it in front of me, then excused himself and left. He had the look of someone who had seen something they couldn't understand. Reynolds motioned toward the food, "Dan, eat please. You look like you might need it. By the way, what is Sarah's last name? I think I might want to get in touch with her."

I was already pulling the sandwich and soup from the bag, having my eyes set to devour it all. "Uhm, Sarah Ruiz. She lives in Redwood City." I un-wrapped the sandwich and took a giant bite. At this point I didn't care what is was made of, could've been dog food for all I cared. I hadn't eaten much real food in a couple of days. I had all my attention on devouring the food and coffee, so that I hadn't noticed that the two lawyers had left, leaving Reynolds and I alone. He had his attention divided between his notepad and laptop as I ate.

Reynolds caught my attention just then, "Dan, I want you to know, I am not charging you with anything yet." He had my full attention after that statement. "At this point, I am just conducting research into what happened. That's why I let the lawyers go. You can leave anytime you want. Just say so. But I would appreciate it if you would continue when you're done eating."

Wait what? Why would he charge me? I'd been fighting for my life, so what I'd been forced to do should be deemed as defensive in nature. "I appreciate that, but what I am about to tell you is going to surprise you and you may not believe me."

Reynolds stared at me with concern written on his face. "Okay, that's fair. Whenever you are ready, just let me know. I've kept the recorder going, so nothing would be missed. You do understand, right?"

I took a large drink of coffee and for once in my life, didn't make a snobbish sneer or remark over it not being my roast. I demolished the sandwich and soup, then sat back in my chair and continued my story.

Chapter 4

Matt had seemed concerned and amazed that I had not heard the news. He pushed himself out of his chair and looked around the floor very conspiratorial and ushered me back to my office. I went along, so as not to upset him further. I took my seat, crossed my legs, and waited for Matt to start. He sat himself in one of my guest chairs on the other side of the desk and closed his eyes, as if he was gathering his thoughts. I drank more of my coffee, enjoying the taste and heat.

"Late last night, the news started reporting on a virus that was spreading, mainly in large cities. New York, D.C., and Boston were the first to get hit, then it took off spreading like a wild fire feeding off of a six-year drought. It presented itself as a common cold, sore throat, runny nose and general aches and pains. It would progress faster into rashes, problems breathing, a high fever, and then death. There is no official name for the virus, but some news reports are calling it "Wild Fire", due to the high fever it causes. I called all the departments in our New York office and finally got someone in the IT department. Gupta, you know, the guy who is always fixing our server issues? Well, he said that Mr. Salazar, the VP of operations, sent everyone home this morning and told them to stay home till more information was released on the disease. Gupta said he was staying at the office, since he had the cafeteria on his floor and a couch in his office. Says he's afraid of what's going on and doesn't want to go home. He described New York as a giant ghost town. No one is on the streets, and the buses and subway have been stopped. He checked with the other offices in Charlotte, Miami, and Boston, and they say the same thing. I have no idea how bad it is on the west coast, but it looks like a lot of people here decided to not come in, and some left this morning before you got here. I heard accounting and HR are empty, too." He rushed this all out almost in one breath. I watched Matt for a long ten count, to see if maybe he was pulling my leg. The guy liked to embellish, but something in his eyes made me believe him. He was sweaty and couldn't keep his eyes focused on one thing. He genuinely looked afraid.

I sat back in my chair and tried to think of something to say. I remembered something about the flu on the east coast, last night on the news as I was shutting the TV off. I came to a decision finally, "Ok Matt, I need your help on this. Go to the first aid station in the supply closet and get all the medical masks out. Then, distribute them around the office and take a count on who is here. Please do not start a panic or talk about what you've just told me. I'm going to make some calls. Come back to my office when you're done and give me the count of attendance and names, if you can."

Matt nearly launched himself from the chair. "Whoa, buddy. I need you to relax. Calm down, take some deep breaths and don't get too excited, ok?" I said. "We don't want a panic."

He took some deep breaths and left my office, looking a little more in control. I opened the company directory on my computer and looked up the number for the head of security. Gunther Friedman was an ex-FBI guy, working out of our headquarters in Denver. I rang him up and he picked up on the fourth ring. "Gunther, speak." The man was very gruff and always to the point. He figured since you'd called him, you had something to report. I had heard he didn't care if it was his boss or the custodian, somehow he got away with it.

"Gunther, it's Dan Welko out of San Fran. I'm in the office today and half of my staff didn't show up. Now, I am hearing about some kind of emergency on the East Coast. Does the company have an official response or process on this?"

"Dan, good to hear from you. Yeah, I've been in meetings all night and this morning about that very thing." He put his hand over the phone and I could hear him yelling at someone. "Sorry, it's a little crazy here. Ok, we do not have an official response right now. Hold on, let me get somewhere private." I could hear him breathing and grunting on the line as he traveled. "Dan, let me tell you something. A buddy of mine at the CDC called me this morning. I've known this guy since we were together at the FBI. He's a straight shooter, someone who would never speak without knowing all the facts and he is one cool cucumber. This time when we spoke though, he sounded stressed out and worried. Said the CDC had no idea what was going on. They have a sample of the damn bug, but have no idea how it works. He said something about RNA and how he thinks it was manufactured. Other than that, nothing. He also said that last night, the President shut down all flights from and to the east coast. So I don't think the bug has gotten to our side of the Rockies, yet. This thing is very contagious though, so I'm sure it's just a matter of time before it shows up. How many do you have in the office? Are any of them showing symptoms of being sick?" Gunther sounded a little scared or at least on edge. Not what I'd been expecting. The guy had always seemed eerily calm and never once, had he ever spoken that much at one shot with me.

"I don't know yet. I just got in. I have Matt Powers going through the office now, handing out medical masks and getting a count. I told him not to start a panic. I'm not sure how many people here know about the flu. Hell, I didn't know until just now."

"Good thinking, Dan. So, what did you see on the streets on your way in to work?"

"This morning, the bus was pretty empty, I didn't have to share my seat, and when I got off, I noticed a lack of cars on the street. For San Fran, that's weird. I thought I was just lucky today, but again my mind was somewhere else at the time. Ok, hold on, Matt just came in. I'm putting you on speaker." I punched the button on the phone and hung up the handset. I pointed at Matt to speak.

"Uhm, so we have forty people, including you and I, on the floor right now. Two people have runny noses and little coughs, But I think they have had them for a couple of days. I gave them all masks," Matt stammered.

"Matt, this is Gunther, head of corporate security. Is anyone talking about this flu or about the news stories?".

"No one is talking about this right now, but Ricky from Technical Writing asked me if he had to worry about anything. I told him no, but he should wear the mask. I think he meant the flu, but I walked away, hurrying to the next person."

"Good job, Matt. Do me a favor, go back to your desk and act like you're working, but pay attention and let Dan know if anything changes. I need to finish this call up privately. "

"Ok, I'll do that. Thanks, Gunther. Bye." Matt left my office and headed back towards his desk.

"Dan, get me off the speaker phone."

"Yeah, Gunther." I picked up the handset and turned off the speaker phone.

"I gotta get going, but do me a favor, pay attention to the office and watch out. If things start to get too much, I want you to take whoever will listen and get out of that building. For now, stay there. I'll call again later and keep you updated of any new procedures," Gunther explained.

"Great. I think I can keep them busy, I don't want anyone to panic and I am pretty sure it's safer here than anywhere else at this time. I have your cell number if it gets worse." I said my thanks and disconnected the call, sat back in my chair and noticed I hadn't touched my coffee in a bit. I downed the rapidly cooling cup and refreshed it from the heated pot. I sat there for a good thirty minutes, staring at my monitor and not really reading the words in front of me. "Well, time to do something, Dan." I grabbed my hot coffee and left my office. Might as well walk the floor.

I caught Matt's eye and nodded my head at the office. He got out of his chair and started to follow me. As I walked around for the next hour, I would stop and say hi to a couple of people, and make small talk. I had this nagging feeling, like maybe, I was making a mistake by not telling these people what was going on. I stopped dead in my tracks, causing Matt to walk into me. I stood there surveying the people I was responsible for.

"Matt, I can't do this. These people need to go home to their families or at least have a choice. Call everyone to the main conference room. I need to talk to them." Matt looked frantic and to tell you the truth, a little sick, like he had a cold. Maybe it's just stress, I thought. Matt nodded yes and took off to round everyone up. I headed to the front to tell Stacey, the receptionist, about the meeting.

I entered the lobby, and found Stacey's station empty, her purse and cellphone missing. I figured she had decided on her own to leave. I went back through the lobby doors locking them up, so no one would come in while we were in our meeting. While coming up to the conference room, I peered through the windows, it was already crowded. I opened the door and made my way to the front of the large oblong oak table. I looked around for Matt and found he was just walking in with two more coworkers. He caught my stare and nodded that he had everyone.

I cleared my throat and took my time looking everyone in the eye. I was taking leadership classes and this was something my trainer had made sure was pounded into our heads. I love data, I love my job, but God, standing in front of people and public speaking scared the shit out of me. I cleared my throat and swallowed the lump that had decided to try and choke me. "Everyone, listen up. I want to give you an update about what is going on inside the company and outside our own doors. After speaking to corporate security and our New York office, Matt and I have been alerted to some pretty scary stuff. It seems that the news has been reporting on a virus or flu going around that is causing some disturbing things. According to the news, the "flu" has a fast incubation period and it is incredibly infectious. Vice President of Operations Salazar closed the New York office down this morning, so they wouldn't spread the bug around. It has also come to my attention that the FAA has shutdown flights from and to the east coast. So, we are not sure if the "flu" has made it out here yet. The popular opinion is that it hasn't yet. As you have noticed, most of the office did not show up to work today. The morning crew has not had the manpower to run their projects last night, and with the New York office closed, we don't have the support we'd need to fix that. I've been asked not to alarm you guys, but in good faith, I cannot lie to you. I'm giving you the decision to do what you think is best for you and your family. I am going to stay here in the office and see what I can do to keep us from falling further and further behind, once we can get this operation back up and running. Anyone who wants to stay, can and whoever wants to go is free to do so. I will not hold anything against you."

I looked around and made eye contact again. "Let me tell you, this thing is bad, according to the news and a couple of sources I have talked to. So that's it, if you want to go, I would suggest for you to get going. Be safe in your decision and we'll let you know when we expect you back. Just sign a sheet that I'll post on my door, and indicate your decision and a contact number. Thanks for listening, ladies and gentlemen and again, stay safe." Matt had already disappeared from the office and I knew he was posting the paper on my door. I watched as everyone started filing out of the room. I took a big sip of my coffee and frowned. It was cold again.

I made my way to the little lunch room down the hall and popped my cup in the microwave. I really couldn't stand reheated coffee, but most of my first cup I'd had to drink cold. It was time for some warm coffee. One minute had passed when suddenly, an alarm went off in the offices and all of the power went out. I was standing there in the dark, shaking my head. "Great, now what the fuck has gone wrong?" I'm really not someone who swears, but my day had started in the crapper and now it felt like it'd just got flushed. A second later, the emergency battery lights kicked on. I opened the microwave and got a small pleasure with my coffee at a warmth I could enjoy. I sighed and stood there for a minute, waiting for the power to come back on. I dropped my head in defeat when it didn't.

I made my way to the main floor and saw people milling about. I strolled over to a desk, picked up the phone handset, but found it was dead. Which was weird, as our telephony system was on a separate power source, and shouldn't have gone down.

Matt shoveled more crap onto my pile of issues, "Big problems, Dan. Whole system is down, even our back up data lines, so the laptops aren't getting a signal and since there is no power, the desktops aren't working either. I can ping our servers, since they are on battery backup, but they are a dead end with no internet. And to add insult to injury, the phones are also down."

Someone was shouting from the lobby. I motioned for Matt to follow. We walked out the main doors and found people standing around the elevators. "They aren't working," Kim a middle aged, short, roundish, Asian girl whined as she kept stabbing at the elevator call button.

"Thanks for the info, but Kim, that's what they are supposed to do. When there is an emergency, they return to the lobby and stop answering calls. The stairs should be fine though," I informed her and the others standing around.

"That's forty-eight floors, Dan. I'm not walking down forty-eight floors," she started whining even louder.

"Kim, there is nothing I can do about the elevators. And think about it, it's easy since you'll be going down." I pushed on the crash bar for the entrance to the stairs and found that it wouldn't open. "What the fuck?" I whispered.

"These stairs are an emergency access and they should never be locked. Matt, use your cell to call security and find out what the hell is going on." I was going to start panicking any second. I mean, the only two ways to lock those doors were by barring them, or turning on the locking system down in security.

"I'm not getting anything, Dan."

"They aren't answering? Fine, call 911. Let's get the authorities here and get this settled." I ran my hands over my bald head. I'm going to need more coffee, and maybe something stronger if this keeps rolling downhill toward the abyss.

"No, Dan. You don't understand. I am not getting anything. I have a full signal, but I'm not able to call out or even getting internet. Anybody else able to get a call out?" Matt asked.

Everyone took their cellphones out, checking them, and apparently not getting anywhere. "Do something, Dan!" Kim whined louder than before and actually stomped her foot.

"What do you think I can do, Kim?" I yelled at her. She shut up and looked stunned that I would talk to her like that. "Ok everyone, let's get back to the office and see if we can't get something figured out." I waved everyone out of the lobby.

"Hey Dan, this is getting weird. Why would everything go down at once? Unless it's on purpose, this cannot be a coincidence. And if it is on purpose, then who and why?" Matt seemed to be on to something. I just did not know what yet.

I pondered for a second, "Well, think about it this way, Matt. We are not the only company in the building. I wonder if something happened and the authorities have decided to quarantine them, and in a fashion, us. Or, if we are just shit balling here, maybe there has been a catastrophe. But let's not go there yet."

I walked past everyone on the way to my office. I stopped suddenly and Matt walked into me again. I looked towards the windows and made a beeline to them. I stood there, looking over the bay and Treasure Island, looking for something out of the ordinary. Nothing though, seemed to be happening. "Someone go over to the other side and look out the windows. See if anything is going on. The bay bridge looks fine, there are some cars moving around out there." Matt and a couple of other people went running to the other side and shouted back that everything seemed fine.

I stood there a while, not really focusing on anything. Just letting my mind run and work on this little mystery. I sighed, stepped back from the window, and walked to my office. Thirty-five names were on the sheet, pinned to my door, indicating they wanted to leave. That left five of us that would stay, including me. I felt like I was out of answers at this point, and out of ideas. "Ok everyone, I don't have any answers right now. Keep trying the phones, cells, and computers. Let's see if the power comes back up. Like I always say, I want solutions not problems or whining. Let's work this out." Everyone seemed to like that and went back to talking and working on the problem.

I sat heavily in my chair and closed my eyes. A migraine had decided to erupt in glorious fashion at this point. Shit, I wish I would've come up with the idea to leave earlier. Then, most of us wouldn't be stuck. I felt useless, no data to work with, no phones and no internet. I had nothing! So I just sat there with my eyes closed and felt myself starting to relax. When I was in college, I'd found if I just sat back and let my subconscious work on my problems, the answers would magically come to me. Twenty minutes flew by, and I opened my eyes in frustration. Nothing was coming to me, except for more pain.

Matt sneaked into my office at this point and closed my door. "Hey Matt, leave that open. I don't want people to think we have secrets here."

"Dan, I've got something I don't think you want anyone else to hear, right now," Matt said with a degree of intensity that I rarely saw from him. He stood there, wiping his sweaty hands on his pants.

I pointed to the chairs in front of my desk. He plopped down and started talking, "You know Marco, right? He's that new data analyst we hired three weeks ago?" I nodded my head yes and gave him the go on sign with my hand. "Well, he is from New York and went home over the weekend, but it seems he got out before they shut down the flights. I saw him this morning in the office, but didn't think about it till I was going over the sign out sheet and didn't see his name anywhere. I also remember him complaining to Stacey, when he came through the front doors that he wasn't feeling very good, but I haven't seen him again. Someone said they thought they saw him heading to the restroom, earlier. I went in there and saw one of the stall doors was shut and locked. I called out to him, but got nothing."

"Shit!" I blew out explosively. I shook my head and couldn't believe all of this was happening. 'This has got to be a nightmare', I thought to myself. "Ok, get me some first aid rubber gloves. Grab some for you, too. I'm going to need your help." He jumped up and left my office in a hurry. I got up and started on my way to the restrooms. Everyone turned to watch me, but I just kept my head low and kept up a non-hurried pace. I got to the bathroom door and waited for Matt to catch up. He handed me a pair of gloves. He put his on while I donned mine. I opened the door to the restroom and stepped in. I saw the stall Matt was pointing at. It was closed. I walked up and started knocking on it. "Marco, is that you? It's Dan, do you need help? Is everything ok? Marco, come on, please answer me."

There was no sound. My heart started to pound so hard it felt like it was going to rip out of my chest. Hell, I could hear my pulse in my ears like someone was playing drums. My hands started to sweat under my gloves. "Matt, look under the door, see if you can see his feet."

Matt dropped down, but I knew he wasn't happy about it. He looked under the stall, duck walked backwards, then got up quickly. "Uhm, yup, he's there. Uhm, I'm not sure if I want to do this, Dan." He kept stepping back. He backed up till he bumped into the sinks and let out a little yelp. He was about to start hyperventilating soon with how hard he was breathing.

"Matt. Relax, please. He needs our help. I can't do this by myself," I said trying to not show my fear, but damn I felt like I was going to faint.

He took a step toward me. A tentative small step, but I was counting on it. He seemed to be swallowing his fear and stepping up. "Good job, Matt. Now, let's get this over." I turned and kicked the door near the latch point, almost knocking it off its flimsy hinges. I looked in and almost started gagging. It wasn't the normal bathroom smell, it was

Marco sitting there, his head rolled back, resting against the back wall, tongue hanging out of his mouth. I could tell he had bit it at some point, but no blood was oozing out and that is never a good sign. Usually, that meant the heart was not pumping anymore. I reached out and touched Marco's neck, like they do in all those medical TV shows, looking for a pulse and not finding one. I tried something else from those shows and opened one of his eye lids. A yelp escaped my lips as I jumped back a step. His entire eye was filled with blood. Now, it was my turn to start breathing hard. Matt reached out and touched my arm.

"I'm ok, just wasn't expecting that. Jesus, I think he's dead. What are we going to do with him? We can't call anyone and we can't leave him here. People have to use the restroom." I was biting back my fear, but couldn't get my mind settled. I hadn't smoked in six years but right now, I could've happily lit up and smoked an entire pack.

Thank God for Matt. It was his turn to step up and take the reins. "Let's put him in the supply closet. No one is going to be going in there, since no one is working anyway."

"Damn good idea. Ok, I'll stay here, see if anyone will come and help. Make sure they have gloves. Actually, just go grab Brian, he's ex-military and I'll explain it to him when he gets here. Thanks again Matt for everything. You have been more than helpful today." I patted him on the back. He gave me an awkward "awe shucks look" and took off.

I decided It was stupid hanging out alone in the bathroom with Marco's body, so I stepped outside the door into the hallway. I tried breathing deep but then noticed I had the damn mask on. I went to take it off and then remembered I had touched Marco's eye and neck. I stood against the door and waited as patiently as I could. "Maybe I can learn to breathe through my eyes."

Soon, Brian came around the corner and down the hall. Brian was a mountain of a man. Easily standing six-feet seven inches and I'd swear he was either a runt Sasquatch or a big bear. He had blonde hair but kept it short. His beard reached down to his chest. The man's forearms made my thighs look small. You would think he'd be a really mean guy, but in reality, he was the nicest guy you would ever meet.

"Brian, Mathew and I need some help. I don't want to freak out the office, but we found Marco in the bathroom. I can't find a pulse and I'm pretty sure he's expired. We need your help to move him to the supply closet. Think you can help us out?"

Brian dropped his head and shook it a little, "Fuck, I was just thinking about how Marco had gone back to New York to see family. I walked by his desk but didn't see him, so I figured he didn't come in. Well, like my Master Sargent use to say, 'nothing to do but get to it.'" Matt came up and handed the gloves to Brian, he was already wearing a medical mask.

"Dan, I grabbed the key out of your office. That way, we can lock the supply closet door and no one can go in and be surprised or get infected, if they could with a corpse." Matt dangled the key at me.

"Ok, go unlock the door and come back here to hold this door for us. We are using the one on this side of the building, right?"

"Yeah Dan, no problem. Be right back." He took off jogging down the hall.

Bryan opened the bathroom door and motioned for me to go first. I walked in and over to Marco, I stood there staring at him. "What's up boss? You seem vexed," Brian asked looking at me, then back to Marco.

I ignored Brian for a second and kept staring at Marco. 'What is wrong with me', I thought, 'what am I missing?' Then it hit me, Marco's head was laying forward on his chest. I could've sworn it had been back against the wall. At that point, Matt came in and I motioned him over. "Matt, wasn't Marco's head lying against the wall when we found him?" I asked

"Yeah, it was. That's weird. Maybe when you checked his eyes and jumped back, his head rolled forward," he answered logically.

"Yeah ok, that sounds believable. Damn, my head is really hurting today. Need more coffee or something stronger. Ok Brian, let's do this thing." I headed toward the body.

"Hey Boss, take his feet and I'll take his shoulders and head. That's the heaviest and well, I am kinda bigger." That was the biggest understatement of the year.

Man, was he bigger! I stood five and half feet tall, one hundred and eighty pounds and he towered over me. I shook my head and moved so Brian could get into the stall first. Once he had a good grip I came in, grabbed Marco's feet and we lifted. Holy shit I thought my back was going to just give out right then. I groaned out loud, but was able to do the job. Brian looked like he was lifting no more than a bouquet of flowers. He shook his head at me and we started towards the hallway where Matt was holding the door for us. After five intense minutes of back-breaking work, we got Marco to the closet. So far, so good, no one had seen us. I let go of the legs and Brian dragged Marco to the back and laid him down. "I suggest we leave these gloves and masks in here with the body. We don't want to risk contamination. Matt, can you get us new masks? And hey Boss, I really think we should tape that stall closed and put an out of order sign on it. What do you think?"

"Ok, you mind taking care of that? I think my back is about to cramp up." Brian smiled, let out a little laugh, and stepped out of the closet. I shut the door behind him and locked it with the key. Just then, Matt showed up with new masks. He handed them out and Brian walked away to do his duty.

"Brian's going to tape up that stall we found Marco in. Don't want anyone to use it, just in case." We walked back in silence toward my office. I collapsed into my chair and turned around to my coffee machine. I stared at the old stale coffee still in the pot. "Fuck it." I poured my last cup and sat back, and drained it, enjoying the caffeine washing over and embracing me into its open arms.

"Damn, that's your last cup, unless we start a fire and boil your bottled water over it."

"Don't think I won't, Matt." An idea came rushing into my mind and I jumped up out of my chair and ran out of my office. "Anyone got a lighter?" I yelled.

Everyone turned toward me and gave me that "What the hell is wrong with him" look. Gwen, one of my analysts came up, she looked a lot like Gemma from Sons of Anarchy, but without the attitude. She handed me a little pink lighter. I looked it over and saw it had a pair of boobies on it. Out of the corner of my eye I saw her blush a little. "One of my friends gave those away to her close friends, when she learned she had breast cancer. She thought it was funny. She made a complete recovery, by the way."

I shook my head and said my thanks. I jumped up on a desk and put my hand up. To find I was about two feet short from my target. Brian came to the rescue as he came into the office, "Let me do that, Boss. You seem a little vertically challenged. This seems like a good idea." I handed the lighter over and he stepped up on the desk.

Before he could lift it up though, Kim yelled out, "Wait! Won't that set off all of the sprinklers? And we are going to get wet!"

"Kim, calm down. Our system is set up so only the sprinkler head that is activated will go off. And best of all, it'll activate the emergency fire system and call out to the fire department who will come and rescue us." She stepped back and sat down at one of the farthest desks.

Brian flicked the lighter on and held it up to the sprinkler head. In seconds it went off, and at first only air came out, then a rush of blackish stinky water gushed out, then quickly cleared. The fire alarms started going off and to everyone's amazement they heard the elevator ding. There was a mad rush as people started running to it.

Chapter 5

When I got there, everyone was stepping back quickly, away from the elevator doors. Brian grabbed my shoulder and slowed me down. I looked up at him, he was looking over everyone into the elevator. "Boss, I think we found Stacey."

I pulled away from him and ran to the elevator, stopping abruptly before crossing the lip. I suddenly wished I hadn't, Stacey was propped up against the far wall. Her blue blouse had been torn open exposing her white skin and an ugly red jagged hole just below her rib cage where her intestines had been pulled out. They were laying on her black skirt and scattered around her. Someone screamed and people started rushing back into the offices. I looked around and found Brian and Matt standing next to me. Brian looked sad, but Matt looked like he was about to lose his lunch. I entered the elevator and went down to my knees. I looked Stacey over and could tell she was dead. I mean, how could you not be dead with all of your blood lying around you and your intestines hanging out? I ran my hands over my head and blew out the breath I had been holding. Brian grabbed me by the shoulders and helped me get to my feet.

Suddenly, someone yelled, "The stair's door is unlocked, let's go!" There was a rush as twenty-five people came running out of the offices toward the stairs, including Kim. Within minutes, we heard screaming coming from the stairway. I turned and ran to the door and looked out. I saw blood spurt up, well maybe more like fountain up onto the first landing. Shadows were thrown onto the wall from the emergency lights and I could see what I thought were people shoving something to their faces. Then I could see the people coming up the stairs. But something was wrong with them, they moved jerkily but quickly, their chests and hands covered in blood. "Move!" I heard a loud roar and was bodily thrown against the wall. Brian grabbed the door handle and slammed it closed, his fingers turning white from the strain of trying to hold it closed. The door would slowly pull open, but then Brian would dig in and close it again using all of his muscles. I looked around and saw the fire hose wound up on the wall. I grabbed it and ran to Brian. He looked at me crazily, then figured out what I meant. He started wrapping it around the door handle and tied it off. He then ran back to the wheel I took the hose from. He took the excess and wrapped it around the wheel jamming it in place and tied it off.

"Now, there is only fifteen of us left," Matt muttered.

I snapped my head to him, "Go get more gloves and masks, we need to move Stacey to the closet with Marco." Matt took off at a dead run. Then he stopped and he reached into his pockets, pulling out a wad of those blue gloves and two folded masks.

"I figured we'd need some more. I wanted to be prepared." He handed them over and Brian and I put ours on.

We went into the elevator as Matt disappeared. I figured he was going to go get the supply room key. "Hey Boss, why are we not talking about this or what just happened on the stairs?"

"Shit, Brian, I don't know. Shock?" I answered. "Let's get Stacey taken care of, then we can talk. Go grab a chair or something to stop the elevator doors from closing." I stood next to Stacey and watched Brian hunt around her desk. He ran back with the rubber stopper that kept our front doors normally open. He shoved that into the bottom of one of the doors and kicked it to make sure it stayed in place.

"That should do it. I can grab her head and shoulders just like Marco." I nodded ok and grabbed her legs. On three we lifted and started carrying her out. As we walked away, some of the office personnel were standing at the lobby doors, watching us do our gruesome duty. I was amazed at how heavy Stacey was. I mean, she was a skinny little thing and was missing at least a gallon of blood and some internal organs. We got her to the supply closet and put her next to Marco. We tore off our masks and gloves and threw them in. Matt closed the door and locked it. He then handed us new masks which we promptly donned.

"Are we now going to start talking about what happened?" Brian asked somewhat impatiently.

"I have no idea what's going on. Since I came in this morning, I have been completely in the dark. I keep seeing bits and pieces of this puzzle, but no idea how they connect. I don't know why, who, or even when Stacey was killed, or why I heard screaming or what those things in the stairway were and all that blood, so much blood. I feel completely unprepared and ill-equipped to deal with today. I should be in a mental facility hugging myself in a white coat, wondering when the nice lady is coming with my green jello and which side of my padded cell smells best. I don't know what to tell those people on the other side of the office. I just want to make it to tomorrow and then the day after and hopefully the day after that. But instead, I don't know if we have serial killers in the building or if it's god damn demonistic fucking yard gnomes!" As I ranted my voice climbed higher and higher.

Suddenly, I realized I was losing my cool and put my back against the nearest wall and slid to the floor, landing on my ass. I covered my face with my hands and shuddered. God, I was sure this was all a bad dream brought on by some cursed enchiladas I'd had the night before and was just hoping I'd wake up. I heard a slight giggle and glared up at the offender. It was Matt, and he had this little smile on his lips as he held in more laughter. "Really think it's demonistic fuckin yard gnomes? Not me, I really feel it might be murderous blue Smurfs who lost it after Gargamel captured and tortured Smurfette," he said through his fingers, still stifling his laughter.

"No, no, no, it's neither. I bet it's the Cowardly Lion from the

Wizard of Oz after smoking a bad dose of bath salts," Brian kicked in with a gigantic smile.

"You know, I am really starting to hate both of you," I slowly pulled myself back together. "Sorry I lost it. Let's get back to the lobby and see what we can figure out. Hopefully, emergency services will be here soon and we can go try to answer a bunch of questions we are ill prepared to answer." At this point, I noticed the fire alarm had stopped going off. I really hoped that isn't a bad sign. I rolled onto my knees, ripped off my mask and took a large lungful of air before standing up. I felt like the mask was choking me. The guys put their masks back on and followed me back to the lobby. As we walked back, I was aghast at the quickly drying blood on our pants and hands. We stopped in the bathrooms and tried to clean up as much as possible.

The elevator door was still open, so I walked in and started looking around. The blood and bits and pieces of Stacey were still on the floor. I looked at the ceiling and saw it had a couple of drops of blood on it. I looked at the control panel and saw a bloody fingerprint. Well, that didn't come from Stacey. There was no way she could've gotten up and pushed the buttons after what had happened to her. I turned to Brian and gave him a shrug, saying I had no idea what I was looking at. That's when I noticed Matt was standing with his ear against the stairway access door.

"Matt, what are you doing?" I enquired.

"I hear sounds like growling. And I swear I can hear someone saying no over and over again. I think it's Kim." Matt said with fear and awe in his voice.

At that, Brian walked over and put his ear to the door. He looked intense as he strained to hear what Matt was hearing. "I think we need to go in there and see if we can help!" Brian said louder than he meant to. Suddenly, something hit the door really hard and we could all hear snarling and scratching.

"Hey, Brian? Hey, Matt? Um, do you mind stepping away from that door?" using my inside voice.

They both got wide-eyed and backed up. Just then, I heard a gaggle of gasps. I looked over and most of what was left of the office personnel was standing at the lobby doors staring at us, demanding an answer. "What is that?", "Why aren't we helping?", "Where are the Police?", "You should get out of that elevator, you're going to ruin the evidence", "What is that hitting the door?", "We really need to get out of here."

I left the elevator, but made sure the wedge was holding the door open. I shooed everyone back to the office. Brian and Matt drifted in behind me and we all gathered around my office door. "I'm not going to blow sunshine up your asses, people or lie to you. Let me catch you up. Brian, Matt and I found Marco earlier in the bathroom, dead from what we think is the flu. He flew in from Manhattan yesterday, and we didn't know he was even in the office till Matt found him. We moved his body to the supply closet and have now added Stacey's body and locked the door. So please don't go over there and definitely do not open the door. Some people ran into the stairway earlier when the door became unlocked and we heard some screaming and saw blood. I also saw something coming up the stairs and so that's why we've secured that door. We think that, that something attacked them. We thought about going in there, but something is attacking the door now, and we have nothing to defend ourselves with. I also have no idea who attacked Stacey, or why she was in the elevator, or when It happened. I know I do not have many answers, just more questions and things seem to be going downhill fast." I stopped and looked down at my watch. "Wow, it's just about six p.m. My hope is that someone will be missing one of us and call the police and they will come and help us. We have no idea when that will be, though. I suggest we all stay together and not wander around without a partner. This is a big space right here in front of my office. Let's move the couches from the lobby into here and bring some chairs from the conference room. We might as well get comfy and ride this out. I am getting hungry, so I know most of you must be too. Why don't we go get whatever is in the fridges or what we brought in today and have a little potluck? Brian, Matt, can you please handle those assignments?" Everyone nodded and Brian and Matt took over and started dividing up the jobs.

I walked back into my office and sat down heavily. Fuck me; can this day get any worse? I grabbed a bottle of water from under my desk, cracked it open and drained it. Then, I grabbed the rest of my water and snacks that I had stashed in my desk, and took them outside my office to be included in our supplies.

Chapter 6

I was interrupted from my story-telling by Reynolds, "I'm sorry, Dan, but I am confused. When we got there, Stacey and Marco were not in the supply closet. The report states that Stacey was found in your office with a metal chair leg in her head and," he flipped through some pages in his notebook, "Marco was found one floor up with his head smashed in.

How and why did this happen if they were dead already and locked in a supply closet?"

"I'm about to get to that."

I drained the leftover coffee in front of me and made a sour smile. It had gone cold. You'd think I'd be used to that by now.

Chapter 7

I stood at the door and watched Brian and his crew, carry the three couches from the lobby and placed them around the space in front of my office. The couches were new, we had just had them delivered about a week ago. Big comfortable chocolate brown couches. They could hold five people sitting on them. We also had three big comfy chairs out there, and I knew Brian would be bringing those over next. By then, Matt and Summer, a young woman around twenty-two, carried a long table we used in the lunch room for special occasions. They brought it over and put it up against the far wall. Two other co-workers, a man named Jesus and a woman named Elisa, followed them pushing a cart loaded with packs of bottled water and placed them under the table. I smiled to myself, we have a great team.

Brian came up to me after sending the rest of his group out to get the chairs from the lobby. "Boss, we need to talk really quick," he said quietly enough for only me to hear. I pointed to my office and we both walked in and stood by my desk. "You know, I'm a little worried about what someone is saying in my group. You know Lisa right? She manages the field database, and keeps us up to date on the customer changes. Well, she is starting a rumor that you and I killed Marco by throwing him in the closet, instead of giving him medical treatment, and that she bets Stacey wasn't dead either. She swears she saw Stacey's body moving when the elevator doors opened. I'm worried about people believing her."

"What does she think you and I could do, even if those two weren't dead already?" I clenched my hands at my sides. I could feel my migraine getting worse, threatening to crack my skull open.

"No idea, Boss. But I thought you should know. I'll keep my eyes and ears open and let you know if I learn more," Brian assured me.

"Please do so. And why don't we get those keys from Matt and secure them. I don't want anyone messing around in there, thinking they can help. All we need now is for that flu to spread like wildfire through what's left of us." Brian nodded and left the office. With such a bad situation, I was just very happy to have both of those guys by my side, taking some of the pressure off of my shoulders.

I stepped back out to the office and saw Matt and his team had laid out all of the food they could find. It looked like a lot of supplies, but I think in this situation that it was going to go fast. Once it was gone, we were going to be in trouble. With the power off, I figured we should probably eat the stuff that could spoil first and then we could ration out the dry stuff. I saw crackers, chips and I had donated all my granola bars and someone looked to have emptied their candy drawer. We had some sandwiches and looked like a good amount of soup and chili, some potato salad, and someone had brought in some rolls, sausage, cheese and looked like a small veggie platter. Matt had even brought out the stale Bagels that someone had brought in this morning for breakfast.

"Alright, people. Let's get comfortable. I know this is no fun and we all are a little stressed out. I'm sure if we can keep ourselves together, we can make it till someone comes and rescues us. And yes, I truly believe someone will come get us. I have no questions about that." It had just occurred to me that I was leaving out something. "You know what? I forgot to ask if anyone had questions, concerns or ideas. I'll leave the floor open."

Lisa was the first to stand up. "Here we go," I said under my breath. Lisa was a short woman about five feet tall, painfully thin, almost elfish in looks, with short hair just ending at her ears. A little tattoo of a fairy was behind her right ear. If I remembered correctly, she'd graduated from Berkley in statistics and feminism. She was wearing a little white summer dress with daisies and stylish bejeweled sandals.

"I want to know what qualifies you, Brian, and Matt, to diagnose someone's medical issues." She was standing on a chair and had her fists balled up and placed on her hips. For someone so small, she seemed so very demanding. The people standing next to her seemed to try and melt into the surroundings, trying their best to get away from looking like they supported her line of questioning. "I mean, are you a doctor? Have you ever dealt with a dead or dying body? What makes you an expert?" Her voice was gaining in volume and accusing. Without letting me answer her questions, she continued to fire more. Each time, wagging her finger at me, demanding answers, "Furthermore, why are you barricading the stairs? Are you keeping us as prisoners? What makes you the leader?"

"Lisa, enough. Let the man answer," Kevin interrupted her tirade. She immediately scowled at Kevin, looking like she was about to explode.

"Lisa, to answer your questions, nothing qualifies me as an EMT or doctor. But I can tell you, no one can survive long, after having their intestines ripped out of their body. And if not, do we have a trauma first aid kit and experience to fix them? How about we call 911? Oh wait, all communications are down. I moved her body, so all of us didn't have to see her and to give her the privacy she deserved. Now for Marco, I checked for a pulse and could not discern one. I also checked his eyes and they were filled with blood. I also checked for breath which I could not find. For the door being barred, well from what we saw and the screams we heard, it was the only option left to us. After we'd moved Stacey's body, something attacked the door and seemed to want to get in badly and I am not going to allow anyone else to be harmed." I'd answered all of Lisa's questions, but she did not seem to like my answers. Her glare was enough to tell me that she wasn't having any of it.

Brian cleared his throat and stepped into the glare of death coming from Lisa. "Ma'am, I served one tour in Iraq and one in Afghanistan with the 26th Marine Expeditionary Unit, which means I saw battle and took fire. I have seen men dying and dead with wounds that looked nicer then Stacey's. I have forced the guts of my friends back into their bellies, while trying to get them medical attention. Unfortunately, I lost more than I was able to save. So, you ask if anyone was qualified to assess Stacey or Marco's wounds, I'll have to say yes, my experience is more than enough. We could not have saved either one, even if I'd had a combat medic available to help. Again, I have seen things that would give you nightmares for years and with what is in that stairway, I would not open it and face it or allow anyone here to face it. So ma'am, why don't you calm down. Dan here, has been doing a fine job trying to keep us safe, fed, and organized."

Lisa didn't look like she even cared or heard what Brian had said, but she did sit down on her chair, crossed her legs and looked away like she was trying to control a tantrum. "Thank you Brian, I appreciate your help and I'm afraid we will need more of it till we get rescued. Now anyone else have something to offer or ask?"

A balding overweight man with a bad comb-over raised his hand into the air, as far as I could recall, I thought his name was Gilbert. I nodded at him to take the floor. He stood up from where he had been sitting. "Dan, I know things have been bad today and I know you are trying to do your best to lead us and I appreciate it. But do we have any ideas about what's going on or maybe a plan to get us out of here? I have two kids and a wife at home waiting for me. I need to get home." His upper lip was sweating badly and he looked very pale.

"I have no idea what's going on out there. I'm as lost as you, but be assured I am keeping nothing from you guys. Again, it looks like Marco had the flu and died from it, just like the news said was happening on the east coast. Things are bad over there and I do not want that to happen here. I don't even know if what happened to Stacey or the people in the stairway are related. My plan is for us to eat, sit tight tonight, and hope for someone to come to our rescue. We have no way to protect ourselves and I am not sending anyone out to the stairs after what happened today." I was getting tired of repeating the facts.

Everyone seemed to shrink back and closed off from questioning. "Why don't we all line up and get us something to eat? Maybe it will help us relax and think of a way out of our predicament." I noticed Matt had moved the crackers and granola bars off the table and stowed them under the table. Smart guy, seemed that he'd had the same idea I'd had, in regards to rationing.

I sat on the floor and finished my sandwich and carrots. Washed it all down with a bottle of water and looked around our little bedraggled group. The first thing I noticed was everyone seemed to be alienating Lisa. 'I'm going to have to watch her. People who are shunned seem to do stupid things,' I thought to myself. Brian seemed to be telling some stories from when he was in the service. He had a pretty good amount of people around him. That was good, he could keep control of these people since they felt assured with having him around. Matt was on the end of one of the couches talking to a couple of people from our team. So far, so good, everyone was relaxing and settling down.

The sun was going down and the office was starting to darken. I looked up at the emergency battery lights and wondered how long they would last. Our offices were pretty high up, and not much light was going to filter in through the windows during the night.

I looked at my watch and saw it was getting close to nine p.m. I yawned and looked over at Matt. I was amazed to see him still awake. He had to have been up for at least nineteen hours, since he'd started at two a.m. His eyes had that glazed-over look, but it looked like he was hanging in there. "Alright team, I think we need to get some sleep. But in order to give me and hopefully you some peace of mind, I'm going to lock the lobby doors." Everyone looked over to me and nodded their agreement. "If someone does come for us, they will surely pound on the windows or hopefully get the phones fixed and ring us up." I walked towards the doors, closed them, and engaged the frame locks. Then, I yanked on them hard to make sure they were secure.

"Uhm, I don't mean to be a pain, but what if we have to pee? Do we have to ask for permission from daddy?" Lisa asked sarcastically.

Brian stood up and fielded that question, "For safety and

convenience, why don't we take turns on watch? I'm not that tired and don't sleep much anyway. I'll take the first watch and then wake Dan in three hours, who will then wake Matt in three hours, and Matt will wake me, so I can take the final watch." Matt and I agreed. He took this as a cue to go ahead and pass out. I found a semi-comfortable place between two of the couches, leaned back my head, resting on the wall, and fell into a restless sleep.

My sleep was fitful and filled with images, not dreams, mind you. It was just a slideshow of images. I saw Stacey and Marco, but not as alive and not really dead either. They both looked as they did when we'd found them, but they looked like they were alive. Open eyes and open mouths as if being caught screaming by a photographer. I awoke with a start, Brian had been whispering my name and gently moving my shoulder.

"Hey Boss, time for your shift. It's been quiet. I took three people to the bathroom, here's the door keys. Mind if I steal your spot?" I smiled up at him and held out my hand. He grabbed it and nearly ripped my arm out of its socket and simultaneously launched me into the air. He caught me before I lost my balance. "Alright Boss, wake me if you need me. I'm used to taking cat naps, so don't worry about it."

"Don't worry Brian, you deserve to crash out. If I can't handle something I'll just scream like a little girl, I'm sure that will wake you up," I croaked out.

He chuckled a little and within seconds was snoring softly. I quietly ambled around the office for an hour, looking out the windows and down at the Bay Bridge and could see the new lights dancing on the wire strands. Everything just felt surreal. 'How could everything look so normal out there, but be so wrong in here?', I thought. I rested my head on the window and tried to think about what I may have missed or could've done differently. I knew I had to lead these people, I was responsible for them. I knew I had a support staff in Matt and Brian, but for the first time of my life, I felt lost, wandering in a fog with nothing to guide me. "Things can't get worse, can they?" I said quietly to myself. I then felt a hand grab my arm and I swung around as fast as I could. Lisa jumped back with a terrified look on her face.

"You're not going to hit me are you?" she said while covering her face and slinking back away from me.

"No of course not, you just surprised me, that's all. What can I do for you?" I said forcing a smile on my face.

"You said if we had to pee you would let us out remember? Well I need to pee," she complained.

"No problem, let me see if anyone else needs to."

I turned to walk away and Lisa grabbed my wrist, "Later, I need to go now! Just take me and you can come back and get the others." She started yanking on my arm pulling me towards the doors. I rolled my eyes and followed her. I unlocked the lobby doors and left one slightly open. I figured since I was here, I would also go and maybe get some cold water splashed on my face. She bounded down the hallway and into the girl's bathroom. I slid into the men's bathroom, headed over to the urinals, and took care of that pressing need. Now that I thought of it, this was the first I had gone all day. I walked to the sinks and washed my face, taking time to wet my head and stretch. I took my time drying my hands; Lisa would just have to wait for me. Suddenly, I heard a guttural scream which tore through to the core of my being. Then, there was the padding of feet running and a door banging open.

"Oh shit, Lisa!" I screamed and slammed the bathroom door open. She was not in the hallway, but the stairway door had been untied and left open. I ran to it yelling for Lisa. I got to the door and looked out, I couldn't see anything through the pitch dark. But I could hear someone, or was it more than one set of feet, pounding on the metal stairway. It sounded like they were headed up not down though. I was tempted to run up the stairs but thought better of it. I couldn't see anything through the pitch black and to tell you the truth I was afraid. More than any other time in my life, I was afraid. I stepped back and closed the door, making sure to retie the fire hose back onto the handle. I ran through the lobby and into the office, leaving the door wide open.

"Brian, get up! I need you now!" I yelled. Everyone woke up with a start and just stared at me in shock. Brian was not one to be shocked awake, though. He came to full awake in seconds and jumped to his feet.

His eyes went wide and he yelled at me to "Move now!" in his best drill instructor voice. I didn't even think, I just reacted. I figured if he was warning me, then I should move toward him since he was safety. That saved my life. I got to him and noticed everyone was running into my office. I stopped and whirled around. What I saw next, I knew would stay with me for the rest of my life. Stacey stood there with her intestines and organs hanging out of her gaping wound. Her eyes were the color of spoiled milk. Both arms out in front of her, hands opening and closing as though she could grab us from there. Her mouth kept snapping open and closed, her teeth clacking so hard I thought they would break.

"Holy fuck Brian, what the hell is wrong with her? She can't be alive right? Holy shit, how can she be walking with her guts hanging out?" I was asking questions in a panic. I couldn't believe what I was seeing.

"Boss, I have no idea how to answer any of your questions. And to be truthful, I don't think right now it matters. Get your ass in your office and lock the door. I'll do what I can do for her." Brian kept backing up slowly toward my office door.

I stopped in my tracks, and looked at my office and door. It would be so easy to chicken out and leave Brian to his own demise. Something inside me shook its head and told me to grow a hairy pair and stand by Brian's side. "Fuck that, I got your back. Matt, close that door now," I yelled. I heard the door shut and then the locked clicked. I looked around the floor looking for a weapon. Nothing, fuck me really? Water? No help unless I could hold her down and drown her with it. Food? Well, if she was hungry that might help. Plastic forks? Yeah ok never mind, that's just stupid. Finally, I saw an old chair that had been dragged from my office. It had these modern looking metal legs supporting its base. I kicked the chair over and was trying to pull the legs off. Suddenly, I was slammed against the wall. Brian reached down grabbed a leg in each hand and pulled inward then outward ripping them free. He handed one to me and turned. Suddenly, there was Stacey in all her gory puss-filled glory.

She grabbed Brian and started pulling him toward her. He dropped his chair leg and put his hands on her chest trying to push her away. I could see the veins on his neck and forearms bulging from the exertion. He had her almost at a stalemate. But then, she started craning her teeth towards him, snapping them hard, trying to bite him. "Stop fucking being a spectator and do something, Boss. This bitch is way stronger then she looks." He was grimacing hard.

I realized I was just standing there with the makeshift weapon hanging by my side. I raised my arm and yelled her name until my voice went hoarse. "STACEY!" I brought down the chair leg and hit her left arm as hard as I could. I heard bone snap but she didn't even yelp in pain or stop her action of trying to get a tasty Brian sandwich. I raised the chair leg again and started hitting her on the shoulder with all my strength. I could've been hitting her with a pool noodle with all the same results. She was now inches from biting down on Brian's cheek. I could tell he was fading, his massive strength at its limits. I lost all control and started hitting her in the head over and over again. Hair and bone exploded all over with each hit I landed. I raised the leg high over my head and shoved the sharper broken side into her head wound that I had created and pushed with all my might. Her body started to falter as she lost her grip on Brian and he was able to push her back. My weapon was still lodged in her head. Somehow she was able to keep her feet under her, yet she seemed only damaged somehow. Brian let loose a guttural roar and stepped over to her. He grabbed the leg ripped it out of her head and using all his remaining strength shoved it back into her pushing it deeper then I had been able to. She finally collapsed, completely as if someone had just turned off her power switch. Brian and I both just stood there, panting heavily, looking down at Stacey's twice dead body.

"Thanks Boss, I know that probably took a lot out of you. But thank you." He reached out gathering me into his arms and giving me a proper hug.

We heard the lock on my office door unlatch and then the door swung open. Matt shakily poked his head out. "We could see the entire thing from the office window. Are you guys ok?" All of them emerged from my office and stood behind us. Stacey's body just laid there. I looked down at her and saw some black looking liquid seeping from her head.

"What the hell is that? Brian, bodies don't leak black shit, right?" I pointed to what I saw.

"Not unless it's a ruptured intestine that was filled with waste. Certainly nothing in the head leaks that color. So by the way, what the fuck happened?"

"Not completely sure, let's go for a quick walk. I need to see something before I can be sure. All of you can either stay here with that," I pointed at the body on the ground, "or you can come with us, it's up to you." I strode from the office back towards the lobby. I didn't have to look back to know they were following. We passed the bathrooms and made a beeline for the supply closet. The door was wide open, that black stuff smeared on the inside and door. The keys were still in the door lock. "Those were on my desk. I know they were. Lisa, that bitch!"

"Dude, Boss man, tell us what's up," Brian demanded.

"While I was on guard, I was staring out the windows at the city, deep in thought about all this. That's when Lisa came up and asked me to take her to the bathroom. I suggested we wake the others and of course, she demanded I take her right then. I didn't want to make a scene, so I took her. I went into the bathroom and did my business and was just splashing cold water on my face when I heard a scream and someone running down the hall. I heard a slamming sound and knew the stairway door had been opened. I ran out to find it open all the way. I stood at the stairway and couldn't make anything out because it's pitch dark in there. But I could hear heavy footsteps running up the metal stairway. I figured there was nothing I could do, so I closed and secured the door and came to get your help, Brian. Lisa must've stolen the keys from the desk, got me to take her to the bathroom, but snuck out and opened the supply closet. Must've seen Marco and Stacey and freaked out and ran. I have a suspicion Marco is chasing her, or probably has caught her by now."

I let out a shuddering heavy breath and collapsed to the floor. I felt like I couldn't get enough air and was choking. Then suddenly, all lights went out as I fell unconscious. That's it, I'm dead. Stroke, heart attack, taken by Aliens? Something finally snapped. I'd like to tell you I was in another land or there was a bright light or had friends and family to welcome me to the other side, but there was nothing like that. I was just standing in the pitch dark, couldn't see my hand in front of my face. Just blackness, crushing down on me, as though a physical force was trying to bury me. Then, I heard voices calling out my name. Someones screaming entered my dark mind, awakening me. I was on an office floor with Brian sitting next to me.

Chapter 8

"Hey Boss, you feeling better yet? You had us all worried," he smiled down at me through his scruffy beard.

"Holy shit, what the hell happened? I feel like I got ran over by a fucking bus," I croaked.

Matt came in and helped me sit up, handing me an open bottle of water. "Drink this, Dan. I know, it's not your awesome sweet ambrosia coffee. Should help, though." I listened and took a swig, man it felt good. It slowly parted the spider webs and allowed me to think a little straighter.

"The best I can figure Boss, is your mind finally just had enough and shut you down. It happens on the battlefield sometimes. Kinda like PTSD, it's an enormous crushing panic attack. You'll be ok. Matt and the rest helped carry you back in here."

I looked around, this wasn't my office, where the fuck am I? "Whose office is this? Why are we not in my office?" I asked stupidly.

"I am getting my promotion tomorrow and was just moving into this office. It's closer to the supply closet, so we just moved you here," Brian answered giving me a little smile.

"Oh, I didn't know you were being promoted. I guess congratulations are in order," I said weakly. I looked into my head trying to figure out if I'd known this or not.

"No problem, Boss. You were going to be told today, no wait, that would be yesterday since it's well after midnight. A new special projects division was going to be opened soon and they asked me to run it," Brian got up and sat on his desk.

"Well then, Brian. Stop calling me Boss, my name is Dan."

"Fuck no Boss, the way I see it, you are keeping us alive and together. This team has no room for two leaders and you are doing a damn fine job. Matt and I will just stay as your sergeants," Brian sketched a rough salute.

"Uhm, I was never drafted. I'm more of a civilian contractor. But yeah, like he said, you're doing a fine job."

"Alright, what time is it and where is the rest of the staff?" I started to get to my knees slowly, preparing to stand up. Brian and Matt both reached out, took an arm, and got me to my feet, steadying me before letting go.

"Everyone is in the conference room since there are less of us and it's pretty much next to Brian's office." He peered at his watch trying to adjust his tired eyes. "It's five a.m. on Wednesday," he informed me.

"Okay, sun will be up soon. Let's get a little more shut eye, then move the food over here."

Matt looked at Brian a little uneasy "You didn't tell him?"

"Dude, you've been in here during the entire discussion. When the fuck did I have time to tell him? Did I whisper sweet nothings into his ear while he was sleeping? Boss, all the food was pretty much splashed with that black shit from Stacey. When you were hitting her in the head, a bunch of the food got covered with it. I'm not that hungry if it means we have to deal with that shit," Brian answered with a sneer etched on his face.

We stood there, those two just staring at me. "What the fuck are you guys staring at me for? I know I'm pretty, but I'm not looking for a new love interest. So, we need food and water. I guess no one is coming for us, so we need to start doing for ourselves. I need suggestions, men." I shook my head and stared back them.

"He's taking this leader thing too far. Must've read too many war novels," Matt said with a straight face.

"Nah, he aint smart enough to read. Probably watched *Saving Private Ryan* too many times," Brian answered back.

"Really? I betcha it was more like *Shaving Ryan's Privates*. I'll bet twenty bucks that he has a giant collection of porn," Matt said trying to hide a widening grin.

"I'm not taking that bet, I'm not a sucker," Brian quipped back.

"Yeah, yeah, screw both of you. So really gentlemen, and I use that term loosely, what do you think our next move is?" It felt good trading quips with these guys. Since I'd gotten out of college, I had changed my entire way of thinking and put on the professional mask as good as I could. It had worked too well. I'd lost that carefree guy that I used to be. My family and old friends seemed to think I had lost my mind or was kidnapped by aliens. Maybe both.

"We have some pretty bad morale, Dan. Nobody has had a decent amount of sleep, on top of dealing with death and being prisoners in our own offices. Bad news on top of worse news makes for a shitty sandwich to have to choke on. Whatever we do, we have to first find a way to get them a win," Matt pointed down the hallway toward the conference room.

"A shitty sandwich? Matt, I think you've seen to many action movies, buddy," Brian's laugh resembled a bear gargling rocks. "You do have a point, though. So we need food, and perhaps either a way out or at least a solid plan showing we are trying to do something more than just sitting around waiting for someone to save us."

"Ok big man, give me some options," I threw a quizzical glance at Brian.

"Great. Just throw me under a bus. Shit ok, the only thing I can think of is to go looking for Lisa to confirm if she is ok," Brian suggested.

"Believe it or not I agree with the big man. I also think we should find a way to secure the stairs and move everyone up to the next floor. That's the executive offices. They have vending machines and a satellite phone in Mr. Heppner's office. It's there for natural disasters," Matt informed. He leaned against the wall and yawned deeply. His eyes looked glazed over.

"Going for a sat phone I could totally buy into, but going to save Lisa after what she did, I'm not so sure I care." I looked into each of their eyes and read the same emotions I was feeling. "Ok well, we have to do something. Big man, you wanna go on a magical trip to the land of unicorns and things that want to eat you?" I said this last part with a modicum of humor.

"You betcha, but I swear if you try holding my hand, I'm going to throw you down the stairs to buy me some time to get away from those things. Matt, you need to be in charge down here. Take care of these people the best you can. I expect you to immediately open that door when you hear us come charging back," Brian said in all seriousness.

"And just like that, we have a plan."

"Wait, I never agreed to this plan. Why do I have to stay back? I think Dan should stay, he's the leader. Brian and I should go. Dan, you're better at keeping everyone calmer than I could," Matt complained and I could see his side.

I knew he'd never wanted the spotlight, that's why he was happy to be a supervisor and not the boss. Yet he knew more about the office and its day to day than any manager or executive member, and that was exactly what I told him. "Matt, you have always been leadership material. I know that every time the team met goals or finished their projects, it was with your guiding hand. Sarah was just good at keeping her chair warm. Many times, I have come to the conclusion that I needed to promote you to her position. I was just trying to find a way to get her out of that office first. I know you can do it. Out of everyone on the team or that I have dealt with, you are the driving force. I believe in you and trust your judgement. You can do it," I reached out and put my hand on his shoulder.

"Everything he said," agreed Brian. "In the military, buddy, it's not the officers that lead, it's the sergeants. And you, my man, are one hell of a sergeant." Brian ruffled Matt's longish hair.

"Fuck both of you. But yeah, ok whatever. Stop kissing my ass and speaking so highly of my virtues. I'll do it, but if I can go on any record, I am not happy with this."

"Your complaint about this decision has been duly noted," I said throwing a mocking salute.

"Are we all going steady now? I figured since we just blew each other that we might as well start dating," Brian announced.

Matt left for the conference room to inform everyone the particulars of the plan while Brian hunted around looking for things to make as weapons and hopefully makeshift armor. That was all Brian's idea, and I was not going to ignore any advice from the big man.

We finally decided on those little metal chair spikes we'd used to take down Stacey. They were only about a foot long and easy to carry. Brian ripped out the last of them and I modified them to make them easier to use. Using duct tape from the supply closet, I made grips to hold onto. I wished I had a grinder so I could sharpen them into a type of dagger, but nothing in the office could be used that way. I did though, remove the plastic tips, which left a little bit of a rougher end.

Brian came back in holding two leather vests. "So, one vest is from my own collection, it's when I ride my Harley to work. I found this one in Carlos' office, he never rode a bike that I know of, but he did like people to think he was tough. So my idea is to cut them in two and wrap them around our arms for protection. We can use your tape to hold them in place. I do have two helmets in my office, but they are full-faced so they have pretty bad blind spots."

I showed him our makeshift tiny spikes. "Well this is the best I could do with weapons. Are we being stupid and throwing away our lives, Brian?" I wiped sweat from my head. "Do we even have a chance in hell of surviving?"

"It's better than nothing, man and we don't have to like it, we just have to do it," Brian said with confidence.

"Is that another stupid military saying?" I sighed.

"Navy Seal, Richard Marcinko was fond of saying that. He's the founder of Seal Team 6 and a pretty scary motherfucker to mess with. I'd rather have a shotgun and a good side arm, but I'm sure more has been done with less." He reached over and grabbed my scissors.

Within fifteen minutes, we had our arm armor and weapons ready. The leather was well broken in, but made moving my elbows a little difficult. Everyone gathered around the stairway door, saying their goodbyes and best wishes and a couple of the staff said thank you. I was overcome at how small our little group had become. Including Brian, Matt and myself, there were only fourteen of us left.

I grabbed Matt, wrapped him up in my arms and gave him a reassuring hug. "I'll be right back, buddy. Hold these people together."

Brian came over and put his big bear paw on Matt's shoulder, "You got this, dude." He winked, "Just remember, when we come back down we are going to be in a hurry, so make sure someone is on guard to let us in. We will knock three times quickly and then two times slower."

"Or screaming bloody, murder or you know, whatever," I said.

"You can trust me, big man. See you two soon. Be safe." Matt stepped over to the door and untied the hose. "On three, got it?" We nodded. "One. Two. Three!" He ripped the door open onto an empty dark stairway, and Brian and I ran in. Once we got through, Matt slammed and retied the door.

Chapter 9

"That was the last time I saw Matt. Can you tell me if anyone from my group made it out?" I realized I had been staring at the table while telling my story. I raised my head and felt tears slide down my cheeks, splattering onto the table.

Reynolds reached over and snatched a tissue box off of another table behind him. He handed them to me and I took one and wiped my eyes. "Dan, I don't have any names, but I was told only one person made it out alive from your floor and is at Saint Francis Memorial. According to this report, the person is ripped up pretty bad. Other than that, you and Brian are the only two who made it out in semi-good shape. By the way, Brian came out of surgery and he'll be fine. They got the bleeding to stop. I have some detectives over there right now, getting his side of the story."

"Just three people made it out of that entire building? With well over a thousand residents?" I put my forehead on the table enjoying its cool surface. I felt like I could fall asleep, but my story wasn't done being told. It haunted me and demanded to be told. If anything, to help this man find out what had happened.

"I know how you feel, Dan. It's the largest loss of life in San Francisco, since the earthquake in 1906. Let's get some more coffee brought in. I think we could both use some." He picked up his cell phone and made a call to someone in the station. "Could you please have a thermos of coffee brought up to interrogation room three, please? Sugar, cream, and two cups. Thanks."

"Reynolds, how long have you been on the force?" I felt like I needed to know more about this man.

"Sixteen years altogether, two as a beat cop, six in SWAT and the rest as a detective. I originally came out of the Army with five years as a rifleman, then two years as an MP. How about you, Dan?" Reynolds put his pad of paper and laptop on the desk and sat back in his chair, taking off his glasses and rubbing his eyes.

"Never been a cop or in the military," I said while my head was still on the table. "But I spent my college years at Chico and got a master's degree in Project Management and minored in Business Applications. I partied a little too much in my first two years, then I lost my mom. She'd always told me I would never make it in this world being 'that guy'. So when she died, I changed everything about me. I buckled down, got my degree and took a job at JP Morgan for five years as an analyst. Then, I came to Next Level and have been here for five years. Was hoping to get into the executive side in another five years."

"Ever been married or longtime partner?" Reynolds asked.

"Nope, too busy with work. No time to enjoy the fun things. Dad moved to Spokane after mom died, and my brother and sister live on the east coast. My sister's an MD and my brother works as a news director. So I just work and usually go hiking, if and when I get time off. How about you? Married?"

"Divorced, no kids. She lives near Portland. We are still friends, but with my work schedule and dedication here, we just couldn't make it work. She never got remarried either," he answered.

Just then, a knock came at the door and Reynolds answered it. Two police officers pushed a cart in with an urn of coffee and some Danishes. He poured us each a cup and put the sweets on the table. I grabbed my coffee and passed on the sugar and cream. The danishes looked good and I attacked one like a kid with a Twinkie at fat camp.

We sat in silence for a couple of minutes, cherishing our coffee. I looked up and caught Reynolds eyes. "Ok, I think I'm ready to continue."

Reynolds put his coffee down, picked up his pad of paper and gave me the go ahead nod.

Chapter 10

Shit, it was dark. Brian reached out, grabbed my arm and we headed towards where we hoped were the stairs to go up. We moved slowly, testing our footing and taking small strides. Finally, we met the first step and we started ascending. My heart was pounding so hard in my chest, I was afraid it was like a dinner bell ringing for those things to come and eat. I never minded the dark, but what we were experiencing right now was oppressive. It smothered me in its confines. It felt alive like it was swallowing us. If not for Brian's hand in mine, I would've been lost in mind, physicality and soul. We made it to the next landing. It felt like a lifetime had gone by, but it couldn't have been more than five minutes.

We stopped and Brian whispered in my ear. I jumped and almost had a heart attack when I'd felt his breath on my ear. "Halfway there, Boss, I hear no sounds, but let's go slowly. I got you, man."

Inside, I was screaming in fear. I felt like we were walking into the pits of Hell and were about to be devoured by some shit-eating, hairy-balled demon named Bob. Yes, my mind goes to stupid places when I am terrified.

We finally made it to the next door and found it unlocked. The door handle was slick with something and took Brian a couple of tries to grip it. He slowly opened the door and light from the creeping sun lit up our position. I heard screaming from below us, so we dove into the hallway and closed the door. I repeated the fire hose trick from downstairs and secured the door with it.

Brian looked down at his hand, it was covered in that black stuff. He wiped his hand on his pants leg, and stood back to back with me, listening for any sounds of life around us. We had no idea if Stacey was on this floor or anyone else infected. I guess, that included Marco. We slowly walked down the hallway toward the bathrooms. Brian opened the door to the woman's bathroom and entered. It was dark, damn it, no power, duh. "Hold the door open so we can get some light. But watch my back. The light right now is our only friend."

I slipped the door open enough to bring light into the bathroom and stood sideways, so I could see down the hallway and into the bathroom. Brian moved from stall to stall and not finding anyone, backtracked to me. We repeated the same procedure on the men's bathroom which was clear also.

"We are going to go left and clear the back office, conference room and those cubes. Then, we will go to the lunch room and cross over to the executive offices," Brian suggested.

"I thought we wanted to go right for that sat phone?" I asked with confusion.

"Well, that's a great idea, but clearing the floor so we don't get our asses eaten is probably a better idea," Brian gave me a 'duh' look.

"I gotcha. Ok, I will watch your back, you go beat some shit up," I answered.

We started down the hallway slowly. I was walking sideways, trying to see what was in front, while covering our rear. We got to the conference room and saw the drapes were open, much to my relief. Brian got to the door and slowly cracked it open. He had his spike raised high and then opened the door all the way till it bumped against the wall, to make sure nothing was behind it. We made our way in and Brian pointed to the door, so I took his cue and closed it. The sun was shining in and lit the room. The table was upended, blocking our view and making a great place for something to be hiding, and the chairs were lying all over the place. Blood was splashed on one of the windows. Brian put his arm out, slowing my pace. He pointed to the wall and gave me the wait sign. He walked stealthily towards the table, moving chairs out of his way as he went.

He reached over and grabbed the table and slowly moved his head over the top to see what was on the other side. He pulled it back quickly and looked back at me with wide eyes. He put his finger to his lips to remind me to be quiet. He then, waved me over. I could hear a slight sucking sound, like someone putting their hands in mud and slowly pulling them out.

I stuck my head over and almost gasped out loud at what I saw. Lisa lay there with half of her face missing, having been torn off savagely. Her lone surviving eye darted over to me. It was pleading, begging for help. I looked lower down her body and saw her shirt had been ripped off, her left breast was missing and her belly was torn open. Marco and another man were kneeling on the floor, slowly pulling her intestines out and shoving them into their mouths. I did not know that disemboweling someone would make that sickening, sucking sound.

I looked up at Brian and he indicated by miming with his spike that he was going to take Marco and then pointed at the other man and then at me. He was saying I'll take this one, you take that one. I nodded my understanding and agreement. I lifted my spike high and waited for Brian to give me the go signal.

"Hey, cock heads! Want some fresh meat?" Brian said out loud.

Both men raised their heads to look at us. Marco let out a high-pitched moan and was about to react by standing up, when Brian brought his spike down into his right eye. I took a page out of Brian's attack and also slid my spike into the other man's eye. I felt things sliding and parting under my spike, but then it felt like resistance. I put all my weight into the spike and pushed down, twisting the spike back and forth. After a while, there was no more movement from him. I pulled my spike out with a disgusting, slurping sound with a pop at the end. I wiped my spike on him to clean it off.

I looked over at Brian and he was calmly wiping his spike clean on Marco's shirt. He then stopped, looked over at me and gave me a small smile. "What do we do with Lisa, Boss?" Brian asked.

"There is nothing we can do for her, she's a big mess."

"Hey boss, I've been thinking about this flu virus thing. Don't you think that when these beasts feed on people that they might transfer something into them. Causing them to go crazy and attack, thus spreading the disease far and wide? Maybe we should put her out of her misery now?" Brian explained his point of view.

"I'll do it, she works for me and I failed her, so I'll put her to rest," I said.

"Boss, cut this 'poor me' crap. She made her own decisions and put everyone at risk. If anything, she should be apologizing to us. If you really think you need to deal with her, then do it," Brian admonished me.

I stood there, rebuked and properly chastised. I would never have been able to do any of this, let alone survive without Brian by my side. "Boss man, it looks like she just let go. I suggest we stand back and see how long it takes for her to come back. But let me take her out when and if she comes back."

I nodded my ok and put my head against a far window looking outside, and felt the sun on my face. Brian stood over Lisa, never taking his eyes off her. He held his spike in his massive right hand squeezing it. "See anything outside, different than usual?"

"No, it looks like a regular day out there, still no real traffic, well for San Fran, that is. Both bridges look half empty. From our height, I cannot see street level. You know a couple of things have been niggling my conscious. First, is this going on all over the city? I mean, if Marco got out of the east coast, how many others have? Next, who the hell locked down the building, shut down the elevators and locked the stairway door access? And lastly, are there any other pockets of life in the building?"

"Yeah, I have been thinking the same things. That and someone must have an inkling of what's going on by now," Brian added.

Chapter 11

Reynolds interrupted my story, "I can answer some of your questions for you now. We actually got a bunch of calls on Tuesday night from people waiting for their loved ones to come home from work. We rolled out a couple of patrol cars and they reported that they could not access the building. All the doors were locked and some were barricaded. All the power had been turned off and no one was answering our phone calls to any phone number we could find."

Reynolds got up, refreshed both of our coffees and eased himself back down onto his chair. He sat back and let out a low sigh, crossed his legs and picked up another folder that had been lying on the table. He leafed through it as I took sips of my coffee. "Once we finally got access to the building, we ran into a bunch of problems. When I arrived on the scene, I was alerted that all access to the upper floors had been booby trapped and locked up tight. We also found that the power had been physically cut to the building, along with the telecommunications cables. It also seemed that someone had reprogrammed the security system to lock out the elevator and all other access." He looked through more pages and came to another section. His eyebrows rose as he read. "According to what we discovered, it was a security guard who did all this. One Garrett Springer. He also had some sort of device that ran on a series of car batteries. That device seemed to be jamming cell phone signals for the entire building. Our tech guys also found repeaters through the stairway once we'd cleared the building. The guy was actually on a DHS list for home grown terrorism charges. How he got a job as a guard and a gun card really makes no sense to me."

"I know him. He has been with the security group for three months. He always made comments about how the government would never be there for us when we needed them the most. I figured he'd meant for the next earthquake and FEMA and how they'd failed Katrina. I usually just let him talk my ear off while I waited for the elevator. I never really paid more attention to him than that."

Reynolds cell phone went off to a ring of the *A-team* theme song. He looked down at the caller id and answered it. "Reynolds. Talk to me." He listened intensely and a look of concentration came upon his face. He took a pen from his breast pocket and started making notes on the jacket folder he'd been holding. "Ok, thank you for the update. Let me know if anything changes."

He looked over at me and just stared for a while, his lips pursing into a thin white line. "That was a friend of mine who's a news director at

NBC. He said he's been monitoring his east coast office since it went down Wednesday. He said he just got an email from his counterpart. It said that the virus was out of control out there and that Washington has just declared a Federal emergency and martial law."

"How are we doing here on the west coast?" I asked

"The hospitals are filled up with sick people. The virus seems to be getting out of control. But it's worse east of the Rockies, for now that is."

"You know what's going to happen with the sick people, right? Just like Marco, they'll die and come back and infect others. This is going to get bad," I explained.

Reynolds put down his pen, file, and coffee cup. He sighed deeply and examined me with his bright eyes. "I hear what you are saying and I'm not believing you or disbelieving you. So far though, we have not had anything like that happen. The hospitals and morgue are not reporting anything. So, unless you are wrong with what you saw, the virus has mutated or we've all gotten lucky so far and have been able to stop this from happening or getting worse. Why don't you continue on with your story? There are more questions I have a feeling that you're going to have the answers to."

Chapter 12

Brian kept a vigilant watch over Lisa's body. I sat down on the floor and rested my head against the window. Brian looked at me, and then did something I thought was strange. He lifted the table up and moved it over, so he could place the edge down on Lisa's body. He then walked over and placed chairs on their side creating a ring around the area I was sitting in. He stepped over the chairs and eased his body to the ground against the windows.

"That's better," he sighed and let his body go limp. "Even big guys like me need to sit down and relax every once in a while. It'll take her a while to change anyway. Let's get some rest boss, since last night sucked all kinds of ass. I'll take first watch, go ahead and get some winks in."

I was too exhausted to argue, so I gave him thumbs up and passed right out. I dreamed San Francisco was on fire, guns could be heard all over and people were running around screaming. I was walking down the Embarcadero towards the piers. The bay was to my right. People would run past me with horrendous wounds, screaming for help before jumping into the bay. Boats could be seen clogging the water, all heading towards the Golden Gate Bridge. I couldn't understand the emergency, I just kept walking, taking in the scene unfolding in front of me. I saw strollers knocked over, cars wrecked into each other, and when I looked up, I saw a huge jet liner go over my head, way too low to make it over the buildings. Suddenly, the plane tipped over on its left wing tip and crashed right into the Coit tower, taking the top half off the tower and crashing into Pioneer Park. The plane erupted into flames, setting more of the city on fire. I stopped and watched the fire grow in intensity. Something was pulling on my arm, I looked down and it was a little six-year-old girl dressed in a pretty white dress. She had her blonde hair done up in big curls. She was trying to say something, but I couldn't understand what. Like her voice was slowed down and echoed back and forth. That's when I looked up and saw a group of bloody people running at us, some missing hands or feet, and their teeth kept clacking while their jaws worked like they were eating something. I picked up the girl and we started running, but there was fire in front of us and these people behind and also now, coming from our left. I cut to the right and ran straight for the bay. A boat was just shoving off and the crew was yelling for me to hurry. I got to the edge of the dock and threw the little girl into the boat. She made it safe into a crewman's arms. I then jumped as hard as I could but missed the boat and was just about to fall into the water, when I opened my eyes and bolted straight up gasping for air. I was back in the conference room. Brian reached out and grabbed my bicep and squeezed assuredly. Letting me know I was not alone.

"Boss, you're fine. Calm down. It was just a nightmare." He patted my back. "You slept for three hours. How are you feeling?"

"Like shit," I croaked out.

Brian produced a half full bottle of water. "Here, I found this and saved half for you."

I sipped at it, feeling the dream slowly slip back into its own world. "Thanks, Brian. I needed that. Did you get any sleep?"

"I napped on and off, I feel pretty good, ready when you are to continue our little adventure," he chuckled seemingly enjoying my discomfort.

"Has Lisa come back yet?"

"No, I think this thing takes a while. Remember Stacey was bitten and infected, at least we assume so. It took her a while to change and I'm thinking this thing takes somewhere around eight or more hours to reanimate the dead. I guess that word is the only way to describe what it does."

"So, do we wait or move on? Part one of our mission is complete with finding Lisa and Marco. So, do we leave her here or should we move on for the sat phone and come back for her later?" I asked as I stood looking over what remained of her body.

"This is going to sound bad, but I think we should go ahead and destroy her brain now. Then, move on to our second objective," he answered truthfully.

I walked over to all three bodies and looked down at them. Right then, I had so much anger built up in my chest and it escaped in a roar as I started stomping on Marco's head. I was so angry over everything and just kept stomping till I ended up crushing it. My shoes were covered in little pieces of black fluid and bone bits. I just stood there staring at what I had done, breathing heavily in and out, trying to control my emotions. I had never lost control before like that and it'd terrified me.

I was trying to process what I had just done when I felt Brian's hand grabbing my arm and guiding me over to the windows again. He handed me a roll of paper towels he had found by the white board. "Here, clean off your shoes and legs. I'm going to take care of Lisa, then we'll need to gather ourselves and move on." I nodded at him and bent down to clean my feet.

I tried to block out what Brian was doing, by cleaning up the mess I had created. I was able to get the beast back into its cage and had locked down my emotions when Brian came back from his gruesome duty. He evaluated both our weapons.

"Hey Boss, I'm a little worried about our weapons. We used them twice and they are already showing some pretty bad wear and tear. Mine is worse than yours, though," he said and flipped my spike to me.

I caught it and quipped, "Of course, yours is worse. It has to deal with your retarded silver-back, gorilla strength." I pointed at his weapon, then at his big arms.

"Yeah well, it's not my fault I do more than work at my desk, then go home and play with myself." He gave me a lopsided grin and flipped me the bird, "Are you feeling better now? Are all outbursts under control?"

I moved to the back door and motioned him over, "Did you put cameras in my house? Never mind. Yes, I feel better, sorry about that. I got a grip on it now."

"Yeah, I got video but it aint making no money on Dorksathome.com. I'll take point, stay on my ass, though. I know you got no problem doing that, just keep your hands off unless you got flowers and chocolate." He walked up and gripped the door knob and turned it slowly. He then swung the door open and stepped back. "Just making sure no one is at the door ready to eat at Brian's buffet." He stepped out, then waved me on.

We turned left and continued down the hallway, clearing offices and closets as we went. It wasn't till we entered the lunch room that we ran into trouble. Two of those things were standing at the far end by the fridge. We stepped back and Brian whispered to me, "There are two of them, and two of us. So, pick the one you want to take care of and I'll take the other. "

I poked my head back in and decided to take the woman and leave the bigger guy to Brian. I pointed to the woman and mouthed to Brian, "I'll take her." I slowly walked in and promptly tripped over a chair, landing hard on my face. Fuck me, that hurt. The two things turned and came for us, but they had trouble with the table and chairs between us. It was like they were drunk and just walked straight into the obstacles.

Brian reached down, grabbed me by my belt and lifted me off the floor. "Alright, rest time is over. You've already taken a nap earlier. Get your shit back in the game. Thank you, by the way, for making this harder. I take it you like a challenge?"

I got to my feet and made sure my grip on the spike was strong. I looked at the furniture and an idea came to me. I picked up a chair and held it like a lion tamer would, with the feet sticking out. Brian looked at me, questioning and gave me the go ahead sign. I moved slowly towards the woman. I waited till she was closer then ran at her, hitting her in the chest. I then kicked her legs out from under her, causing her to fall to the ground. I pinned her to the ground with the chair and took a deep breath to calm down. I raised the spike over my head and brought it down, intending to slam it down on her head, but she moved her head to the side. My arm went numb from slamming the spike into the floor. I couldn't tell if she'd moved intelligently or if it'd been just a fluke. She tried moving out from under the chair, but there was no way I was going let her. I got mad, lifted the chair and slammed it back down, but this time, forcing two of the legs into her, one in the throat, the other into her chest. I looked over at Brian and he had already finished off his thing and was now sitting on one of the tables smiling at me.

"Need help?" he asked. I gave him the finger and put my foot on her head. I then slammed the spike down into her eye socket, finally finishing her off. I wiped my spike off on her brown-crusted dress and walked over to Brian.

"Fuck you. I'm new at this shit. You were trained professionally;

70

I'm learning on-the-job." I was breathing hard and trying not to lose my lunch from the rotten smell coming from the two bloody bodies. The smell was like nothing I have ever experienced. It was as if you picked up fresh dog crap, microwaved it with rotten broccoli and garbage. Yeah, never mind, that smell I'm sure doesn't even come close. In fact, that sounded heavenly.

"Boss, they don't teach you how to kill these things in the Marines." Brian patted me on the back, we got up and headed back toward the elevator lobby.

We arrived in the lobby without meeting anyone, or should I say, anything. I grabbed my keys out of my pocket and unlocked one of the doors. "Thank God I remembered my keys, huh? That would've sucked." I held the door open and waved him on, "Beauty before brains."

"Really, Boss? I mean, first you like my ass, now you tell me I'm beautiful. We need to have a deep talk after all this." Brian walked into the hallway.

This floor was laid out differently than the one we worked on. Instead of an open area of cubicles, this one had a big lushly carpeted hallway with offices on the window side. This was where the bigwigs worked. Their secretaries sat on the other side in cubes by the break room, which we had already cleared. I could see most of the office doors were open.

We walked up to the first one and Brian poked his head in. "Clear. Move onto the next one. I'll follow you."

"Brian, don't you think we should check the entire office, like behind the door and desk? You know, just to make sure?" I pointed out.

"Damn, you really are the brains in this operation. Good job pointing that one out. I'll make a soldier out of you yet." Brian slowly moved into the office as I kept a watch on the hallway. We talked in hushed tones so we did not alert anyone or thing to our presence. Brian looked behind the door and then travelled behind the desk. He even moved the chair and looked underneath it. "Clear."

I smiled, then moved onto the next office. I poked my head in first and saw it vacant of anyone or thing. I walked in further and checked behind the door and mimicked Brian's pattern from the other office. "Clear," I said.

We repeated this for the next two offices and found nothing; the doors were open and inviting. We came upon the first office with a closed door and Brian motioned that he would take this one himself. He pointed to the other side of the door and told me to watch our backs. He reached out and tried the door knob. He found it locked. He hunched his shoulders at me as if saying, "Now what the fuck do we do?"

"Let's move on and try the other offices. Opening that door is going to make an awful racket." Brian smiled at that.

We moved on to the next closed door and Brian tried the handle. It moved, so he unlatched it and pushed the door open, stopping it before it could slam into the wall. He walked in taking slow measured steps. He was checking behind the door when it was pushed back at him. A man stumbled out, grabbing Brian's forearm and taking a big bite. Brian closed his eyes, taking the pain in, but took his spike and shoved it into the thing's eye. Brian moved the arm being bitten closer to him like doing an arm curl with weights, helping the spike to dig deeper into the eye socket. He jiggled the spike back and forth, then pulled it free with a pop. He used the spike to pry the things mouth open, releasing his arm. I moved forward to help, but he stayed me with a look. He examined his arm closely and then sighed out loud and sunk to his knees. "The skin is not broken, but fuck me, that hurt." He flexed his hand a couple of times, testing out his grip and I'm sure, trying to regain his composure.

While Brian sat on the floor and took a breather, I walked around and finished the sweep for any more of those things. "You know what? I don't even know what to call these damn things. I mean they can't be human anymore, not with guts and stuff hanging outside their bodies."

"Why don't we call them exactly what they are, Boss. Zombies! I mean, they are impervious to pain, dead, oh, and they tend to try and eat people," Brian pointed out.

"Ok fine, Zombies. I haven't watched one of those movies since my freshmen year in college. Kind of wish we had guns or something other than these damn chair leg spikes," I said while sitting down on the edge of the desk.

Brian got a giant beaming smile on his face and stared past me. "What got you so excited? If there is a six-foot, naked, hot, and alive woman behind me, I call dibs and you're going to have to give us a couple of minutes," I quipped.

He got to his feet, walked past me and took down two bats. He handed one to me and weighed the other bat in his hand. "Oh thank you, God. They are real Louisville sluggers. I say we use these bad boys to take down the next zombie."

I stepped back and took a couple of practice swings. "I like the way this feels," I pointed at the door with the bat.

Brian took lead again and I stayed on his heels as we left the office. I frequently looked behind us as we went searching for zombies and cute live women. Hey, a guy can wish, can't he? We stopped at the printer alcove and Brian stuck his head in, found nothing and we continued down the hall, coming to the last office in the hallway. It was the regional VPs office. I had been in there three times in my entire career with the company. "If I remember correctly, there is a private bathroom to the left rear of the office. It's a corner office, so it's the biggest so far," I informed Brian.

He turned to me and gave me an awkward smile. "I've been to this office a dozen times, in the last month alone. This is where they told me I was being promoted. Sorry to pop your self-important bubble there, Boss." He snickered and patted my head, "You're starting to get a little fuzzy there."

"Yeah, fuck you, jolly green giant. I'll shave when we get out of here." I reached around him and turned the knob. The door opened easily. A shot rang out, just missing me. However, Brian was not so lucky. As I squatted in the hallway, I looked over to Brian and saw that he had been hit in the upper bicep.

"Don't shoot, we're alive!" I screamed and yanked on Brian, pulling him back into the hall beside the entrance. I poked my head in and saw a man standing behind a huge oak desk, pointing a gigantic handgun at us. "It's Dan Welko and Brian from operations."

"I don't fucking care who you are. Get off my floor. I'm not sharing anything with you. You can't have my supplies and you'll only take this gun from my cold dead hands." He shot again. The bullet shot down the hallway, hitting the closed lobby door and shattering it into a rain of safety glass.

"What do we do, Brian?" I asked, looking around for cover. I spied the open office we'd just come from. I could probably get there without getting shot, but not Brian. I would not leave him. I'd grown close to the psycho bear. "We need to get into that office," I pointed to the adjacent office.

Just then, I could hear pounding on the locked office door down the hallway. I looked at Brian and found him looking up at me. "I can make it. Just stay down and move to the left after you enter the office. Once I pass you, slam the door and lock it," Brian said, wincing at the pain in his arm. I could see the blood soaking through the leather. If we didn't stop it soon, he could bleed to death. Brian held up three fingers and started silently counting, dropping a digit as he counted. When he got to one, I stayed low and made a mad dash and dove into the office, I came up on one knee and then jumped to the side of the door just as three things happened simultaneously. First, shots ripped down the hallway, too high to hit either of us. Secondly, I heard the door down the hall crash open. Thirdly, Brian with an unbelievable roar. dove into the room colliding with the chairs in front of the desk. I lurched to the door and slammed it shut and threw the bolt. I could hear grunts, moans, and gunshots echoing in the hallway.

Chapter 13

The guy with the gun would scream, before he fired each shot. There was a brief lull, then he started shooting again. Since the first shot, I'd counted about twelve more. Next, there was a blood curdling scream which I assumed came from the shooter, followed by moans and grunts. I looked to Brian, who had removed his leather arm covering to examine his arm.

"Fuck me, what a douche bag. You ok, man?" I got down on the floor and started looking over his arm. He had a five-inch-long by one-inch-deep gouge across his left bicep. He had found a souvenir golf towel on the desk and kept dabbing at the blood with it. I looked down and saw that the bullet had hit the same arm that the zombie had bitten. He had two big half crescent bruises almost coming together to make an oblong circle. The bruising was blue and purple and looked bad.

"I'm good, been hit worse while in Afghanistan. Here, help me make a bandage or something. If he aint dead, I'm going to choke the living shit out of that selfish ass monkey." Brain looked more annoyed than pissed.

If I had been shot, I would've been into throes of anger that would equal that of a scorned woman walking in on her husband fucking her own sister. I know, I've got issues. I believe I said that earlier. "Here, let me look through the office. Most of these guys are afraid of germs and there might be something in here. Just hold that towel and put pressure on it."

"Really? Put pressure on it? Nah. Fuck, I was just going to sit here and squeeze it to see if I can't get it to spurt. Fuck, I'm not new to this, man," he said through clenched teeth.

"If you can get it to spurt, try getting it on a big piece of paper. Maybe, we can sell it as a new Jackson Pollock. Get enough money and we can retire. Now just hang on a sec." I rifled through the desk and found an unopened first aid kit. I brought it over and opened it for Brian.

"I doubt this kit can handle this wound, but since you went through all this trouble, let me see the damn thing." He took out the small bottle of saline and a couple of the antibiotic packets. Then, he pulled out the three rolls of gauze and medical tape.

I sat there and watched him go through the motions of cleaning and dressing his wound. "Are you going to be able to keep fighting, big man? Cause if not, I don't think I can handle whatever is on the other side of that door alone."

He stopped, turned his head to me and gave me a look that said 'are you stupid, insane or both'. "Hey Boss, I'm good, don't worry about me. Like I said, I've been hurt more than this before." He wrapped all of the gauze around his arm and then used the medical tape to secure and cinch it around his massive bicep. He moved his arm up and down, and in and out, and gave me thumbs up. "I'm just gonna have to do the brain bashing and depend on you to do the brain pulping. So, we work as a team now, unless there are more than two that is, then we just wade in and kick some ass." He stood, grabbing his bat and hoisting it onto his shoulder.

"I'm in no hurry, Brian. Let's sit here and catch our breath for a bit." I sat in the executive chair and swung my feet onto the desk. "I always knew someday I would have an office on this floor." I leaned back and closed my eyes, trying to summon a relaxed posture.

Brian harrumphed and sat in one of the guest chairs and swung his massive size-sixteen feet onto the desk. "Damn, this feels good. How long do you want to hang out here, Boss?"

"Fuck, I don't know. A little while, I guess." I shrugged my shoulders at Brian.

"Good enough answer for me. Hey, did you notice all of the vending machine food was missing?" he asked.

"Nope. Never looked. I was busy with that zombie bitch, remember?" I answered back.

"Oh yeah, you and that chair. You had me in stiches, man. What were you thinking?" He gave me a hearty laugh.

"Yeah, I have no idea. I figured I could hold her to the floor between the legs of the chair and just brain her more easily. I guess I didn't think it all the way through, but I'm glad I could provide some levity with my awesome prowess and fighting moves, giving you the laughter you so deserve, asshole." I kicked his foot softly with mine. Ow, that fucking hurt. Did this guy have feet of steel, too?

I stared at Brian for a while as he was sitting there with the bat resting on his shoulder and it finally hit me. "You look like a younger, massively bearded Mark McGwire. I didn't see it till you picked up that bat!" I was laughing and pointing at a picture of Big Mac on the wall in all his A's glory.

"I always thought I looked like a bigger, more ripped Jason Momoa. Of course, my hair isn't as dark as his." He gave me a giant grin and hitched his shoulder in a silent laugh.

"Yeah, I guess. If Jason Momoa got hit in the face by an ugly stick. Well, more like the entire tree, then you two would look alike." I laughed harder than the quip deserved. "I'm going to take lead on going through doors, from now on. You ok with that?"

"You aint no Brad Pitt, either and yeah, I'll be happy to cover your skinny ass now."

"Really, you like my ass? I have been working out, thanks for noticing," I gave him a wink.

"Dude, you need help."

We sat there shooting the shit and talking about sports and music. He was into country music, and I was into eighties and nineties hair bands. He rooted for the Baltimore Ravens, and me the Oakland Raiders. We sat there for an extra hour and were kind of hoping the dude who'd shot at us was dead by the zombies. If he was still alive, this would give him time to calm down.

Brian pointed toward the door, "Shall we get going?"

I got off my chair with a sigh and had to rub the knots out of my back. I opened the door just enough to peek out. I peeked left first, toward the lobby and saw it was clear. Then I looked right, and two dead zombies lay at the entryway to the office. I stretched my head out further, but couldn't see all the way into the office. Slowly, I started walking and Brian put his injured arm on my shoulder to let me know where he was. A few more steps and I could see in the office. No one was shooting, so that felt like finally something to put in the win column. I stepped into the doorway and scanned the room left to right. It looked clear, so I stepped further in. Brian moved his right hand to my left shoulder and closed the door with his left hand. He didn't move his hand from my shoulder or make a sound, so I figured nothing was behind the door.

"I'm going to move to the left side and clear that side, you take the right," he spoke softly in my ear.

I nodded and moved off to my right and carefully made my way over to the far wall so I was not close to the desk, but was able to see around it. There was a pool of blood and three zombies. Two were not moving, but one was still alive. It looked like its left knee had been blown apart. It noticed me and started to moan and crawl toward me. Suddenly, its head was crushed under Brian's bat. "Left side clear."

"Sorry, uhm yeah, right side clear." Suddenly, two shots came out of the bathroom door. Brian dropped to the floor and I slid into the side of the desk. "Why the fuck, are you shooting at us, you stupid, privileged, piece of shit?"

"It's your fault they got in here. And you want to take my stuff. It's mine, go find your own," he whined through the door. "Did I get any of you?" he asked.

"No, you, stupid waste of skin," I yelled back.

Four more shots came through the door and buried themselves into the far wall.

"Stop antagonizing the man with the gun."

"I think he might be running out of bullets. Why don't you crawl over to the left side of the door, I'll piss him off so he will keep firing. When you hear him run out, kick the door open and I'll charge him."

"That sounds like a stupid fucking plan to tell you the truth. And why do you think he may be running out of bullets? Do you know what kind of gun he's using or how many bullets he has?" Brian asked incredulously.

"I don't know guns, but I can read and there is an almost full box

80

of bullets on the floor over here and a magazine. It says .45 ACP." I showed him the magazine and box and ammo. It gave him a big grin.

"Okay, your plan has more merit. But if I take another bullet, I'm going to shoot you in the ass," Brian said back. He then crawled his way slowly to the left side of the door. He nodded to me and slid to a standing position, careful to keep his body away from the door.

"Hey fucktard, when you going to come out and give me a handy?" I taunted.

"Fuck you, man. Why don't you come over here and let me shoot you in the face?" he yelled back.

I grabbed a stapler from his desk and hefted it in my hand. Nice weight, must be loaded is the thought that went through my mind. "Fine, asshole. Here I come, and be prepared cause I'm going to kick the shit out of you and take your stuff." I stomped my feet, then threw the stapler underhanded at the door. Before it rebounded to the floor, the guy started firing off shots.

He got about four off before you could hear an empty clicking sound. Immediately, Brian stepped to his right lifting his big foot and kicked the door clear off its hinges, which collided on top of the gunman who was squatting on the floor. I roared and took off running. When I hit where the doorway was, I launched myself into the air, landing on top of the door. I saw the gun come up, reloaded with a fresh magazine and pointed towards me. Without thinking, I reached out with my right hand and twisted the gun back with all my strength. I could hear and feel the man's trigger finger crack and collapse from the gun. I threw the gun out of the bathroom and stayed sitting on the door, bouncing it against the guy under it.

Brian was there in a flash. He reached out, grabbed my hand and pulled me to my feet and out of the way. Brian was mad and I was glad to be away from him. He grabbed the door and launched it back into the office, out of his way. He reached down and lifted the man off the floor and slammed him ruthlessly against the bathroom wall. Brian then used a towel to secure the guy's wrists with some specialty knot. All I can do is a bow when tying my shoe, so I had no idea what kind of knot he used, probably something he'd learned in the Marines.

The man was yelling in between sobs of pain. "Shut the fuck up before I break your scrawny little neck in half," Brian whispered into his ear. That shut him up quick. Hell, it shut me up and he hadn't even said it to me. He'd just said it with so much venom that I figured, you never know. "Hey Dan, look this fucker over and see if he was bitten." Brian lifted the man off his feet turning him around in the air, then planting him back down on his feet so I could get an all-around look.

I saw a bite on his right wrist up high. He had pulled his shirt sleeve down trying to staunch the blood. He had another one on his left calf muscle. I informed Brian and he threw the guy against the wall hard, shaking the whole bathroom.

"Look, you piece of whale shit, I'm not very happy that you shot me in the arm and I took that very hard. So I'm not gonna be very nice back to you. Answer my questions, and I'll end your life quickly. Lie to me, and I will take you to realms of pain you never knew existed. Now, all we want is the sat phone and maybe some water," Brian said this in a voice I had never heard from him before. Shit, I would've given him my grandmother's safe number if he'd asked with that voice.

The guy took a little too long to answer, so Brian reached out and twisted the man's left wrist, sounds like corn popping issuing forth. "I said I was not in the mood right?" The man screamed out loud and Brian smacked him lightly in the back of the head. "Stop being a pussy. Hell, you shot me and you don't see me crying, do you?"

"The sat phone is broken. I tried to use it yesterday, but it wouldn't turn on," he squealed out.

"How did it break?" Brian asked.

The man squirmed in obvious pain. "I was pouring some bourbon and I knocked the phone off the desk and it fell into my garbage can. Then, I lost hold of the bottle and it fell into the can, submerging the phone in its contents. It was wet when I turned it on, it flickered for a second and now it won't come back on. I was mad, so I threw it back into the can. See? It's over there by the far side of the desk." He was really starting to squirm now, "Hey, if you guys help me get out, I'll pay you a lot of money, I'll even promote you to vice presidents. What do you say?"

I looked at Brian with disgust on my face and nodded at the guy, "I'm sorry, but we tender our resignations, ass hat." With that, Brian broke the man's neck and laid him in the shower stall. "You want to do the honors?"

I nodded yes and grabbed my trusty bent spike. I squished through the eye and made brain pudding. We both walked back into the office and lowered ourselves onto the leather couch by the door. We were both lost in our own thoughts.

"So, what the fuck do we do now?" I asked.

"I've got no idea, Boss, I'm out of ideas. We have nothing to take downstairs to share as a win like we'd set out to do. We did find Lisa, but that does not have a happy ending," Brian intoned.

"We could go up to the forty-eighth floor. It's a much smaller floor plan, has a nice conference room looking over the entire bay and it has access to the roof wings on the sides of the building." I got up and started rifling through the guy's desk and pulled out an LED flashlight that I turned on to be greeted with a bright light. I also picked up the gun and ammo and handed them to Brian, then headed over to the wet bar set, "What's your poison?"

"Scotch, bourbon, and whiskey, in that order." He gave me a smile and started checking out the gun. He chambered a round, then dropped the magazine from the magwell to top it off and now he was loaded and ready. He got up and retrieved the empty magazine off the floor by the desk and the one in the bathroom he had noticed after ending the man's misery. He reloaded each one and put them next to him and the gun on the couch.

I handed him a large bottle filled with an amber liquid. "That's Macallan 1939, it's like forty years old and priced around $10,000 a bottle. I guess I will be drinking fine tonight. What did you find?" Brian said appraising the bottle of amber liquid.

"I have no idea; it says Taylor Fladgate 1965 single harvest port. Sounds good, oh and I found these." I held up four big cigars with rings that proudly announced Cohibas.

"Hell, yeah! That's what I'm saying." He smiled wide and reached out for the cigars.

I handed him two and put mine in my breast pocket. I went back and grabbed the hurricane lighter from the bar. "I wonder what this fucker was eating."

Brian got up and starting going through the desk and cabinets, "I found a small bag of jelly beans and a box of crackers."

"It's only been like thirty hours, Brian. Maybe, he was just drinking alcohol. That would explain why he wasn't thinking right," I suggested.

"I'm not going to drink or spend any more time in here. Let's move back to the other office. There is less blood and corpses in there. You can have the executive chair in there, I'm taking this guy's throne chair." He got up, walked over and placed his gun, ammo, scotch, and cigars on the chair. He lifted it over the bodies and then wheeled it out of the office.

I just stood there and watched him go. I grabbed my bottle, the bag of jelly beans and crackers and followed him to the other office. I placed my newly found treasures on the desk, turned around and shut the door, locking it before taking a seat on the leather chair by the window. "I figured you never know, right? If I get drunk, I don't want to worry about someone coming in to eat me."

I took the foil off the top of the bottle and sat staring at a cork. Brian started laughing at me, then reached into his pocket and took the cork screw out of his pocket and flipped me off. I threw a pen at him, that he dodged easily. "I figured you would need it." He pulled the cork out of my bottle, then his and took a healthy swig.

I sat on my chair, lit my cigar and put my feet on the desk. Took a puff, a big swig on my bottle of port and let all the day's stress go. I looked over and saw Brian mimicking me.

"So Brian, I never got a chance to know you very much till today. Did you join the military right out of high school?" I eyed him over my cigar.

Brian took another couple of puffs off his cigar and a big swig from his scotch. "I usually don't talk much about my life." He took another puff and stared at me for a hard five count. "My father was in the forces and we moved a lot. I was always getting in trouble because I was always the new kid. So, my mom took me out of public school and home schooled me, instead. I studied and learned more than I ever would have at school. When dad came home from work, he would take me out shooting and took me to the base gym. He said other kids joined sports to stay in shape, so dad had me lifting weights and running with him. By the time I was thirteen, I was running five miles a day keeping up with the old man. At seventeen, I had enough credits to graduate from homeschooling. I refused to take the SATs and instead, had Dad sign a letter allowing me to join the Marines a year early."

He stopped his story and took another big hit off his bottle and cigar. I could see a little glazing covering his eyes. "Since Dad trained me in military history, tactics, guns and physical training, I sailed through boot camp. Afterwards, I joined my platoon and was pretty much immediately shipped out to Iraq. I trained with my team and did some things, was involved in some firefights. I came home, was promoted, given my own fire team and was sent out to Afghanistan. While there, we climbed through a bunch of mountains, explored some tunnels, shot some people, and got shot at. When I came home, I took some college courses and got my Bachelor's in Project Management. I was tired of being shot at so I got my discharge, came here to San Fran and got this job. I know, not much detail. I really don't like talking about my time over there." He took some more puffs of cigar and drank more of the bottle.

I sat back and thought about what he'd said. "So, you are really only like twenty-six or twenty-seven?"

"I'm twenty-six, you are correct. I tend to read a lot and am pretty fast at learning." He smiled and took another big swig of the bottle.

I had been taking drinks off the bottle of port and puffing on my cigar. I was starting to feel very warm and had that wonderful buzz going on. I wasn't a person who liked to talk about himself, so I gave Brian a quick edited rundown of myself, "You told me, so I'll tell you. My dad worked for Lockheed and did some classified stuff there. Mom was the perfect mom who also worked at MCI when they were still relevant as a telecommunications company. I have a brother and a sister who are both professionals and don't live here. While in college, mom died of cancer and that's when I took her advice and changed my life. I used to be kind of a party guy and didn't really have a direction. So I buckled down, got my degrees and well, I work here. I never served and never even thought about serving. Never been married or even thought of it. All I do is work. Dad lives up in Spokane, so I have no family here."

I took a big swig of my port and puffed more on my cigar, enjoying the taste and smoke. Brian opened the crackers and jelly beans and we enjoyed our feast. Seemed that our pairing of alcohol and food worked just fine. We told stories and jokes and laughed. Just at the edge of our conversation was our situation, which sat like a pregnant hippo. The last time I looked at the clock on the desk, it showed 8pm.

I woke up with a headache and my eyes hurting. The office was bright and I felt stiff. I looked over and saw Brian holding his bottle of scotch like a teddy bear, lying back on his chair and snoring so loudly, I thought the windows were going to break. I got to my feet and bent over, trying to stretch and knuckle out the knots in my back.

"You are not a pretty sight to wake up to, man. I feel like something shit in my mouth," Brian had a grimace on his face as he stretched back on his chair.

I continued to stretch and work out the aches I had gained from sleeping in the chair. Brian finally gained his feet and was doing stretches, getting limbered up. "I think I need to take a leak, you coming? I think wandering alone around this place is a stupid idea."

"Yeah, I need to piss like a race horse, grab your bat. If it's ok though, I'd rather not use that private bathroom next door. The dead guy might spoil the mood," I suggested.

"I totally agree, man." He grabbed his bat and walked to the door.

I was looking at his arm as we walked to the door, his wound seemed to have stopped bleeding at some point. "That looks a little better," I said pointing at his arm.

"It feels a little better, but I am bringing the rest of scotch as a rudimentary antiseptic. I have more gauze in my pocket to give it a fresh bandage." He opened the door and stuck his bat into the hallway. Then his head came out as he looked around. "All clear, let's hurry though, before I end up pissing in my pants." He walked away with the bat on his shoulder looking even more like a major baseball player.

I followed in his wake, nursing my new and improved migraine. I only got hangovers from fricking wine, so I guess that's what the port was made out of then. I massaged my neck with my free hand then thought better of it, since I was walking with my head down. We got to the office that had been locked the day before and glanced inside. The place was a blood bath; there was blood on the walls and window and some even on the ceiling. I walked in to look around; all of a sudden, having to pee was just not a high priority anymore.

I found three dead men and one woman, well dead as in being in pieces. The woman had the most damage to her body, her pelvis and abdomen were basically eaten down to the bone. Her spine and hips could be seen, half of her chest and most of her face had also been eaten. The three men had their faces, chest, and abdomen also eaten through to their spine. These four just didn't have much left on them to be mobile enough to be part of the attack yesterday. I had forgotten my spike, so I took my bat and bashed in the head of the male zombie, who was trying to crawl toward me. I looked over and Brian had used his bat to take out one of the other men. I turned toward the woman and watched as Brian moved towards the last male. We took them out quickly.

"Looks like they were trying to hide in here, but one of them must've been bit. You ever notice how some are really slow while others move very fast? I think it has to do with how badly they are messed up. At least, I'm hoping that's it. I really don't want to worry about too many of them being fast and strong. Now, can we please go take that piss?" He walked out the door without checking to see if I was coming.

I followed him as fast as my aching back would allow. We got to the lobby doors and found one side open all the way. "Wow, I must've been in a hurry yesterday because I never secured them. Whoops."

"I think the floor was secure, so no harm no foul," Brian said as he took off jogging toward the bathroom.

I got there and opened the door just as it was closing. I could hear Brian already relieving himself, so I stood there holding the door open, keeping watch on the hallway.

"Oh, that feels so much better." He finished up and came towards the door. "If you can wait a second, I'll go grab something to prop the door open."

I nodded my agreement and did the pee pee dance while waiting for Brian to come back. Finally, after what'd felt like ages, Brian appeared with another rubber door stopper from the lobby and shoved it under the bathroom door to keep it open. Once he did, I ran to the urinals and barely got my zipper down in time. I reached out to flush and Brian interrupted me, "Just in case we only have a limited amount of water pressure left, let's use it for cleaning up and drinking."

I zipped up and moved towards the sinks. Brian handed me a nice clean white cotton towel. I looked at him questioning. "While I was grabbing the stopper, I ran to that guy's private bathroom and grabbed these towels that I'd seen yesterday."

I turned on the faucet and was rewarded with some water. I quickly whipped my shirt off and splashed water on my chest, arms, face and neck. I pumped at the soap dispenser and worked up a lather on my exposed skin. I quickly rinsed off and cupped my hands to drink my fill of water. The water felt great going down my throat. I filled my belly and then put my shirt into the sink and using some soap, started washing it. I looked over and saw Brian had his shirt off and was doing the same things. His chest, stomach, and arm muscles bulged as he worked, along with thick scars on his stomach and back.

"Dude, put your shirt back on, you're making me feel very self-conscious," I said while wringing my shirt out. I was thinking of doing my underwear next, sweaty unwashed undies are gross.

"Not my fault you are a girlie man. You are so pale I could use you as a way to reflect the sun the next time we enter a dark room. Now shut up and clean your crap," he laughed and finished wringing out his shirt.

He took the bottle of scotch opened it and took a small drink. He removed his bandaging and looked in the mirror at his wound. It looked encrusted, but in certain places was still oozing blood. Brian took the bottle and while holding his arm over the sink poured some of the scotch onto his wound. He hissed and gritted his teeth, "Holy shit, that'll wake you up in the morning. Also a great hangover cure." I shook my head at him. He added more antibiotic cream to it and then dug the rest of the gauze and tape from his pocket and bandaged it back up.

"You are crazy. You know that, right?" I walked away and popped into a stall where I removed my pants and underwear, then popped my pants back on commando style. I exited and went to the sink to wash my boxers. Brian eyed me and started laughing, "You a little shy dropping trow in front of other men, Boss? How did you shower in high school?" He laughed while taking off his pants.

"Oh man, now you are gonna make me cry, Brian. I don't think we are this close, man." I averted my eyes to concentrate on washing my boxers.

Brian chuckled as he stood there, buck ass naked washing his boxers and pants in the sink. I just kept my eyes on my chore. "You are a giant idiot, Boss. Do what I did, use the towel to cover yourself, unless you like dirty bloody pants." I looked over and that was exactly what he had done. My pants most definitely looked like they had seen better days. I took them off and covered myself with the towel and started washing my pants as well.

I was amazed the water was still on and said so to Brian. "Might be nobody else using the water. Since the pressure was built up, we might be good a little while longer. But drink as much as you can. Never know when we will find more."

I finished washing my pants and wrung them out and then drank my fill again of water. I wished I had something to eat, though. Brian gathered his clothes and started to walk away.

"Where are you going, big man?"

"Going to hang my clothes by the nearest window and hope they dry a little before I put them back on," he said over his shoulder.

I hurriedly grabbed my possessions and jogged to keep up. I could feel my towel trying to slip, so I had to grab and hold onto it while also holding onto everything and jog. Finally, I found Brian in the lobby, laying his stuff out on the couches. I followed his lead and watched amazed as he walked over and unlocked and rotated the two lobby windows open. "I didn't know they did that!" I said amazed.

He gave me a strange look and shook his head, "How do you think they clean the windows? The slope outside is too sharp for them to use the sleds or swings." He laughed at my expense again.

"Oh, cool," was all I could manage to say as I laid my clothes out.

The open window allowed the sun and breeze to dry our clothes. We went back to the office we were using as our temporary home. I sat behind the desk in my chair and Brian did the same in his chair.

"I think we need to plan out our next steps," I said.

"I've been thinking about that. Since we have already moved up one floor, why don't we go through each floor one by one upward, till we hit the top. Then, we can either go downward or stay up there, depending what we find," he concluded munching on a couple of crackers we had left.

I took a couple crackers also and just stared at them as I spoke, "I can agree with that plan. Hopefully, we'll get lucky and find some food for Matt and his merry band of office dwellers." I crunched away on my breakfast. We sat in silence for the next twenty minutes or so, lost in thought of happier times.

"As soon as our clothes are dry, we will go ahead and move up to the next floor. We have the gun and our baseball bats. I wish we had a new way to gouge out eyes and mush the brains, though. I don't want to use the gun unless it is absolutely necessary, since we have a limited number of bullets," Brian concluded chewing on more crackers.

"I've got a great idea. Follow me." I jumped out of my chair and grabbed my towel before it could fall to the floor. I rushed to the door and down the hallway back towards the elevator lobby. To the right of the elevators, before you reached the stairway, was a narrow door that was the same color as the wall. I used my keys and opened it. Inside was the janitor's closet full of chemicals, brooms, and mops. I grabbed a broom and handed it to Brian, "If you can break this in half, we'll have two new spikes and then we can break the mop and have another two as reserves."

Brian looked at me for a second, then flexed and broke the broom in half leaving jagged edges. "Sometimes, Boss, you surprise me with your imagination."

I reached in and pulled out a roll of silver duct tape and smiled. Brian reached behind me and pulled the mop out. Easily, he snapped this in half, put the mop side against the wall and using his bare foot, kicked the mop head off. I handed him the broom side and he did the same for that. We made our way back over to the clothes and I sat in one of the lobby chairs and started using the tape to wind the smooth ends of the spikes, so we would have a better grip.

Brian checked the dryness of the clothes. "Hey, your underwear is dry." He threw my boxers and they landed on my head. I laughed and tugged my boxers on under my towel. Brian laughed, dropped his towel and slid his boxers on. "You are such a prude, boss. The rest of the clothes are just damp, but I think we need to put them on and get moving before we lose our light."

I put my new weapons and tape down and followed suit pulling on my clothes and shoes. The pants were a little damp, but the shirt was fine. Brian got all his clothes back on and his shoes tied. "I'll be right back. I'm going to go grab our supplies and stuff. Why don't you finish taping these up?"

"No problem, and grab more alcohol from the bar and while you're at it, look for more cigars."

I sat and folded the towel, thinking of how I could bring it with me on our trip upstairs. I looked down the hallway and here came Brian pushing his executive chair with all our supplies on it. He got to me and smiled, "I found backpacks in that guy's office that we'd missed. Guess what is in them?" He threw a black one at my stomach, knocking the air out of me. Quickly, I unzipped the bag and looked inside. It was packed with protein bars and dried fruit and beef jerky. Pumping my fist in the air, I asked, "Where was he hiding these?"

"I decided to check under the bar for more liquor and found these two shoved behind some empty bottles of liquor. I think we need to make some room in the bags for some of our other supplies. Mainly the alcohol and these." He picked up a small box off his chair and opened it, displaying a full box of the Cohibas we had smoked last night.

"Ok, so I think we need to divide all this up to fit all of our stuff in the bags." I up ended the bag, spilling its contents onto the couch. At the bottom of the bag was a small first aid kit. I picked it up and threw it at Brian. "Might want to keep this close, just in case you get bit or shot again," I laughed.

He gave me a blank look and dumped his bag out on the couch. He looked through the contents and started sorting it out, putting everything together into small piles. I sighed, mostly because he had not reacted to my little bit of sarcasm.

We worked quickly and had all the food in small sorted piles. I did the inventory and came up with twenty-five small bags of Jerky with a couple of pieces inside each, forty-five protein bars and sixty small bags of assorted dried fruit. We also had two small first aid kits. For alcohol, we had a quarter of a bottle of scotch, two full bottles of some tequila I had never heard of, another bottle of port from the night before and lastly, a bottle of vodka. Our weapon inventory was four spikes, two baseball bats and one gun with twenty-one bullets. We both shared a package of jerky, snapped a protein bar in half, and devoured a package of dried fruit each.

"This is the best I have felt in a while. You ready to get moving?" Brian asked.

I tucked my spikes into my belt and shouldered my bat. I slung my bag onto my back and cinched it tight. I stared down at the leftover straps hanging and walked over to the receptionist's desk, digging around in her drawer to find a pair of scissors. I came back and I cut the excess strap because I didn't want to leave anything that some dead fuck could grab onto. I handed the scissors to Brian and he did the same. Brian tucked the extra magazines into his pocket and the gun into the right side of his waistband.

Chapter 14

Brian untied the fire hose from the stairway door. I reached out towards the door handle and waited for Brian to give me the go signal. He looked at me, gave me a nod, and I opened the door while holding out my bat, but it was all clear. Brian took lead and flipped on the little LED flashlight we had found. He narrowed the light to a tight, narrow beam. I put my hand on his right shoulder so he'd know where I was at all times. We slowly took the first three steps and stopped for a second. Brian shook his head and kept moving upward. Every time Brian's foot left a stair, I replaced it with one of mine. We made it to the first landing and I found I was stretching my senses to their limits, trying to hear, feel, or see something coming our way. Brian stopped again and I looked forward where the small beam of light lit up a dead unmoving body. So much of it had been consumed that there was not much was left. We gave the body as much room as we could and we skirted by. The next set of stairs went quicker and easier. The next landing was empty, but I squeezed Brian's shoulder when I heard something below us.

"I think something is below us, following us slowly. I hear a thump and a scrape every once in a while," I whispered in Brian's ear, "shine the light slowly this way."

Brian did as I'd asked and after a lifetime of waiting, the flashlight lit up a zombie missing its legs and slowly pulling itself up each step. It had no lower jaw and that could've been why it had never moaned or made any other noise. I looked closer at the zombie and recognized him as a member of my team who had run out the door earlier yesterday. It was Sam, someone who had been with us for three years. I remembered he had just gotten married and was waiting for his first child. I removed one of my spikes and held it tightly in my right hand while keeping the bat in my left. I used the bat to roll the body over and hold it down as I shoved my new spike through its eye, pulping its brain to mush. I wiped the spike on the body's leftover remnants of clothes and shook my head in shame.

Brian turned the flashlight back up to the door in front of us. He reached out and slowly opened the door. He looked both ways and signaled for me to move inside. I did and moved to the left. This floor was much smaller, since the building was built like a pyramid. This floor and the rest above us did not belong to my company, so I had never visited them before. I did know, by working in the building for a while, that these floors were occupied by the building's management team. Brian closed the door behind us and used the firehose trick to secure it.

Brian came up beside me and surveyed our immediate area. He

proceeded down the short hall to our left and together, we cleared the bathrooms using the flashlight. We had not come upon anything so far. We turned at the end of the hall and came back toward the elevator lobby and moved around the receptionist desk. The big glass doors in front of us were wide open. So far, everything seemed to be in place, with no damage or signs of a rushing evacuation.

We made our way down the hallway, checking off empty offices. Only five offices were located on this floor, but they were slightly larger than the ones on our floor. Each office had its doors wide open. We entered every office and found each one empty. We looked at each other, hoping the other might know what had happened to the people and why this floor was untouched.

"Not much here, Boss. Why don't we go ahead and move up to the next floor? We've found no supplies to add to our bounty or weapons. The phones are dead here, too."

"Let's go." I followed Brian back to the stairway door and untied the fire hose. Brian gave me the flashlight so this time, I could take the lead. The stairway had stayed the way we'd left it, with the one twice-dead zombie. We moved quickly up to the next level, running into nothing; no zombies, no bodies and no signs of anything.

At the next door, I unlatched it and pulled the door open. Brian stepped in quickly, keeping his bat in front of him. Suddenly, he stopped and then, slowly took a half step back. He waved at me to come forward. We both stood there at the doorway and saw that the entire floor had been upended and the floor was littered with bodies. I swept the light over the bodies and made a quick count. "Eight dead bodies, Brian. I don't see any head damage and I really don't want to stay on this floor. I have no idea what has happened and I don't want to know."

Chapter 15

Reynolds interrupted my story and took out another file. "Which floor was that?" He made a note on his file and waited for my answer.

"Forty-fifth floor."

He wrote down something and leafed through the file. His eyebrow went up as he read on. "According to this file, we found twenty-five bodies on that floor. The lobby alone had eight bodies, six in the women's bathroom and the rest scattered through the offices. I don't have a report from the morgue yet, but preliminaries showed lots of what were labeled as bites and some even had no outside damage on them. We believe they died from the flu. We think that whoever did the killing made it off that floor."

The door opened and a uniformed officer came in. He handed over some files and a note on yellow legal paper. Reynold's read it and studied the officer. "Has this been verified?" The officer looked at him, then at me. "You can answer my questions in front of Mr. Welko, it's ok."

"We've been having problems all day keeping in contact with the morgue. Now, when we call, no one is answering. The night Sergeant has sent two cars over, but they are having problems getting through the crowded streets. We're not sure if it's a protest. The Captain has sent out the riot squad and hopefully, we will have some answers soon." The officer looked harried and kept looking towards the door.

"Let the night Sargent know to keep me updated the second any more information comes in." Reynolds started going through the folders he'd just been handed. The officer looked like he wanted to salute but instead, nodded towards me and left the room.

Reynolds ignored me for a bit while he continued to leaf through the files. Finally, he tossed them all on the table, removed his glasses and massaged the bridge of his nose. He grabbed our coffee cups and refilled them again. Taking a long sip, he made a sour face and finally looked at me squarely in the face.

"These reports have some strange facts and some have glaring inaccuracies. The more we delve into your story, and with these new reports being delivered, I find you to be not just believable, but truthful so far. I also have an inkling that by this time tomorrow, we might have some pressing issues going on in this town," he stated.

"I truly believe that by morning, the entire police force is going to be overwhelmed and this city will be close to falling if you guys don't start being proactive." I stared straight into Reynolds' eyes and made sure he saw I was not joking around. "If I could ask for a favor?"

"Go ahead and I'll see what I can do," Reynolds answered.

"If Brian is stable, can we get him moved here? I think he can back my story and to tell you the truth, we have been through so much that I would feel better if he was nearby," I asked almost embarrassed.

Reynolds stared at me for a while, reached out and grabbed his cellphone off of the table and made a call. "Hey, Tony. Are you and Cheryl still on protection duty for Mr. Leeder?" He listened for a second, "Is he stable? Oh wow, he's doing that good, and asking about Mr. Welko? Do me a favor, pop him into your car and bring him here. Do not go by Folsom Street, looks like the riot police have been called out and the streets are packed with people. Great, thanks!"

"Thank you, Detective Reynolds," I smiled at him warmly.

"Don't thank me yet, just continue. Do you really think the city is in trouble?"

I thought the best way to answer his question would be to continue.

Chapter 16

Brian and I backed up into the stairway, closing the door and turned on our flashlight to make our way up the stairway towards the next floor. Brian took lead again and I followed him. No bodies or zombies blocked our way, but I kept hearing sounds behind us. We got to the door, opened it, and I watched the stairway, while Brian stepped in and surveyed the area to ensure our safety. He reached out and tapped my shoulder. I stepped in backwards and closed the door. Brian handed me the hose and I secured the door like before. I turned around and took in the scene.

The lobby was empty and pristine, not a single body part lying about. We turned left together and headed down the hallway to the restrooms. I entered the women's bathroom while Brian held up the LED, bouncing the light off the mirrors. I looked to the far end and saw a body on the floor. I walked over and rolled it over with my foot. Then, I stepped back quickly as I examined the woman, I saw no wound to her body, I waited a couple of seconds. The eyes opened and a moan escaped the throat. I didn't know why I was hesitating. I lifted my spike as if my arm was fighting syrup. I aimed for the eye and right before I'd delivered the killing blow, she spoke, "Please." The voice was hoarse and quiet. I stepped back and looked over at Brian.

"Did she just say something?" Brian inquired, as surprised as I was.

I put my spike back in my belt and knelt down closer, "Speak again, prove you are human or I will finish you." I made sure my body was prepared to move, in case she lashed out at me.

"Please, I need help. Don't hurt me," she said in a voice full of concern and lack of any energy.

"Have you been bitten?" I asked her, preparing to take her out if she answered yes.

"No, not bitten, I've been really sick," she croaked out.

I stood up and moved back and thanked God I hadn't gotten too close. I walked over and cupped my hand under the sink, filling it up with water and came back to dribble some water into her mouth without touching her. I retreated back to Brian, "I don't know what to do. If she has the flu, then she is going to die and come back as those things and then we'll just have to kill her anyway." I was ashamed of myself for considering terminating her life, but it might be the only right thing I could do.

Brian made his way over toward the girl, "Ma'am, my name is Brian and I need to ask you a couple of questions. I will try my best to keep them brief, but I need the truth so I'll know how to help you. If you understand, nod." She nodded. Brian turned to me, "Find a cup. We need to get her some more water so she can talk. Be careful, be slow, and watch before you do anything."

I left the bathroom and made my way back towards the receptionist desk in the main lobby. It seemed to me that most of these desk occupants were people who would keep a water bottle or coffee cup near them at all times. Success! There was a full, unopened bottle of water, so I snatched it off the desk and headed back to the bathroom.

As I entered the bathroom, I witnessed Brian getting off the floor and wiping his spike on some paper towels. He had a deeply sad look on his face. "Her name was Olivia. She had flown back on the same plane as Marco, they were actually boyfriend and girlfriend. I thought I'd recognized her from the picture on his desk, but I had to make sure." He walked over to the sinks and ran some water over the spike. He toweled it dry and inserted it back into his belt.

I leaned against the bathroom door, suddenly feeling even more exhausted. "You did the right thing. Let's clear the rest of this floor and then find a place to hunker down. This has been such a long day and the sun is starting to set."

Brian agreed and we cleared the next restroom and made our way to the set of offices occupying this floor. We found only one zombie and he was in the first office we came to. Brian hit it with the bat and held it down, while I dispatched it by spike. We found a little bit of snack food here and there and some warm soda in a mini fridge under the desk of the big office. While Brian explored the office, I checked the suite bathroom and found it empty.

When I came back into the office, Brian had shed all his gear and had secured the door. I walked over to the desk and laid my backpack and weapons on it. I looked longingly at the two couches and saw Brian was, too. I ignored the larger one and collapsed on the shorter one, "Since you are a moose, you might as well take the bigger one."

Brian chuckled more than the joke warranted. He walked over and laid down on the couch, letting go of a deep sigh. He looked over at our supplies and sighed again. I got the point and went and retrieved the liquor. I brought him his scotch and I decided to sip vodka tonight, instead of the port. Brian smiled wide when I handed him his bottle.

"Much obliged, Boss, much obliged." He pulled the cork out with his teeth and spit it across the room, took a huge gulp and looked to be in heaven. I could see he was hurting, but not from his physical wounds. What he'd had to do to Olivia was heavy on his mind. I sat there watching him while I sipped from the vodka. "Whatever is on your mind, just spill it, Boss. No reason to dance, we've gone through too much together to worry about hurt feelings," he looked over at me, winked and then closed his eyes.

"I just want to make sure you are ok, big man. Something like that stains the soul. I know you killed in the war and you've killed zombies. But she was alive and her only crime was getting the flu. I'm hurting, so I know you are hurting," I said not trying to sugar coat it too much.

"Dan." Brian got my attention right away with that. He had never called me by my name, it was always 'Boss'. I looked over to him and gave him my full attention. Brian opened his eyes and I could see the unshed tears watering his eyes. "This is hurting me, you are right. But not for what you are thinking. I killed her cause she would've died and then would've come after us and I could not let that happen. The reason I am hurt, is because she and Marco had gone back east to celebrate their engagement.

Such a happy occasion but instead, they came back sick and Marco turned and killed Lisa. Olivia did nothing wrong, but now she will never experience the rest of her life, by Marco's side. The disease took that away from her and I took her life, but I did it to give her peace and respect." He drank a deeper gulp of his scotch and let a couple of tears flow down his cheeks.

"I get that, Brian. I do. But you did what was right and what happened to them was no one's fault. I would've ended her life also." Although, I was secretly relieved that Brian had put her to rest because I don't know if I could actually have done it. I took a large gulp of my vodka which burned terribly going down my throat, but once it reached my stomach it became a warm glow. I could feel the alcohol flood through my system.

"You ever fall in love, Boss?" Brian asked now just sipping his scotch.

"Just once, Brian. I met her my first year in college. Her name was Julie, and she and I spent all our time together. I had planned to go to Europe with her that summer. Then, my mom died and I didn't feel like the same guy anymore. At the funeral, I told Julie that I needed some time alone. I'm sure she'd felt like I was rejecting her, but she'd said that no matter how long it took, she would wait for me. I'm sure she has moved on by now, probably a great career, married and has kids. But some nights when I am alone, I think about her and wonder if she is still waiting. There has never been another for me and I miss her, man. That was close to ten years ago," I choked up, but covered it by taking a slow sip of vodka. "How about you, Brian?"

"I didn't tell you why I left the military, right?"

I shook my head no and he smiled, "Well, they found out that I am a homosexual and I was pulled aside by a pretty high officer. He gave me the choice to be discharged from the service honorably, or be outed and probably leave the corps in shame. I chose honorably. I'd like to think that the guys I'd fought alongside wouldn't have cared a rat's ass about my sexuality, but I didn't want my parents to find out. Hell, I even dated a woman for while in my late teens, so I could hide who I really was. I'm no pansy and can fight with the best of them, which kinda scares guys away. There was one guy I'd met in the corps and we'd spent some special time together. Turned out, that he was so afraid of what would've happened to his career if others found out, that he reported me. So, I guess you could say that I loved him so much, that I fell on my sword and moved on with my life. I've been out on some dates, but none are him." He finished the scotch and belched.

I handed over my bottle of vodka and we shared taking drinks off of it. "I'm not sure how to read you, Boss. I mean, I just told you I was gay and you've said nothing." He passed the bottle back to me.

I weighed his words while taking a bigger then normal sip. "Honestly, Brian? I couldn't give a shit if you're gay or not. You have saved my ass so many times and I feel like we could be brothers. So you being gay has nothing to do with anything. I'm not going to cuddle with you, but honestly like I said, you have become my brother." I looked over and Brian was sitting up on the couch staring right at me. "Dude, if you're planning on kissing me, I wouldn't. That would be incest and I will scream rape," I said with a smile.

Brian reached his hand out to me and I put the bottle down and grasped it. "I would be honored to call you my brother. Don't worry, I don't find you attractive at all. I like muscular, outdoors kind of guys," he winked at me and let my hand go. "Now, if you don't mind, I'm going to fucking sleep. Stay on your couch and do not even think about trying to take advantage of me." He rolled over and was almost instantly asleep.

I took a couple more drinks from the vodka bottle and then put my feet up on the far couch arm, laid back, and drifted off to sleep. I dreamt again of that night. This time, I was walking along Folsom Street, having to fight my way through a crowd, full of all kinds of people. I tried to focus on faces, but they were blurred. I could hear people chanting something that got louder and louder, almost hurting my ears. I couldn't hear the words, but it was now so loud and the people were becoming more and more crazy. I had to push and pull through the people to make it to the side of the street. I saw a parked car and made my way to it. I climbed up onto the hood, then onto the roof. I stood erect and could now see above the heads of the crowd. I focused on the front of the crowd and saw police cars and fire trucks. A row of riot guards stood there with shields and their shiny armor.

Abruptly, the crowd surged forward and the riot police took two steps back and went to their knees. The fire engines had their nozzles pointed at the crowd and let loose with a torrent of water, knocking down the front ranks. Now, I heard screaming coming from the back of the crowd. Not screaming to get attention, but screaming like people were being tortured. I turned and looked that way, but I had to try to refocus because I can't really be seeing what I think I am seeing. The crowd is going down in clumps by zombies biting, gouging, and tearing into them. With zombies in the rear and police in the front, this was turning into a slaughter fast. I was hollering till my throat turned raw, pleading to the cops to let the people escape.

The zombies were up near the car I was standing on, yet they paid me no heed. They kept attacking other people. Something else was happening, something terrible and made no sense, like zombies made sense, I know. The people they had attacked in the beginning were already getting back up and joining the zombies in attacking the others. I watched men, women, and children being torn to pieces and eaten. I tried closing my eyes, but they wouldn't respond. I heard my name being screamed above the din. I searched for the source and found it had come from a little girl, standing next to the car. It was the same little girl from my dream before; dressed the same and with the same hairdo. She looked into my eyes with a desperate pleading look. I dropped to my knees, grabbed her arms and lifted her off the ground. I held her in my arms, turning her head into my shoulder, shielding her from the scene going on around us.

She was sobbing into my shoulder, begging me to promise to protect her. Begging me to find her and protect her, to make that promise. I found my voice, and looked down to her angelic face and made my solemn vow to find her and protect her till the day I died.

I felt someone grabbing my foot and shaking it. I looked down, but no one was there touching me. Yet my foot kept being yanked off of the car and shaken. I was confused over what was going on. I looked down at the little girl and she was gone, but I heard someone yelling my name, a man's voice this time. A deep, grumbling man's voice.

I awoke with a start, sitting straight up on the couch. Brian kept his distance, but kept his hand on my foot. This time though, he held it firm instead of shaking it. "Boss, it's morning and let me tell you, you must've been having some horrendous nightmare, man. You were screaming and kicking. You ok?"

Most dreams leave me like smoke dissipating into the surroundings, but these dreams I've been having lately have been holding on like memories, instead of subconscious thoughts. I looked at Brian and shook my head to clear it. My heart was pumping so hard it felt like it would break my ribs. "Yeah, I'm ok, man. These nightmares are kicking my ass." I stood and walked to the bathroom and relieved myself. Then, stopped at the sink and took a whore's bath. What more can you ask for; A rag, some soap, and a sink of water. I came out cleaner then I'd gone in and smelled a slight bit better, too.

Brian had already repacked his gear, but had left out a small amount of food for our breakfast. I sat down and put on my shoes, tying them up tight. I really wished I had worn sneakers, instead of these damn dress shoes. I walked over to the desk and geared up. I sat on the desk and ate my jerky, protein bar, and dried fruit in silence.

"I want to push all the way to the top, today. If we can get there by this afternoon, then let's head down to our floor so we can get this food to Matt and his team," Brian informed me.

"I agree. So what are we waiting for? Let's rock and roll. That is a military saying, right? I'm trying to act all tough and manly, so you'll feel comfortable around this stupid, girly civilian," I said with a smile.

Brian moaned, grunted, and walked away down the hall toward the lobby. I laughed out loud, grabbed my baseball bat and shouldered it, jogging off to keep up.

I met him at the door. "Alright, you get the door. I'll clear first, then you take rear guard. No more dumb jokes or I'll kick your ass," he admonished. But I could tell he wasn't mad.

I untied the door and opened it quickly. As the door swung open, a red-haired, female zombie, missing her shirt with her chest covered in bites fell through, but before she could make it across the threshold, Brian had pushed her back with the bat and followed her into the stairway. I made sure the flashlight was shining on them to provide Brian with illumination. Brian pushed her back further, gaining some ground then swung his bat going for a homerun. He crushed in her head, then placed his right foot on her chest and pushed her backwards down the stairs. I made sure the light shone down the stairway and then up. We were clear. Brian backed up to me, and I placed my hand on his shoulder and we worked our way up. No other attacks came. The black 47 on the wall, let us know we were almost to the top. We quickly cleared the next floor with no surprises. The floor was under construction, bare concrete on the floors and plastic sheeting as walls. No tools were present, but there were buckets of dry wall mud and paint.

Chapter 17

We left the floor and made our way up the last flight of stairs to the forty-eighth floor. Before we got to the top, I heard scratching and thumping. Brian took each of the last steps glacially slow. When we got to the top, we found two zombies, both males. One was missing an arm, but the other looked untouched. Brian pointed to the armless one and then pointed at me. He pointed to the other and then to himself. Now I knew which one to go all Babe Ruth on. We moved side by side to our victims. I lined up for a hell of a hit on the zombie. Brian brought his bat down off his shoulders and gave me the go ahead motion. I pulled the bat back and then let out a low whistle. Both zombies turned their heads towards me. I swung with all my strength and made contact with the middle of the zombie's face, hitting him in the nose and eyes. His head made a cracking sound and he dropped to the floor.

Brian was so quick that the second my zombie dropped, Brian had swung with his zombie's head all but disintegrating into a haze of black fluid. We both stepped back and waited to see if they were truly dead, again.

Neither moved, so I grabbed the leg of the zombie I'd killed and dragged his body over to the wall away from the door. Brian's zombie had been pushed back from the force of Brian's hit, so I didn't have to move him. We tested the door handle and it was locked. We hadn't expected that.

"What the fuck?" I said aloud.

Brian knocked out, *'shave and a haircut, two bits'* on the door and stood back and waited with his massive arms crossed. I was shaking my head in the negative about to say we should move on, when the door handle moved and the door creaked open a touch. The person tried to shut the door and Brian moved in quick and popped the door open with his left shoulder. I came in right behind him and shut the door quickly. Finding a chair that had been used to wedge under the door thus keeping it closed, I used it for the same reason and effectively locked the door.

Brian was standing in front of someone lying on the ground. It was a woman, blonde and dressed in a rumpled skirt suit. Her hair was a mess and she looked scared out of her mind. I guess a guy and a bear wielding baseball bats would scare anyone.

"Who, who are you? Are you going to kill me?" she said in a high voice and started crawling backwards towards the windows.

"No one is here to hurt you. My name is Brian, this is Dan. We have been looking for supplies since we left our floor on forty-two. Have you been bitten or are you sick?"

"No. I've been here since Tuesday, um my name is Magdalene, but I go by Maggie. I was setting up the conference room for a big meeting when I got locked in here. When the stairway door unlocked itself, I tried to take the stairway but heard a lot of screaming. I looked down and saw a bunch of people being attacked. Blood was everywhere. I gasped out loud when I heard a door slam and then, those two things chased me back upstairs. When I got back up here, I secured the door. I've been here all this time living off a cart of food that'd been sent here for the meeting. It's all moldy and stale now."

I reached into Brian's pack and removed a protein bar. I showed it to her and then tossed it to the floor in front of her. She grabbed it, ripped the wrapper off and devoured it in what seemed like one fluid motion. Brian pointed at me and then gestured to the room. I got the idea and started walking around, checking the supply closet and the two small bathrooms which, unlike the other floors had windows in them, so I didn't need the flashlight. Everything seemed clear and I came back to alert Brian to the fact. I found him down on his haunches talking to the young woman. I moved to my left and glanced at his hands, but I found no weapon in them. I could hear him talking to her in quiet tones.

"You are ok, now. We have other survivors on the forty-second floor. Dan and I can take you down there and then you'll have other people to be around. We have a little bit of food that we are going to take to them down there. What do you say, Maggie?" Brian spoke in a calm voice and was holding her hands, making sure to keep eye contact.

Maggie looked us both over and nodded her head, "I would like that a lot."

"Great to hear, are you strong enough to walk?" I asked.

With Brian's help, she was able to stand up. She looked a little shaky at first, but firmed up. I smiled at her and handed her one of my spikes. "I always feel stronger and more calm when I know I control my own destiny. You take this and stay in between us. I may ask you to step over and gouge out the eyes of the zombie we have to put down. You push hard and don't stop till you feel a pop, then move the stick around, pulp that brain to mush. Make sure not to get any of the fluids on you. Wipe off the stick on their clothing, if possible."

She held the spike tight to her chest, smiled and nodded to me. I could tell she'd taken in every word and would obey if asked.

"Alright, let's get going. I will be in front. Maggie, stay behind me and put your hand on my left shoulder so I'll know where you are at all times. Dan will be behind you and he'll hold your right shoulder. If something attacks from behind, Dan will take care of it. If something attacks from the front, I will handle it. If we get overwhelmed, I want you to run back upstairs and wait for us to come get you. You also have an important job. Here is our flashlight. Make sure you light up the front at all times, unless Dan tells you to check behind us. You understand?" Brian lectured.

Maggie nodded yes and he smiled at her. I walked to the door and pulled the chair out and caught Brian's eye. He winked at me and lifted his bat so he could use it to push a zombie back if needed. I pulled open the door and stood back. Maggie walked over, put her hand on Brian's left shoulder and shined the light around him, since he was too tall for her to shine it over his shoulder. I took her right shoulder in my grasp and held my bat at the ready. The landing was clear, so we started moving down the stairs, pausing on every landing and listening for any movement or sound. We did not need to tell Maggie how important it was to be as quiet as possible.

We went past landing after landing, floor after floor, without running into anything. We stopped just above our floor. Brian motioned for me to come up next to him, "Something isn't right. There is a dim light down there."

I shook my head, "I wonder if someone left the floor door open. How do you want to handle this?" I was getting antsy, wanting to rush to our people.

"We need to secure that floor. We have no idea if something is in there or not. Ok, we all go in together. I don't want Maggie to go upstairs. She needs to stay with us," Brian whispered in my ear. He then turned around and spoke to Maggie quietly, "We think something is wrong here. The door to our floor seems to be open. We don't know what's going on, but we need to get back in there. We are all going to go inside, then secure the door and sweep the floor of any zombies. You stay between us at all times unless we say otherwise. Got it?"

Her eyes got enormous and you could smell the fear coming off of her. But she bit it down and steeled herself to follow us. We got back into position and made our way to the forty-second floor and yes, the door was wide open. Blood was smeared on the inside of the door. Brian entered first, then Maggie, and once I'd entered, I shut the door quickly and Brian handed me the firehose. I tied it off and checked to make sure the door was secure.

I stepped up behind Maggie and looked over the lobby as Brian headed down towards the bathrooms. The lobby didn't look that bad and the doors were still locked and secured from what I could see. I turned and caught up to our little team. I squeezed Maggie's shoulder to let her know I was there. We popped into the women's bathroom and checked each stall; we were clear. We backtracked out and did the same for the men's. It was also clear.

We came out back into the hallway and made our way to the conference room. The shades were up and we could not believe what we saw. The room was a mess. The table was upended and the chairs were thrown about in a tangle with blood coating two of the walls. Brian shook his head and then made a bee line to his office. We found it empty and entered. "This is what is going to happen. Maggie, you will stay in here while we clear this floor. I want you to lock that door and keep it locked until we come back and alert you that everything is ok."

"Yeah, no problem. I'll stay here," Maggie said in a stronger voice than what I was expecting from her. I gave her a pat on the shoulder and walked back into the hallway. Brian gave her a little reassuring hug and stepped out to me. She shut the door and we heard the lock engage.

Brian motioned towards the lunch room and we entered, finding another mess. All of the chairs and tables had been thrown around, but the room contained no zombies or bodies of any kind. We checked the cubes and found them all to be empty. "I guess we need to stop dilly-dallying and go check out the conference room."

We walked back and opened the rear door, stepping into the chaos of the conference room. I spied two bodies right away and nudged Brian. He nodded his head, assuring me he'd seen them. We both moved towards the windows and found another two bodies that had been torn to pieces. They were missing skin and muscle. Brian's shoulders slumped as he reached into his belt for his spikes. "I got these two. Just wait and we will do the next two together," he said in a soft voice soaked in pain.

He made it to the two bodies and pushed them back with his foot. I identified the two as Robert Pagano, and Sarah Condish. They both had worked in my department. Brian took a spike in each hand and drove one into each of the bodies at the same time. I could tell it hurt him because it hurt me. These were our co-workers, people we had celebrated holidays, birthdays, and good times with. I know what you're thinking. We'd already killed three of our own, but two of them were already monsters and Lisa had made her own decision, which had caused so much pain.

We walked over together to the other two. I didn't recognize the black male, who was covered in blood from his face down his chest and onto his hands and arms. He was not one of my people and I was sure he hadn't worked for our company. The other was Sherry Aguilar, one of our accountants and estimators. She had bites on her face and left arm. We spiked them both with no problems. I stood there studying the two bodies. After a full five minutes, I walked back to the other two and examined them as well.

"What's up, Boss?" Brian asked.

I pointed to the two in front of the window, "I think they were attacked first and torn to pieces. Sherry must've come in while the new guy was attacking them. She then tried to pull him off of them and he started biting her. What I really don't get is why was that black guy not trying to attack us when we came in? Where's the rest of our group?"

"Good eye, Boss. I was thinking the same thing. No scenario I can come up with makes any sense to me. Let's go clear the rest of the floor. Maybe we will figure it out later." Brian motioned to the hallway.

We left the room and continued down the hallway towards the lobby. I took my keys out and unlocked one of the doors. Brian stood in front of me and entered first. I followed and left the door slightly open, so we could get out in a hurry if needed.

We looked over the cubes from where we stood and saw that they were clear. We made it down toward my office at the end and checked the printer alcove. I walked to my office door and waited for Brian to take position next to me. I opened the door and Brian entered quickly, scanning the room.

I walked in after him and went right for my desk. A sheet of paper was sitting there that I had not left. I picked it up and read it. My heart sank and I felt sick to my stomach. I handed the letter off to Brian.

I watched him read it, his shoulders slumped and it looked like he lost some of his hope. He dropped the letter onto my desk and sat heavily in one of the chairs. I put my bat on the desk and dropped into my own chair.

The note read:

Guys, we've waited two days but have not heard from you. Some of the group think you have abandoned us. They have taken a vote and have decided to take our chances on the stairway. I've decided to go with them, since I am responsible for them. Sarah, Sherry and Robert have decided to stay behind. They are afraid to leave and believe you will be back soon. We took in a guy named Gary who was pounding on the door last night. We thought it was you. He says he came from the 41st floor. There is something wrong about him, he just doesn't seem right. Anyway, I know you two will come back for us. I just wanted to tell you where we went and hopefully you will follow. I tried my best to lead them Dan, but they had no trust in you like I do.

Matt

Chapter 18

I picked up the letter and held on to it. I didn't know what to do or say, so I sat there staring at the wall behind Brian. I felt numb, our entire sacrifice meant nothing. "So Brian, what do we do now?" I asked.

Brian stared out the window behind me, a haunted look in his eyes. He ran his hands through his hair, tilted his head back, closed his eyes, and sighed deeply. "That is an easy answer, the easiest ever. We get our butts together and go find our people. We know they didn't go up, so there is only one way to go."

I looked at the clock on my desk. It was 1 pm with plenty of light left. "Well, shall we go find out if Maggie wants to come with us?" I stood up, grabbed my supplies and headed out of the office. Brian was close on my heels. We sped our way back to Brian's old office and Maggie's new hideout.

Brian knocked on the door and said out loud, "Maggie, it's us. Everything is clear, open up." The door opened and Maggie peeked around the door. I waved at her and she smiled and came out of the office.

"Did you find everyone?" she said with hope in her voice.

I tapped Brian on the back, giving him the job to tell her what was up. I walked down the hallway to the bathroom. The door wedge was on the floor, so I used it to jam the door open for light. I went into the far stall, sat down and took care of business. I finished and came out of the stall. Brian was at the urinal taking care of his business. I took off my shirt and started taking my prerequisite whore's bath, which I was becoming good at. Brian came up and started using a sink two over from me. I ignored him while I washed up, but stopped when something caught my attention.

Maggie had come out of one of the stalls and was standing next to me, stripped to her bra and doing the same as I. "Hope you don't mind, but I am not letting you guys out of my sight anymore. So, look if you have to, but deal with it." She continued to splash water on her face and neck and moved to the soap.

I laughed hard and looked over to Brian, "Hey Brian, do you have a problem with this?"

He stopped what he was doing, looked over at me and shook his head. "Hmm. Let me think. A beautiful woman is shirtless in nothing but a flimsy, lacey, red bra. Yeah, I am offended. Please stop," he retorted sarcastically, then started laughing so hard that he had to bend over to catch his breath. "I've already seen Dan naked so yeah, feel free to do what you need to do, girl."

Maggie looked at us both and shook her head in confusion, "You two have been friends a long time, I guess?"

"Nope. He used to work for me and we never really spoke much. I guess all this has pushed us together. Now, I can't get him to stop following me around," I said with a smile. Brian groaned and just continued washing up. Maggie and I laughed at Brian's expense.

We all finished and got our gear together. Maggie dropped her suit jacket on the counter and took her high heels off. "I don't need the jacket, and those shoes are gonna kill me on the stairs. I wish I had some tennis shoes right about now."

"I know Sherry has tennis shoes on, but do you really want to wear a dead person's shoes?" I caught her eye when I spoke.

"No thanks, I'm good. I'd rather walk on broken glass infected with Ebola," she said seriously.

We gathered at the stairway door and Brian explained how we were gonna stack up the same again, move slow, and pay attention. He gave Maggie some batteries and she replaced them in the flashlight. She still had her spike and seemed ready to go. I untied the hose and prepared to open the door. Brian stepped up, getting his bat ready. I yanked the door open and stepped back. Maggie quickly moved back and Brian advanced into the stairway.

He raised his hand to show we were clear. Maggie moved quickly behind Brian, took his shoulder and positioned her light. I stepped behind her and took her right shoulder. We took the first flight down and ran into what I imagined hell would look like. The stairs and walls were coated in dried and in some places, sticky blood. Twelve bodies were lying on the ground, bodies almost entirely stripped of skin and muscle. We walked around and took in the next flight of stairs. I detached from Maggie, climbed back up the stairs, took my spike and started destroying the brains of the people I thought were my co-workers. I could feel tears falling down my cheeks and running down my neck, coating my shirt.

Brian waited until I was finished and we continued downward toward the door of the forty-first floor. Brian stepped aside and took the other side of the door and motioned for Maggie to open the door. She reached out and took the handle, it was slick with blood. Maggie though, proved to not be squeamish one bit. She unlatched the door and opened it quickly, stepping back to allow Brian and I to enter. I stepped to the right and Brian to the left. Maggie stepped in behind me and shut the door.

"Movement left. Stay with Maggie and secure that door." Maggie grabbed the fire hose and handed it off to me. I tied it around the door and went back to the wheel and tied it off there. Maggie watched the entire time and I could tell that she was taking in everything and learning. I moved down the hallway towards where Brian had gone. I stopped and waited, I had no idea if he'd gone into the bathroom or somewhere else. I put my hand out and Maggie stopped and put her hand on my shoulder, squeezing it lightly.

Brian popped out from a cubicle area and gave us the hold sign. He jogged back down the hallway, "I took three out in the cube farm. We need to clear the bathrooms and the conference room next door."

We took our positions at the door of the women's bathroom. Maggie reached out and opened the door wide. Brian and I stepped in and took turns checking under stalls. The bathroom was clear so we moved on and repeated the process with the men's restroom. In the last stall, I saw a pair of feet. I checked the ground around it, but didn't see any blood or movement. I signaled to Brian and he raised his bat. I kicked at the side of the door about where the latch was, the door burst open and I stepped back quickly. Brian stepped forward and waited, the body never moved. Using his bat, Brian poked the body in the chest but again, nothing. Brian then tapped it on the head with the bat, this time the head moved slightly.

"I'm not sure what's going on here. Could he just be sick?" Brian walked backwards toward me.

I squeezed past Brian and by using my bat, held the chest in place. I reached out to the neck and Brian's bat appeared, pushing the head back and holding it in place. I put my fingers to the neck searching for a pulse. I thought I'd found one, but it was very faint. I also noticed the heat radiating off it.

I stepped back to Brian, "I think this one has the fever and is not long for this life. I'm not sure what the right move is."

Brian took his spike out and looked at me. I took it and moved in closer while Brian reached out with his bat and tipped the head back again. I got my fear in place, set the spike closer and just as I was about to push in, the body began to shake. "Hurry! It's happening."

The spike disappeared out of my hand and a big meaty hand grabbed my shoulder, pushing me back hard. I could hear the crunch and squishing sound as Brian did what was necessary. I moved past him and made a bee line for the sinks. I turned on the cold water and started splashing my face. I tried to control my breathing but the room started moving on me. I ran and made it to one of the stalls just in time to see the precious amount of food that was in my stomach pouring into the toilet. I collapsed to my knees and worked hard at catching my breath. I sat there for what seemed an eternity, dry heaving, shoulders hitching.

I felt a hand on my back, and could tell it was not Brian's. A paper towel was handed over my shoulder. I grabbed it and pressed it to my face. "You're gonna be fine. Come on, let's go clean you up." She put her hands under my shoulders and helped me keep my balance. I washed my face and gargled some water trying to clean out my mouth. I opened my eyes and felt a ton better.

I turned off the water ,turned around and leaned against the sink. I looked around and noticed that Maggie and I were alone. "Where's Brian?"

"He told me to take care of you and went to clear the floor. How are you feeling, hun?" She had concern etched on her face.

"That person still had a heartbeat and I've never killed a living person. Something inside me just wouldn't let me do it."

"I'm glad you still have that reaction. Brian's had to kill people while in the Marines but you have never had to, so this proves you have not become jaded." She wrapped her arms around me and gave me a reassuring hug. This was not a sexual hug, but a hug to help me calm down. She stepped back and looked me in the eyes. "Feeling better?" she asked.

"A lot, thank you for being here for me," I said blushing, a little embarrassed. "By the way, when did you find out Brian was a Marine?"

"He told me during our little conversation, while you were getting me some water."

I walked toward the door and noticed Brian had used our handy rubber stopper to keep the door open. I picked it up and secured it in my pocket. I shouldered my bat and moved out into the hallway with Maggie hot on my heels. We headed towards the lobby and Brian came around the corner. We stopped and waited for him. He came up and put his hand on my shoulder. "You ok, Boss?" concern etched on his face.

I gave a weak smile, "Yeah, I'm good to go. Sorry about that."

Brian gave me a frown and hugged my shoulders with his giant python-like arm. "No need to apologize. I told you I'd always have your back. This floor is clear, but found no supplies. We still have sunlight, so let's move on." I nodded and we moved on to the door. Maggie opened the door and fell back as always and this time, I took lead on the landing. It was clear. Brian came up on me looked around and shook his head, "Should we try and go all the way down or skip a couple of floors and go to thirty-five while we have a chance?"

"Let's skip some floors and go to thirty-five. We've been locked in this building way too long and I want out faster," I answered and Maggie agreed.

We took our positions and slowly made our way down the stairs. As we came upon bodies, we pulped their brains to give us security. Maggie made a point that she needed to help more and took a couple herself. On her first one, Brian stood guard and I walked her through the process.

She was reluctant at first but sucked up the will and shoved home the spike. I told her to push harder, and she leaned into it till she felt something give way. She stirred her weapon and then pulled it out, wiping it on the remaining clothes of the dead body. I noticed she didn't show any emotion, but this had to have eaten a little part of her soul. I know because my soul seemed a little bruised from the things I'd had to do. I patted her shoulder and gave her a thumbs up.

She gave a little smile and we moved on. We ignored most floors and continued to move on. We had yet to run into anything alive or a zombie trying to attack us. Once we'd got to the thirty-fifth floor, we stacked up and prepared to enter.

Maggie walked up and took the latch, but it would not open. Brian then reached out and gave it a shot, "Locked up tight. Let's move on."

Floors 34, 33, and 32 were also locked up tight. I checked my watch and noticed it was getting late and the dark would be encroaching soon, making it difficult to clear floors.

"It's getting late and we may need to move on faster. Floor clearing is about to become a lot harder with just a flashlight." Brian grunted his agreement and we picked up the speed to the 31st floor. Brian reached out and the door latch moved.

He opened the door quickly and moved in. We were lucky that this floor was also under construction. We piled in and secured the door quickly and cleared the space. Which was not hard to do, since it had just been demolished and only one wall was left standing. There was a man's urinal only with no concealment.

"Well, a girl's gotta do what a girl's gotta do. Why don't you fellas go first?" Brian and I took care of business and walked away to give Maggie some privacy.

We found a stack of sheetrock on the floor and a couple of bags of insulation. We moved them around to make our new little haven just that much more comfortable. Maggie came back looking a little sheepish. She sat down on our new little nest and gave us a smile, "So, what do you think we should do next?"

I opened my bag and handed out some food to everyone. Brian

disappeared and came back with a case of bottled water. "Found this when we first came in. Union rules for construction says water has to be present on job sites."

Maggie grabbed one and drained half of it quickly. We all sat down and rested our weapons in a pile nearby. Brian put the gun down and I was shocked, I had forgotten that we had it. "You guys have a gun? Why aren't you using it? It's gotta be easier than using these spikes and bats," Maggie inquired.

Brian smiled at her, "A gun is very loud and would be like a zombie dinner bell. Plus, we only have twenty-one bullets, so we don't have that much."

Maggie blushed, "Yeah ok, I got it. Sorry, I'm not really into guns."

I burst out laughing and punched her lightly in the shoulder. "Maggie, after what you have done, I would not call you a little girl. You got that Linda Hamilton from the Terminator kinda thing going on," I said as a compliment and she took it as what it was.

She raised her arms and showed off her biceps, "I do work out and I am a blonde."

Brian laughed and shook his head at us. It was getting dark fast, and as soon as we'd finished our meal, we each found a place in our nest to bed down. We turned the flashlight off to save the batteries. I used my backpack as a lumpy, crappy pillow and soon was sound asleep.

This time I didn't dream. I was very grateful to say the least. When I woke up, Brian and Maggie were both fast asleep. I rose and found my way to the urinal. I relieved myself and walked over to a window near our nest. I placed my head against the window and watched the city below. From our floor, I could see more of the street finally. It was covered in rescue and police vehicles. Hope blossomed in my chest.

I ran back over and tapped Brian's foot. He came awake instantly. He looked over at me, questions in his eyes. I motioned for him to follow me. He did and we made our way to the windows. I pointed down. His eyes widened and the biggest smile I have ever seen lit his face.

"Holy fuck! That is what I was hoping to see. Should we wake Maggie and show her?"

A voice made us both jump slightly. "Show me what?" A sweet melodious voice came out of the dark.

I walked over and took her hand and led her to the windows. I pointed down and she cupped her hands on the window looking to the direction I indicated. "Oh god, finally!" She jumped up and down doing a little happy dance.

"We're not saved yet. We have no idea how long the responders have been here already, or how long it will take them to get to us," Brian informed her. No matter what he'd said, Maggie kept hanging onto her joy and hope. I, on the other hand, agreed with Brian. Why hadn't they made contact? What kind of roadblocks were they facing? Too many questions, not enough answers.

"Let's go sit down and have something to eat and drink. Maybe we can keep going down until we run into help," I suggested and hurried everyone over to the nest we had built.

We all ate breakfast and enjoyed some more water. We stayed quiet and in our own heads until Brian spoke up, "So, what does the group want to do? Stay put and hope we get rescued soon, or get our shit together and rescue ourselves?"

The sun had just broken the horizon and its rays started shining onto the floor.

Chapter 19

Reynolds stopped me at that point of my story, "You keep talking about this person, Maggie, but I have nothing in my files or reports about her. What happened to her?"

I stayed quiet for a bit, staring at the table with unshed tears coming to my eyes. "That is in my story. I'm getting to it. Can you tell me though, what's the status of Brian?"

Reynolds picked up his cellphone and made another call. "What's your ETA with Mr. Leeder?" Reynolds listened for a while and got a thoughtful look on his face. "Understood. Swing west, then north and get here. Run the sirens." He turned off the cell and placed it on the table. "Another twenty minutes or so. The streets are becoming hard to drive on. Seems this riot on Folsom may be growing and spilling out on to other streets. This is sounding eerily like one of your dreams. Let's just hope it doesn't end the same way." He looked at me over his glasses.

"I am afraid all of this is going to get worse and worse." I looked Reynolds in the eye and asked the question that was on my mind, "If this does happen, the way I'm sure it's going to happen, do you have any plans to get us out of here? Or do Brian and I need to find our own way out of this city, as it falls down around our ears?"

Reynolds did what he always did when I confronted him. He put all of his stuff on the table, took off his glasses, rubbed the bridge of his nose and closed his eyes. "Dan, I don't have an answer for you right now. But if things go down, I will do what I can to help."

"Like weapons?" I pushed.

"I'm not supposed to give out weapons to civilians, but if things get as bad as you say, we will look into it then." Reynolds stared at me for a while making me uncomfortable.

Chapter 20

"My choice is to keep making our way to rescue. If they have been here for a while and still haven't gotten to us, I suggest we keep going," I drank some water and looked over our little party.

"I'm new to this group so I will follow you guys, but it seems safe here on this floor and we could just hang tough," she said and hid her look behind her water bottle.

We both looked over to Brian. "You know how I feel. The sun is up, so let's stop being lazy little rotten crotch Susie's and get a move on." He stood and geared up.

While I geared up, Maggie took off to the urinal to take care of business. I stretched out my back and shoulders and met Brian's eyes. He said a lot with that look. I saw fear, something I hadn't seen before. "What's bugging you, big man?" I asked.

"The more we go down, the more we are going to run into zombies and maybe other people. That means something could go wrong. Just keep a sharp eye out and let's move slowly," he answered before Maggie came back.

She walked up and I whistled out loud and smiled. She had wet and brushed her hair out using her fingers and with a piece of string she'd found, had put it up in a ponytail. She was also wearing a pair of old work boots she must've found, which looked silly since she was still wearing a blue skirt that rested just above her knees.

"Thank you, Dan. I'll take that as a compliment. Oh, and someone here has small feet like mine, so I have new boots!" she kissed my cheek and giggled.

I shook my head and started towards the door. Maggie caught up to me and showed me her new weapon to add to her spike. It was a big iron claw hammer.

"Now I can go all smashie on these things, too," she winked and stepped back. I shook my head and rolled my eyes at her.

We lined up and I opened the door and Brian shot past me into the stairway. A zombie male had been standing right there and was about to take a bite out of me before I could even react. Brian booted it in its chest so hard, it flew back and landed on the stairs going up. Brian moved quickly and bashed its head in easily using his handy bat.

I stepped out and guarded the down stairs access and waited for Brian to come over so we could form up. Maggie snapped on her light and Brian took my position as I stepped to the back. Maggie moved in front of me and we took our assigned shoulders. We moved down the stairs a little faster than I thought was smart. We walked through another killing ground and we all took our time to take out the fifteen dead bodies. Maggie even took a couple out by herself.

We reformed and worked our way further down the stairs. We stopped in front of the door on the next floor. Brian put his back to the wall and brought us in so we could talk quietly, "I say we keep going as fast and as far as we can, thirty more floors. I say we stop on the twentieth and see if we can take a break there."

I nodded yes and Maggie shrugged her shoulders saying sure. We reformed and walked further down. When we arrived on the twenty-fifth floor, I could hear growling and moaning coming from below us. I reached forward and tapped Brian. He nodded his head, agreeing with my unspoken word. We went to the door on that floor and made our way into the offices.

We cleared the lobby, but the floorplan looked so different than the rest we had visited. No lobby doors and it looked like a cube farm with maybe two offices at the far end. Time to change our rules of clearing the floor. 'This has got to be a call center,' I thought. Brian stood tall and could see over the first couple of rows of cubes. "I'm going to take the left side. You and Maggie go over to the right side by the windows and clear that area. We can meet up over there, by the offices. The doors are closed, so let's assume someone or thing is in there."

Maggie and I nodded our understanding and Brian cut left, walking away from us. I gestured Maggie to get behind me. I walked to the right and walked down the last aisle. I stopped in mid-step and whispered to Maggie, "I'm going to be looking down the rows. I want you to keep looking forward, so you can warn me if something comes at us." She squeezed my shoulder in understanding.

Each row we went past, I stopped and paused for a second to verify nothing was on the floor or hiding under the desks. We would then move on and cleared each one the same. We came to the middle row and I put a hand out to stop Maggie. There was a body lying on the ground, face down in a puddle of blood. I made my way over slowly and when reaching the body, poked it in the head with my bat. It was a woman in a short black skirt and a tan tank top. She didn't move or twitch. I stuck my bat under and tried to roll her over, but was having a hard time moving her. I dropped my shoulders, handed my bat to Maggie and reached down to grab the woman by her shoulders and slowly roll her over. Her eyes popped open and a scream exploded from her open mouth. She reached up quick and grabbed my shoulders, trying to pull me down to her mouth. I couldn't grab my weapons and knew I wasn't strong enough to fight back. Suddenly, a spike appeared and jammed into the zombie's eye. I closed my mouth and eyes and turned my head to stop any fluids from getting in my face. Suddenly, the zombie let go and fell back to the floor. I reached down and pulled the bottom of my polo shirt up and wiped the side of my face clear of any fluids. Immediately, a bottle of water was being poured down my face.

"Thank you, but you need to make sure we are ok. I got this." There was a sweater on the back of the chair and I used it to clean my face completely. I looked down and saw the zombie was missing its nose and one cheek.

Once my face was completely cleaned, I stood and took my bat back from Maggie. I nodded my thanks and Maggie offered me a beaming smile. So, lesson learned, no rolling bodies over. Just go all bashie on the head with the bat. We slowly started walking again down the aisle. I looked up and saw Brian was way ahead of us. Everything else was clear and we met up with Brian who was leaning against a wall.

"How many did you have to take out?" he asked while staring at my face.

Maggie spoke up, "Just one. It sprayed all over Dan's face when I staked it, so he had to get all cleaned up. How about you, big boy?"

Brian shook his head over his new nickname. "Only two. One must've had screwed up legs because it couldn't stand, so I kicked it on its back while I was dealing with it. Then, another came out from a desk nearby. Not too hard. Let's take this office first."

Maggie stepped aside to watch our backs while Brian and I went in quickly. There were two clawing at the window. We got closer and Brian whistled out loud. They both turned towards him as I came in from behind one and knocked it over the head as hard as I could. It went to the floor and I finished it off with another swing. I got back up and saw Brian holding the thing by the back of the neck. He swung it around and shoved a spike into its eye and pulped its brain. He looked over and winked at me.

"Keep that up, Brian and I'm going to get all sweet on you," I winked back.

"I told you, I don't find you attractive," Brian laughed out loud.

Maggie popped her head in, "Are you hitting on poor Dan again,

Brian? He's mine, so don't mess with him or I'll kick your ass." She smiled and blew a kiss at me. I caught the kiss and planted it on my cheek.

"I'm going to throw up!" Brian walked out of the office and toward the next one.

I followed him out. We cleared the next office quickly, finding it empty. "How about the lunch room?" Maggie asked inquisitively.

"I already cleared it out before we moved onto the offices," Brian answered.

We walked over to the windows and looked down at the streets. "Looks like more emergency vehicles," Maggie informed us.

I walked away to the lobby and sat on one of the two couches, stretching my legs out, but coming up short of being able to rest my legs on a nearby table. Brian came over, plopped down next to me and stretched his legs out, he was able to reach the table easily, resting his feet on it. I know he did that on purpose to put me in my place. "You're an ass hat, anyone ever tell you that?" I said to him.

He chuckled and thumped me on the chest. Oh man, that hurt. I think he bruised my sternum, but I wasn't going to complain out loud. Maggie came over and plopped on her own couch. Tucking her legs under her, like only girls can do. "So, what are we going to do now?"

"Well, I am thinking of heading out to the stairs alone to check out what is going on. A little recon, I guess you could say. But first, we never checked the bathrooms, so let's do that now." Brian stood up reached down and grabbed my shirt and lifted me to my feet, "Stop being lazy. Let's get this done." He made me feel like a toddler every time he did something like that.

Maggie jumped off the couch turning on her flashlight. We entered the women's first and cleared it quick since it was empty. The men's had one male zombie on the ground trying to get up, once our light shined on it. I walked up and swung my bat as hard as I could. The head smashed in, came off and hit the stall door. "Homerun!" Brian called out.

"Uhm, guys? I need to tinkle, but I am not using this potty. Let's go into the women's. I told you I wasn't doing anything alone," she walked away and entered the bathroom next door. Brian looked at me and shook his head.

We followed her in and used our own stalls. "Yeah, toilet paper!" Maggie yelled out and whooped.

I smiled and finished my business, came out and went to the sinks. I washed my hands and face. Brian appeared next to me smiling, "At least one of us seems happy over little things." He washed his hands and started cleaning his bat and spikes, I followed suit.

Maggie came out all smiles and came up to the sink. "I have to do something kinda gross, sorry." She tossed her black satin panties into the sink and started washing them with soap and water. Brian and I started to laugh.

"We did that a day or so ago. So, no problem," commented Brian.

"Yeah, Brian was upset his lacy, pink, thong was becoming brown and not pretty anymore." I laughed and jumped backward fast, just missing Brian's outstretched hand as it flew by. With how fast it went by, I felt like if it had been able to connect, I would've ended with a broken rib or ribs.

135

Maggie laughed, then ran back into her stall. "You would look sexy in those I'm sure, Brian," she yelled.

I left Brian and Maggie in the bathroom to finish what they needed to do. I made my way over to the lobby and dragged the table closer to the couch to use as a footstool. I sat on the couch again and stretched out, propping my feet up. Man, that felt good. Brian and Maggie came out laughing over some comment or joke I never did hear. Maggie plopped down next to me, and stretched her legs out onto the table and smiled up at me. Brian grabbed his weapons, the flashlight, and geared up.

"Well, you two look like you need some time alone. I'm going to go do that recon I'd talked about. Someone keep an eye on that door and open it quickly when I pound on it." He walked over, untied the door and disappeared.

I looked over at Maggie, as she rested her head on my shoulder. "Just need a place to rest?" I asked.

"Something like that," she purred and snuggled in.

After ten minutes, I started getting worried over Brian and excused myself from Maggie and the couch. I grabbed my bat and stood over by the door. We had never retied it. Another three minutes crawled by. I would wait another five, then go looking for him. Two passed and someone tapped on the door. I opened it quickly and Brian stormed in, slamming the door behind him. As he retied our little security lock, I looked him over for any new damage. He looked whole and ok, except dirty and a little more tired.

"I don't know if we can go any further, there's forty or so crammed in the stairway. We need to stay here for a bit and wait to see. Hopefully, they'll disperse."

"I have an idea," Maggie said raising her hand.

"What's that, kiddo?" Brian asked.

"Two ideas kinda opposite of each other. First, we could light some garbage cans on fire and throw them down the stairway. Maybe we can burn them out."

"No good. The smoke would come up here and choke us to death. But I like the way you are thinking," I said.

"So, the other is with water. We have a fire hose. Why don't we crank it up and stand on the top stair and shoot them down further? The pressure should be really strong," she added.

"Now that's an idea I can get behind. Blonde, brains and beauty, the whole trifecta," Brian answered.

Maggie stood there and smiled wickedly, batting her eyes at us. "And so much more," she said biting her bottom lip and staring at me.

"Well, you know me. Let's just get to it. No reasons to stand around with our fingers up our asses," Brian said.

"You'd like that though," I said jokingly.

Brian even broke out in laughter. "Now, that is a good one!" He pounded my back with the flat of his hand.

Chapter 21

He untied the hose from the wheel and screwed it back onto the spigot. He handed me the gun. "No way, man. You take the gun. I've never fired one before. I'll take the hose and Maggie can take my bat." Brian stood there staring at me for a while.

"Okay, it's a plan, grab the hose, I got the gun. Maggie, grab Dan's bat and spikes. You are going to have to protect his rear."

She jumped off the couch and ran over, grabbed my spikes and bat, then kissed my cheek. "I'll cover your ass, don't worry," she winked at me.

Brian opened the door and was stunned to see four zombies on the landing. Maggie cranked the water and I opened the hose nozzle. The water came out so fast that I almost lost my grip on it. I fought with it, just in time to bring the water down and directed at them. The water pressure blew them off the steps and down to the next landing. I followed the bodies close behind and Brian pulled the hose all the way out so I could move freely.

I kept the water on them pushing them further and further as I descended the stairs. I finally hit the full crowd pushing them into each other, and then down they went too. I kept moving and at some point, was on my own. Brian was further back and I couldn't concentrate on what was happening back there. I heard the gun go off and was stunned. I tried re-climbing the stairs to get back to the group. The pressure was so strong, I had a problem keeping my feet under me as it was pushing me back. I finally made it to our landing and saw Brian carrying Maggie back into the offices. I turned off the nozzle and followed them in. I shut the door and ran over to turn off the water shut off valve. Finally, I had to empty the hose so I could bend it. After another minute, I was able to tie it at the wheel and at the door latch to secure the door.

I turned to Brian and found him holding Maggie down on the ground. I ran over and fell to the floor on my knees next to them. I looked over Maggie and saw blood pouring from her stomach. I ran and gathered napkins from the bathroom and came running back. Brian was sitting back on his ass with tears running down his face.

"What the hell happened? Is she?" Tears started pouring down my face and I started having problems breathing.

"While you were moving down the stairs, I was covering your butt. Maggie must not have been paying attention to the upper stairs, I heard a scream and turned in time to watch three zombies tackle her to the ground and start tearing at her. I pulled my gun and shot all three in the head, but then I slipped on the water while trying to lift her and hit my back on the stairs. When you looked back, I had finally gotten her up and was pulling her into the offices when you started coming back. They did so much damage. I can't fix this. They tore her belly open and I…..." he stopped and just stared at Maggie's lifeless body.

"Oh fuck. Oh fuck. Oh fuck." I reached over to Brian and took his hands, so I could clean them of Maggie's blood using all of the napkins I'd had in my hands. I then pulled him close and hugged him. We both sat like that for a while, just holding on to each other.

Weak moments happen to the best of us and even though we had been surviving in a living nightmare; to lose the one person we had actually saved was devastating to us. I stood up wobbly and went into one of the back offices, leaving Brian to watch over Maggie. When I came back, I noticed Brian had taken care of making sure that Maggie would not come back as one of those monsters. I gave him a weak smile of thanks for his thoughtfulness. Using a full length overcoat, I had seen earlier. I draped it over Maggie to give her peace. I said a few words over her and started gathering my weapons.

"What are you doing, Boss?" Brian asked in a whisper, instead of his cock-sure voice.

"To do what we had originally planned. I'm sick and tired of being locked up in this place, afraid and never knowing when our end is coming. I'm taking all of that into my own hands. I will find a way out of here. You coming?" I headed toward the door.

Brian came up next to me and patted me on the back. "Let's do this thing then," he stated.

"We will use the water again. You need to cover me though, and make sure to not get killed. If the water pressure dies, maybe we can get down another floor, at least," I planned out.

I untied the hose from the door latch and the wheel. Then, I spun the wheel, bringing our pressure to full on the hose. Brian opened the door quickly and I opened the nozzle and shot a full stream over the landing. Nothing was there, but I kept it up anyway. I walked towards the stairs and started making my way down. I still hadn't run into any of the zombies, but I kept advancing. We made it to the next floor and I figured I had enough hose to go for one more. Where had all the zombies gone? They had been packed in the stairway tightly. We kept going and I thought I knew where they had gone. The door at the next floor landing was open. I ran out of hose at this point, so I turned off the nozzle and turned to Brian.

"I bet if we move fast, we can make it to the bottom," I said.

"Finally, we can get out of here," he said with relief written on his face.

We heard screaming coming from the open door. I didn't even think, I grabbed my bat that I had stuck into the straps of my pack and headed for the door. I felt Brian next to me and knew he had his gun ready.

We made entry and immediately turned and secured the door. We made our way into the lobby and stayed on alert for more screams. We heard someone yelling and we took off in that direction. We found at least twenty zombies trying to break into an office. Brian used six quick shots from his gun and took a zombie out with each one. He then replaced the magazine with a new one, stuck it into his waistband and we waded into the crowd using our bats to make room. I had just caved in a third zombie's head and my arms felt like Jell-O, but I wasn't going to stop, I hit another one that was fresher and I didn't crack the skull. I grabbed a spike off my belt and shoved it home into the zombie's eye and pulled it back out as it fell to the ground. I noticed the zombies had turned their attention to us, so I moved back making them come to me, giving my poor arms a rest. I saw Brian had knocked down six and was copying my withdrawal method.

We only had four left, thank god because I didn't know how much longer I could keep this up. I watched as three came my way and only one turned to Brian. Fuck me, they must be able to sense I was the weaker prey. Just then, I thought about Maggie lying dead upstairs. I felt a surge of anger swell up inside me and I roared in anger and moved forward. I booted the first zombie in the chest, knocking it down to the ground. As the next one reached out, I swung for the fences and its head came apart like a piñata at a Mexican birthday, but instead of candy and prizes, bits of bones, brains and that black shit came exploding out. I sidestepped the one on the floor and shoved the last one against the wall. I came down hard to my knees, using the momentum to crush the Zombie's head on the floor to mush with the bat.

I pushed myself to my feet and went after the last one again. My vision was turning red from anger. I yelled out every obscenity I could think of and went at it as hard as I could. Next thing I knew, Brian was pulling me back. I had taken the zombie down to the ground bashing its head on the floor with my hands. Its head was a mass of fluid, bits of hair, and broken bone. It had ripped the bottom of my polo shirt and my pants were soiled with blood and fluids. I was breathing heavily and my vision was slowly coming back, the red crimson subsiding.

"Boss, you ok?" Brian asked quietly.

"Yeah, sorry man. I just went a little crazy for a second." I lowered my head and continued to try and catch my breath.

I looked up and saw the office door opening. Three people came out, all male and all with bites in various places. I sunk to the floor onto my knees with a sinking feeling, Brian just sighed lifted the gun and shot all three in the head. Really, what else could he have done? We had just done all that we could and yet, were still too late and there was nothing more we could do to help in the end.

Brian grabbed me by my arm, helping me to stand up. I really felt pathetic and worn out, exhausted beyond belief. My body was hurting, my emotions felt grated and raw and my eyes were red and bloodshot. "Let's start moving out of here and head down again," he pushed.

I grabbed my bat and followed him to the door where we

unsecured it and headed down the stairway. It was clear, so we moved quickly but on automatic, like robots. Before I knew it, we'd hit the fifth floor. So close to getting out of here.

Out of nowhere, we had lights shined in our faces and someone was screaming at us. Brian took the gun out of his waistband and as he was dropping it to the floor someone hit him from behind, where he fell and bounced his head off the floor going unconscious. I was kicked in the back of my knees and forced to my stomach, onto the ground while lying there, being flex cuffed, I looked over at Brian. He was lying in a pool of blood. I nearly lost it and started fighting against the two holding me down. Right then, I felt electricity explode through my system, all my muscles froze up and my head felt like it was going to explode. I stopped fighting and went limp.

Chapter 22

"You know what came next, so now you know my story from beginning to end and how things happened. I understand why the officers did what they did, but we were the victims, not the aggressors." I looked at Reynolds and gave him a sad smile. "The question, I guess, is if you believe me. If the reports, files, and facts you have, jive with what I've just told you." I sat back and drained the rest of my cup of, you guessed it, cold coffee.

Reynolds finished writing on his notepad, then put everything down and stretched. He crossed his legs and stared at me with no expression. I couldn't read him. He sat like that for five long minutes just going over his thoughts. "Dan, a story about dead people coming to life, attacking and devouring people sounds like a bad, made for cable, late night movie. For a cop, it's hard to swallow something like that." He stared at me again, this time for what felt like an eternity. I was too tired to show emotion, I was running on empty and had nothing else to give. "But I'm a detective. not a cop, I can read facts and see through the reports. I can deduce when someone is lying to me. I can read people, and know when they are making something up. In the beginning, I must admit, I had no belief in you or your wild story. I let the lawyers go, so I could make you feel more comfortable. It's a trick I use sometimes, so I can see how a suspect reacts."

Reynolds shook his head then, "It's been a long story and frankly, one I believe every word of. That's the reason I ordered to have Mr. Leeder brought here. Too many things are happening in my city tonight for me to completely ignore or chalk up to coincidence. The question is now, what do we do? If this thing is already out of control as you've suggested, then there is nothing I can do to help my city, and that doesn't sit well with me."

"I told you, there is nothing we can do to help. Except to warn people, then get out. I'd like to get Brian and just boogie, but I can't do that. If there is something I can do to help I will, but I hope you are as smart as I believe you are. When you see the balance start to tip, we need to have a plan. We need to move fast and be ferocious or we will become one of them," I explained.

"First things, first. Let's get you some clothes and a pair of shoes, you look like shit. Then hopefully, Mr. Leeder will be here. Follow me." He stood and walked to the door, opened it and stood back, allowing me to walk into the hallway. The floor felt as cold as a meat locker, since I had no shoes. The lights were so bright they hurt my eyes, as I tried to focus after the dim interview room. I followed him down a couple of hallways and into a room whose sign read Men's locker room. "Why don't you take a hot shower? I'll be right back with some clothes. What size shoe do you wear?"

"Eight and a half," I stuttered out. I was stunned at the turn of events. "Thank you, Reynolds. I appreciate everything you are doing."

"No problem, Dan. There are fresh towels on the hooks outside the showers and here is a plastic bag to put your clothes in. Who knows what kinds of bacteria are in all those stains?" He handed me a big plastic bag with a zip top on it and then walked away.

I tore my clothes off, pushed them deep into the bag and zipped it up. I put it on the bench next to me, rose and walked towards the showers. I almost collapsed when the warm water flowed over my body. I could feel the pressure and stress of the last couple of days roll off my shoulders and go down the drain. I used almost all of the bar of soap and scrubbed every part of my body till it turned a raw shade of red. I rinsed off and stumbled out to the towels. I happened to look into the mirrors and saw a haunted looking man staring back. His eyes were red rimmed, he looked like he had seen too much and was ready to give up. I realized it was me. I looked closer into my eyes and that anger I'd felt in the tower came back. It told me to become stronger, to not be defeated, to stand like a man. To fight for what was mine and to take care of those who would stand by my side. I stood straighter and saw a glint come back into those eyes. I refused to give up, to let a bunch of bad events define who I was.

I saw Reynolds' image in the mirror behind me, smiling. He was holding a set of black clothes with a pair of black boots on top. "Feels good to shower and clean up, doesn't it? These are some of our SWAT BDUs, or for you civilians, Battle Dress Uniform. They should fit you. I added some socks and boxer shorts. When you're dressed, come look for me. Go left down the hall onto the main floor, ask someone and they will direct you to me. Brian has just arrived and should be in here soon." He put everything on the bench and turned to leave.

"Reynolds." He stopped and looked back to me. "Thank you for all you've done, I appreciate it." God, I really must be thankful. That was the third time I had thanked him, he must think I'm a dolt.

He threw a smile my way, nodded and left. I dressed into the SWAT clothes. They fit almost perfectly, Reynolds must have a good eye, I thought. I put on the socks and laced up the boots. I stood and looked in the mirror. A different man looked back at me. Someone that looked confident, someone who looked strong. I dismissed my image and left the locker room, following Reynolds directions to the main floor, which was crowded with police officers; some in suits, some in uniforms, some dressed like me. I approached one, "Excuse me, officer-" I read his name badge, "Allen, I'm looking for Detective Reynolds?"

"Yes sir, he said you would be." He pointed towards the other side of the room to a small row of offices. "The middle one over there is his. He's waiting for you."

I thanked him and made my way through the throng of officers. I noticed that some seemed to be exhausted, others on edge and jumpy, yet others calm, cool, and collected. I made it to Reynolds' door and knocked. "Come!" announced a voice. I opened the door and entered.

I was almost knocked over when a giant of a man picked me up off the ground, crushing me in a hug. "I can't breathe, you overgrown

Neanderthal."

He put me down on my feet, stepped back and took in my clothing. "Wow, give a boy some manly clothes and he thinks he's a soldier. Glad to see you're ok, Boss," grumbled Brian's deep gravelly voice.

"Glad to see me? Hell, last time I saw you, you were unconscious in a pool of blood!" I looked at the bandage on his head.

"Just a scratch, head wounds bleed like a bitch. The officer taking me down was just a little over zealous. I did have a gun and they had just heard gunshots, so I can't blame the guy. Like I always say, I've had worse. Detective Reynolds was just informing me of the story you've told him. He asked a couple of questions about it and I filled in some gaps and told an abbreviated story."

"Reynolds, what do we do now? Any news on what's going out there?" I asked.

He removed his tie and threw a report in my direction. "The report is in there, but let me give you a quick rundown of the facts. Those two cars that were sent to the morgue never answered, so we rolled a third car. When he arrived, he found the cars empty. He went inside the building and reported to find the two cops down and mutilated badly. He said the place was painted in blood and he could not find the staff. He retreated to his car and called in that report. He is still on station, waiting for a CSI unit to roll out. I also have a report from the three hospitals of patients being aggressive and attacking others. They've had to restrain a bunch and lastly, the big riot on Folsom has gotten worse. It's grown in size and the National Guard has been called in to support with riot control. Everything you'd said is coming true. I made some calls to my friends in SWAT and told them about what we think is happening. Most won't listen and laughed me off, but my old team hasn't rolled out yet. They are standing by if we need them."

"Do you have any of those SWAT pajamas in my size, Reynolds? I don't think my clothes are going to be able to stand up much longer," Brian asked.

"No idea, but we can go look. Oh, and stop calling me by my last name. The name is Victor or Vic, choose one. Dan, why don't you stay here? I'll take the gorilla and see if I can't get him some clothes, I also need to change." Vic and Brian left me alone in the office.

I looked at his desk phone and made a decision. I picked it up and tried calling my father. He didn't answer, so I left him a quick message explaining what was happening, to get his guns and how to protect himself. I would try to come there, so he should stay and protect himself. Next, I called my sister but her phone never even rang, just went straight to voicemail. I left her a quick message saying I loved her and hoped she was fine. I also tried my brother, but got nothing, not even voice mail.

I moved Vic's mouse on his desktop and was greeted with his desktop. 'No password?' I thought. I opened a browser and logged into my Gmail account. I had a ton of email. I navigated till I found one from my dad. It said he was ok and not to worry, he had armed himself and was sitting tight and if I could, to try and make it to him. He had just finished fencing his acreage and was making it secure. He had plenty of room for friends. I smiled at that, leave it to the old man to be ready. No emails from my brother or sister. But one from Julie? I'd had this email address for a long time and she would know it. The email spoke of the disease and flu and how she was at her house in Fort Bragg. It listed her number. I almost knocked the phone over with how fast I grabbed at it. My fingers shook while I dialed her number.

She answered on the second ring. "Julie! Is that you?" I just about cried out.

"Oh God, it's you! Are you ok? Caller ID says you're calling from a San Francisco police number. Are you in jail?" she asked. Her voice was raw, but sounded like an angel to me.

"Long story, sweetie. One I hope to tell you, but relax I am not in jail. Are you in the Army? Why do you have a number in Fort Bragg?" I asked.

"Wrong Fort Bragg. I live in the city of Fort Bragg, off the Pacific Ocean, well north of San Francisco. Listen, Dan. Some bad things are being reported on the TV. I'm scared and the only person that makes me safe is you. I know it's been a long time, but I need to know you're ok," she started to cry a little then.

"Listen to me, Julie. San Francisco is about to fall soon, but I am safe. I want you to get as many supplies as you can and hold tight. Do not go outside after you supply up, do not go near any sick, or injured people. If someone attacks your house defend it, but you must destroy their brain. Just trust me, do you have any firearms?" I asked. Her crying was tearing my heart apart.

"You forgot, you big dummy? I was brought up in Nebraska around guns. So of course I have guns, and I'm pretty good at using them too, if I'm being truthful," her crying had slowed as she explained this to me.

"Oh shit, sorry. I forgot. Listen, I don't know how long it will take for the phones and stuff to go down. But I promise Julie, I will come for you. I have a lot to apologize for and make up for. If you'll have me, that is." I was starting to get emotional and had to fight down a small sob.

"I've been waiting for you for a long time. Be safe and get your butt here, then we can start on your apology. Hurry, my love. Please hurry." I saw Brian and Vic coming through the offices back to me.

"Listen babe, I have to go, but I promise you I am coming. I will not break that promise, just be safe and be alive when I get there." We said our goodbyes and hung up.

Brian walked in and stood there staring at me. "You ok, man?"

"I'm fine. Just got off the phone with Julie. You remember me telling you about her?" He nodded yes. "She's alive and living in Fort Bragg, California. It's a city to the north, not the military base."

"I know that, you moron. So, are you and I headed out to gather her up?" he asked.

"I am, but you don't have to come. You owe me nothing," I explained.

"Of course I owe you nothing, except we are family now. If you need to get your girl, I will help you," he promised.

"By the way, what the hell are you wearing?" I asked. He was dressed in a pair SFPD sweat pants which seemed one size to small and a SWAT T-shirt that was stretched to its limits, trying to hold onto him. He was also wearing combat boots like mine.

"It fits and it's what they had. Not my fault, they don't make clothes for real men," he complained.

Vic walked in next, dressed in what I guessed was his old SWAT uniform. They looked like mine, but much better fitting and he had a holstered gun. He had been listening to our conversation.

His desk phone and cell phone went off at the same time, and we heard all the phones on the floor go off at once. He grabbed his cell, stuck it against his ear and listened intently for three minutes. He hung it up, and looked out to the floor. Officers were grabbing their equipment and running out to their vehicles. He looked at his phone and dialed a number, then put it to his ear. "It's happening. Stay in the garage and pack up those supplies I told you about. We will be there in a bit, there's a couple of things I need to deal with first." He hung up, then dialed another number. "Hey hun, it's me. Do me a favor. Take out that handgun I left you. Put it in your purse and go stock up on supplies. Then go down into the basement and lock yourself in tight. I'll be there to get you as soon as I can, baby. I may run into a couple of problems, but I promise I'll come home to you, for good this time. Be strong, see you in a couple of weeks. I love you too, hun." He hung up one last time and slipped the phone into his chest pocket and velcroed it closed.

Chapter 23

"Alright, gentlemen, the first call was an emergency call out to all officers from the Chief. It seems that the riot is getting worse and all emergency services are being called out. Reports of multiple attacks and murders." He looked at me. "Sounds a lot like that dream, doesn't it, Dan?"

"Yes, it does, and I think maybe you know what comes next. So what's your plan, Vic?" I stepped forward.

"I have a SWAT vehicle with its six shooters, all friends of mine. I say we get you two something to protect yourselves with, then move on to my friends and get out of the city. Sounds like you have a friend you need to get to, and it could be on its way to get my ex-wife," he stuck out his hand to me.

I grabbed it and shook it hard, "Thank you for believing in Brian and I, and thank you for agreeing to get my Julie." I turned to Brian and he put his arm around my shoulders. "And thank you, big man, for having my back."

He shook his head and smiled at me. "Boss, I wouldn't have it any other way. Now can we get going please? When this city falls, it's going to fall hard and I'd rather not be here when it happens."

Vic walked away and we followed him, like good little children. He took two flights of stairs and passed multiple secure doors. We then went through a door marked *SWAT Armory Authorized Personnel Permitted Only*. Past that door, another sat with electronic locks on it, standing in our way. Vic pounded on it three times, the door locks were disengaged and the door opened slowly on well-oiled hinges. The door was pure steel and had to weigh two tons, yet swung effortlessly. Six officers dressed in SWAT BDUs stood around, seemingly waiting for us.

Vic walked in and shook the oldest man's hand and then embraced him like a long lost brother. "Guys, come meet my family. This old guy is team lead, John "Iron" Kuppers. He took me in when I was brand new, taught me everything I know, and then kicked me out and made me become a detective. The short stocky guy next to him is little Jonny. He's a mean little Irish man and ex Green Beret. The stocky guy, over there is Anthony or as we call him, Cupcake. The little Asian guy is Kenji Komatsu. He is Japanese American, but we call him "Senshi" which means warrior in Japanese But don't get him wrong, he was born and raised in Topeka, Kansas. I speak more Japanese then he does. The cowboy at the end is John Henry Holliday, we call him Doc, I'm sure you can figure out why. Last but deadliest of the bunch is Lozen. She is named after her great, great, great, grandmother who fought with Geronimo. We just call her Apache."

Apache jumped off the counter and walked over to us. She stood about my height, with long black blue hair down to the middle of her back. She had a body that even her loose SWAT BDUs could not hide. She could easily be mistaken for the comic book goddess Wonder Woman. But her eyes were the one feature which grabbed my attention. They were the color of milk chocolate, but glittered like the stars in the winter sky. "I also graduated from Cornell University in linguistics and then played with the Army for a bit. But I'm a nice person, good to meet you guys."

Brian shook her hand, "Brian Leeder, former Marine with the 26th expeditionary force."

I shook her hand and she almost crushed it. "Dan Welko, middle manager for Next Level Analytics, girly man and plain old civilian." Lozen laughed and patted me on the back.

"I like him," she said.

The rest came over and shook our hands. "Ok Vic, so what the hell are we doing here? Since we are ignoring direct orders, we'd like to know why?" Kuppers asked.

"Dan and Brian here, are the only known survivors of the Transamerica Tower yesterday. Believe it or not, they know what's going on out there and better yet, they have already had to fight and kill their way to safety. Dan, do you want to fill everyone in?" Vic pointed at me.

"I don't know what to say. Brian and I were trapped in the tower with our office mates. The "Wild Fire" virus got into our office from an employee sneaking back in from New York. One of our secretaries was attacked and mutilated, and somehow reanimated. I had to kill her with a metal chair leg by driving it into her head. We had to fight numerous ferocious people who all in all, looked, acted, and died like the zombies from all those horror movies. Brian and I got out of there barely, and lost everyone we'd tried to help. Now the police have lost contact with the morgue, hospitals are having hungry patients and I don't think Jell-O is going to satisfy them, and now that riot out there is turning bloody," I looked to Brian.

"He said it best ladies and gentlemen. We are going to be neck deep in flesh eating zombies very soon. I know you don't believe us, probably think we've lost it. But we have been fighting those damn things over the last couple of days. Seen a lot of deaths of friends, coworkers, and someone we tried very hard to save. Very soon you are going to be face to face with these things. Don't let your guard down, that's all I can ask of you," Brian informed them.

"Well said, gentlemen. Ok, what kind of weapons can we arm these guys up with?" Vic pointed at us.

Kuppers scratched his chin and looked over at Doc, "What do you think, Doc?"

Doc smiled wide and walked back to a cage, unlocked it and opened it wide. "What's your poison, boys?"

Brian walked over and pointed at two weapons. "I'm checked out on all of those weapons and proficient as hell with that M4 and the M14."

Doc nodded his head, reached in and took out the weapons Brian had indicated and also handed out an M1911 .45 sidearm. "Sorry, but we don't have any armor to fit your gorilla-like physique, but here's a narco zip up jacket. It's size XXL, so it should fit you." Doc handed him a black vest that said SWAT across the back. Brian backed away to load up and check his gear.

Doc waved to me and I meekly walked over. "I'm not a gun guy. Never held one, never used one. I've had no use for one, but I'd be happy with a steel collapsible baton and a night stick." Doc looked me over and nodded his head.

"Tell you what, son. If we make it out of here in one piece, I will teach you all you need to know. But if you leave here with nothing, then we might not be able to tool you up later. So, I'm going to arm you up. Just leave them alone until we teach you, but you are going to carry your own weight. Got me, boy?" Doc stabbed his finger into my chest.

"I'm more than happy to be a mule, Doc," I said meekly.

Doc looked me over, then handed me a blue vest looking thing that you see most SWAT members use in movies. "Like you care son, but that there is a second chance tac vest. The pockets will carry ammo, a radio, and some other great pouches. It also has a chest plate and a back plate. So if you get shot, hope it's in one of those places. It's heavy, but keep it on and don't screw with it."

I shrugged into it and Apache helped me settle it properly, zipped me up, and velcroed over the zipper. "Looks good on you, Dan," she winked and stood back.

Doc frowned at the weapons in front of him, then started handing things to me. Thank God for Apache; she just started filling my pouches up. "Don't touch any of that stuff till we show you what to do with it later." He then took out a weird holster and handed it to Apache. "This is a 6004 SLS tactical leg holster. You wear it on your thigh, there. This here is a M1911 .45 sidearm, it fits in that holster. The magazine is loaded and the gun is ready to fire. So don't touch it, unless told to do so." He handed it to me, butt first. I carefully slid it into its holster and snapped the strap over it to keep it snug.

Doc removed a wide belt and told me to snap it around my waist and adjust it tight. He reached back into the locker and took out two collapsible batons. "These are Smith and Wesson twenty-one inch collapsible batons, they open up and allow you to kick some serious ass. These? Feel free to use without supervision. I also have a normal police baton or night stick as you called it, if you want it." I nodded yes and he handed it over.

"Hey Doc, I know this is a stupid request, but do you have any knives I could carry? Gouging out eyes and pulping the brain has become kind of a staple for me," I asked with surprising strength in my voice. I felt out of my league with all this stuff, but I felt confident in what I needed.

He reached to his side and unbuckled something off his belt. "This here is my daddy's Marine Kabar. He carried it with him almost his whole life. The blade is seven inches long and sharp as hell. I want this back at some point." I was stunned he would give me something like that. I promised him I would make sure he'd get it back.

"One last thing I have for you. It's very dangerous so don't touch it, hell, don't even look at it. This is a Benelli Nova tactical pump shotgun, with pistol grip. You will wear it over your shoulder on your back. We may need it, so you get to carry it." Apache took it and slung it over my shoulder and tightened the strap so it wouldn't bang against me when I moved.

"These are tactical gloves with Kevlar reinforced knuckles and palm. I take it you know how to put these on?" He smiled when he handed those over.

I slid them on and jumped up and down making sure everything fit right. I felt overloaded and to tell you the truth, a little like that pack mule I'd talked about earlier. Brian came up and patted my back. "You look good, Boss. We'll make a soldier out of you eventually. Just stay by my side like in the tower and we will be just fine. These guys are professional and look competent enough to me."

"Mount up guys. Vic, do we have a plan? How about a route? Or even a direction?" Kuppers inquired.

"Well, the Bay bridge is out, we'd have to go around the riot on Folsom to get there. Think south is the way to go?" Vic asked the group.

"If I may put my two cents in?" I raised my hand.

"Put your hand down, for God's sake we are not in fifth grade. Now, what do you have to add?" Vic motioned toward me.

"We need to go north. South and east just get us into denser cities and probably more trouble. West is the ocean and that won't work either, unless we have our own boat and lots of food and supplies. But you guys are free to do what you think is best. I am going north, my father and someone else is that direction. Plus, going that way has woods and lakes and it's probably easier to hunt and survive out there." I noticed I had spoken too much and shut my mouth, leaning against a table. Brian came over and put his arm on my shoulder.

"You heard the man," Vic announced.

Kuppers looked at each of his teammates and every one of them nodded their agreement. "North it is. So, the Golden Gate then? Let's hope it's not choked up by the time we arrive to cross or we are going to be royally fucked."

Cupcake walked over and opened two double doors at the end of the room and we all followed. After a short walk, we came to a garage big enough for four fire engines. What sat in the middle was a big black military looking vehicle with SWAT painted in white on its flanks. It exuded roughness and assurance. Cupcake walked over and slid his hand down the side, "Gentlemen, this is a 1999 Lenco BearCat armored personnel carrier. She has a 300 hp Caterpillar turbo diesel residing under that hood over there, she has hardly any mileage on her and I baby her. I do all the work myself. This is my girlfriend and she treats me very well. We've stacked some basic supplies and strapped some fuel containers on top because she is a thirsty girl. Mount up and let's get the fuck out of here already." He opened up the back, then went up front and climbed in behind the wheel.

Little Jonny took my arm and loaded me in first, "In the front, buddy. If we have to dismount, let us go first, since we can use our pretty toys. Before you sit down, swing the shotgun around in front of you and point it at the floor. Got it?"

I stammered out a yes and made my way to a seat. I swung the shotgun around, pointing it down and made sure my hand was nowhere near the trigger. I strapped myself in and swallowed my apprehension. Brian got in and sat across from me, his monster-like knees pressed up against mine. Apache was next and she sat next to me and Senshi slid in next to her. Little Jonny sat next to Brian and Doc next to him. Kuppers entered last and took the last seat near the rear doors. Vic took the front "Navigator" seat next to Cupcake. The doors closed and the engine rumbled to life. Darkness enveloped us then and a red light snapped on pushing back the dark.

Finally, I thought, time to move, no more wasting precious time. I thanked God, which I rarely did, for the warriors surrounding me, for giving me the chance to go to Julie, to give me the second chance I did not deserve. I made a promise right then that I would never give up, I would not die and I would do everything possible to find Julie and to never let harm come to her.

Apache looked over at me, then placed a helmet on my head and strapped it down. "Don't want to scramble your brains, Danny boy." Her smile seemed like it was etched on her face.

I examined our enclave and noticed everyone else was wearing a helmet. Brian's looked like it was a tight fit, but he had it on and that was important. He winked and threw a smile my way. He looked like he belonged with these people. It brought out the real him.

We rumbled out of the garage and turned right on Jones street and then right on Turk Street. Cupcake was running the sirens and was driving very offensively, almost pushing cars out of his way if they didn't move quickly enough for him. We made another right onto Franklin and were stopped dead in traffic. Cupcake laid on the horn and whooping the siren, trying to get people out of the way. "No good, Vic. This must be people trying to escape the riots. They had the same idea as us. Which way now?"

Vic looked back at me. "If this is that bad, I promise you the bridge is probably packed too. Any ideas, Dan?"

"Anybody got a cell phone?" Apache handed me her iPhone and unlocked it. I opened her GPS program and was terrified to see the traffic in the city. "Everything to the bridges is gridlocked. We aren't going anywhere."

"The Ferry," announced Little Jonny, "We used them once to go to Napa that one time we worked with DHS. If we can commandeer one, we can make it across the bay to Sausalito, disembark and head inland or at least over land in this beast."

"Don't call my girl a beast. Unless it's *sexy beast*," Cupcake admonished. Everyone ignored him. Seemed like a normal thing for them.

"Ok, let's get to Market and take that to the Embarcadero. The ferries are south a little bit, but we are going to be close to that riot," I answered.

"Okie dokie, my man." Cupcake threw the APC to the right, blew over a sidewalk and skidded onto Eddy Street.

He continued and I lost track of the turns. I had turned inside myself, I felt like I was missing something. Every time I thought I was going to be able to catch the thought, it would float away.

I was pulled out of my private thoughts by Brian as he tapped my knee with one big finger. "Boss, you ok, man? You seem a little distracted." I could see concern etched onto his normally smiling face.

"Yeah, I'm good, brother. Something is just nibbling at the edge of my thoughts. But I can't seem to focus in on it," I answered shaking my head to clear it.

"Ok people, we've decided to bypass Market Street. It seems to also be out of control," Vic recited.

"We are going to get stuck in more and more traffic, human and vehicle, the closer we get to Folsom. I say go north over to California and then west to the Embarcadero. We should be able to ride on the fringes of all the chaos. Then, with our sirens and some sidewalk driving, we should be able to get there faster. Just my opinion, but risk assessment is what I do best." This came from Brian.

"You heard the Sasquatch, back north to California. Do some of that crazy driving shit you do, Cupcake, and get us where we need to go!" ordered Vic.

The APC rocked on its suspension as Cupcake made a fast left and somehow pulled out a U-turn in the beast, without flipping it over and killing all of us. Apache saw the fear on my face and laughed, "Don't worry, Dan. Cupcake drove bigger APCs in the Army. I trust his driving and he knows this thing like the back of his hand or in his case, inside of his right masturbating hand." Apache made the hand job motion using her right hand and giggled. Humor seemed to be her natural disposition.

"Hey, I heard that. I'm primarily a lefty when it comes to satisfying myself. The right is for pulling the trigger on my trusty M4. Now hold on guys, and by guys I mean Apache, we're going airborne!" I grabbed onto my seatbelt and closed my eyes as somehow, the crazy bastard actually got the APC to leave the ground, if even for just two seconds. I felt my stomach trying to go out through my mouth and clamped my jaw down tight.

"Ok, I'll swing right onto California. I see an opening so I'm gonna get the girl up to sixty, so hold on tight," Cupcake shouted back to us.

While Cupcake pushed his rig up to a wild and crazy speed of sixty, Vic looked back to us, "Ok, we just passed Montgomery, so we will be slowing down to take a left on Market. Prepare to get out and protect the truck, if we get overwhelmed. Dan, you stay in the vehicle at all times and hold on. Let the professionals do their jobs. Apache will stick by your side, got it?"

I nodded agreement and Vic turned around to watch us swing on to Market through two cars. I could hear the wrenching of metal as Cupcake may have scratched some paint off of them. I had a feeling there was no damage to the Beast, as I'd decided to name it. Almost immediately, we braked hard to a jolting stop.

Chapter 24

"We got a problem, Kuppers!" Vic shouted back.

Kuppers hit the door release button, opened the back door and stepped out to survey the situation. The man never seemed to just stand in one place. It's like he planted himself to a spot and dared anyone to knock him down. He closed the door and I couldn't see him anymore till he walked to the front of the Beast. I witnessed out the front windshield, a blockade of emergency vehicles standing in our way. Vic popped open his door and last I saw him, he was jogging toward the ferry's dock.

Kuppers swaggered his way to the front and started shouting orders to the officers manning their stations. I could see them wilter from this one-man storm. They started moving vehicles and Cupcake drove the Beast through the opening out to the rear, taking up station near the Ferry building. The rest of the men in back disembarked from the rear door and took up defensive positions nearby. Apache, Cupcake and I stayed where we were.

Vic came back and sidled up the rear of the Beast so everyone could hear him. "Ok, here's the situation. The ferry that can handle our rig is not here and won't be back for a long time. But they do have a flat barge with a crane that can lift the APC onto it. They are going to pull it into position in twenty minutes." He stepped back and Kuppers marched up.

"We can't move on yet, guys." I noticed Apache never batted an eye. I guess she felt like one of the guys, so had no problem not being singled out as the woman of the group. "These poor bastards are ordered to hold the line and there are only ten of them. A lot of overflow from the riot, is on its way. We probably have about five minutes till it gets here."

"What can we do to hold people who are just trying to get out of here, too? We can't shoot everyone. That's not human," I said.

"I have an idea, but it may not make a dent in the crowd coming,"

Vic said covering his eyes from the sun, while looking out to the ferry building. "There are three ferries sitting at the dock right now. Each one can carry about 450 people. I bet if they squeezed them in, they could carry close to 600. Maybe get them to the old alameda air station, then come back for more. Let's operate on that idea. I'll go talk to the captains of the boats and make them see the light." Vic grabbed a radio from the back of the Beast and put it into his tac vest, and took off toward the ferry's docks again.

Doc grabbed radios and started handing them out to everyone. Apache grabbed a second one and put it into a special pouch on my vest and threaded an ear piece up through the vest and rested it into my ear. "Dan, if you want to talk, just push this button here. It'll open the channel and transmit whatever you say to the squad. Thumbs up, if you understand." I gave her a thumbs up and stayed seated where I was.

I could hear the crowd coming down the street. At first a roar, but soon I was able to pick up individual voices.

Then Kuppers' voice came over a loud speaker, "I am Lieutenant John Kuppers of the Tenderloin Department of the San Francisco Police. Please calm down and stay civil. We are working on ways to help you. First, we need to know which of you is sick or injured, and who is healthy. We will move the non-infected to the Alameda air station using ferries. We cannot handle everyone in one shot, so be patient, be orderly and we will get you out of the city."

"The NG are here, guys," Little Jonny announced. Later, Apache informed me that NG meant National Guard.

The radio in my ear clicked open and a voice came over, "This is

Vic. I have all Captains in agreement to ferry people out of here, but they will not take anyone infected or that looks unhealthy. I think we can accommodate them on this matter. The Barge is here, Cupcake. We can start moving the APC over and get her loaded and secured. Dan, stay with Apache and the rest of the group. Over."

I got out with Apache and she made sure I stuck to her side. Cupcake got the Beast started and moved off in the direction of the ferry building. I looked around and saw five large trucks pulling up and dispersing military personnel. Kuppers left the officers at the barricade and approached what I figured was the leadership of the National Guard contingent.

Apache and I moved closer so we could back up Kuppers and listen in on the conversation. "I am Lieutenant Kuppers of the SFPD. Who are you guys?" Kuppers seemed to always be so gruff. I was amazed when they answered him, deferring to his position.

"49th MP Brigade out of Fairfield. I am second Lieutenant Rodriguez and this is Master Sergeant Janikowski. Nice to meet you, sir. Are you in command of this area?" The short Latino held his hand out.

Kuppers took it and shook it once and nodded at the Master Sergeant, "I am the highest ranking official here from the SFPD, so I guess I am in charge. How many men do you have? And how in hell did you get here from Fairfield so fast?"

"Actually, we were working at the old armory on the west side. We were called up by the Governor about three hours ago and we fought our way through horrendous traffic to get here. I have one platoon consisting of Military Police, so guess it's at a hundred men, primarily armed with lethal weapons only. No non-lethals available for us to use," the Master Sergeant answered.

"The San Francisco armory hasn't been used in a long time. What were you doing there?" asked Apache.

"This is Sergeant Lozen." Kuppers introduced her, but left me out of the conversation. Which was fine by me.

"We were over there moving some old files and helping out with a movie shoot," the second Lieutenant explained, "I do have one favor to ask, sir. We were sent over here from the shoot, but we have no ammo. Mind letting us borrow some?" The young soldier looked down and kicked at a small pebble.

"You've got to be kidding me!" Kuppers shook his head and mumbled quietly, "Of course, it's the fucking military." Then louder to the men around, "We have a small pallet worth. I'll have it pulled out and you can help yourselves, but you will owe me, boys." He clicked on his radio. "Doc, bring that mini pallet of 5.56 out here, seems our NG buddies have dry weapons. Yes, I know that's all we have. Stop your bitching and do as you're told."

"So where do you want us, Lieutenant Kuppers?" the Master Sergeant asked.

Kuppers stared at him for a while. "Once we get you ammo, the plan is to separate the sick and injured from the healthy civilians. We secured transport for the healthy to go on the ferries to just across the way to Alameda air station. We want to get them out of the city, so we can deal with anything else that pops up," Kuppers instructed. He then turned his attention on the Second Lieutenant, "Are you in contact with the Red

Cross? Also, you wouldn't have any medics, would you?"

"Yes on both fronts. I will also see if I can get in touch with the Red Cross group over in Oakland and get them to meet the ferries." He saluted Kuppers and walked away.

"That kid must be out of his comfort zone. No need to salute me, I'm not in his command structure. Oh well, he seems competent enough. Apache, take Dan away from the action and send over that Sasquatch with the rest of the team that's not already busy." Kuppers turned and walked away, back toward the barricade. In the distance, I could see Doc pulling on the mini pallet of 5.56 ammo, dragging it over towards the NG.

Apache steered me over to the guys, "Alright boys, Dad says he wants you with him, even you Sasquatch." Apache punched Brian on the arm and I actually saw him wince. Wow, she must be one tough chick. They trotted away and we headed back to a safe area where we could watch the action but still get away quickly.

I could see the crowd growing in size. The NG troops formed up and broke off into smaller groups and assigned different areas in front of the barricade. "Looks like we are going to sit here for a while. Tell me how you joined SWAT, if you don't mind."

Apache looked at me with a weird look, then gave me a big smile. "I got bored with the Army, but missed the guns and fun stuff. So I started looking around the country for the best team and decided on these guys. A friend of mine knew Kuppers from their days on the force and said I would fit in good with him. So, I showed up and he took me to the range and handed me a bunch of guns. He wouldn't interview or really talk to me till I shot. So I set a new record on all weapons at the range and he comes up shakes my hand and says congrats you're hired. He gave me one week to move here and settle before he introduced me to the team. Each guy on the team was handpicked by Kuppers, even Vic."

"Sounds like you guys are more family than a team," I commented.

"You have no idea, Dan. We've fought side by side and rely on each other more than with our real family." She never took her eyes off the team while she'd talked to me.

A hand fell on my shoulder and I turned, startled. Vic was standing there smirking, "Relax, Dan. You're going to have a heart attack." He then clicked his radio on and announced over the channel, "Team, the ferries are ready to roll. Once they have been checked, start sending them in. One thousand eight hundred for the first wave only. They will be back in one hour at the most to start this all over again. What do you say we hand this over to the NG troops and get out of here?"

"Not yet. We will help with the first set to evacuate, then we will move out. The NG are calling in another platoon and won't need us anymore soon," Kuppers radioed back.

"I want to see the front. Can we please move up?" I asked.

"Apache, why don't you take Dan to the front, but be ready to get to the APC at a moment's notice," Vic looked in her direction.

She took my hand and we walked away to just behind the barricade. I could see faces now and just how big the crowd was becoming. The sea of humanity must've counted eight thousand and growing steadily. I became afraid because any minute now, I knew this could all fall apart. Once the zombies appeared, this place would become one of panic and disorder. The NG had their medics on the front line checking temperatures and doing physical checks of the civilians. It was a slow process, but at least something was happening and the crowd could feel that. They were calm for now.

"Do you have any binoculars, Apache?" I asked her.

"They are called glasses and yes, here you go." She handed over a small but powerful pair of black ones.

I climbed up onto the truck in front of me and started looking around the edges of the crowd. "What the hell am I looking for?" I mumbled more to myself but Apache heard me. She didn't miss much I'd noticed.

"When you find it, let me know," she answered.

I took the glasses and started scanning their faces. I kept at it for a long hour till I came upon a little blonde girl in a white summer dress standing on a car waving at me, trying very hard to get my attention. I was floored. I was shocked. I was sure I was seeing things. "The girl from my dream," I whispered. I clicked my radio like an old pro, "Vic, I need you now."

"What girl? Show me." Apache held out her hands for the glasses. I handed them over and pointed in the direction of the little girl waving at us.

Vic came running over to me, "What's up?"

"That little girl from my dreams. She's out there." I pointed in her direction.

Vic jumped up onto the truck. "She knows we are here, how? I have no idea. Her little eyes shouldn't be able to see us." Apache handed over the glasses to Vic.

He looked where I pointed and I could see the color drain from his face. "How can this be real?" he asked out loud.

"I don't know, but I promised her I would protect her and there she is. I have to go get her." I was getting agitated. I had to calm down or Vic would never let me go out there.

Brian made his presence known speaking loudly enough to surprise everyone. For his size he was fucking ghostly, with how stealthily he was. "I'll take him. Have Apache set up over head protection. The faster you agree, the faster we can be back," he growled out.

Brian reached up took my hand and helped me down. Vic seemed to be chewing on the idea. Finally, he made a decision. "Apache, grab your long gun and get visual on these two. Anyone impedes them or attacks them, you take care of it." He walked away towards Kuppers to explain the situation.

Brian and I slid between two vehicles into the crowd and made our way over to the left edge. I could feel the crosshairs from Apache's gun on my back as we made our way through the crowd. Brian dealt with the people in our way, speaking with authority to get them to move or just down right manhandling them out of the way. We stepped onto the sidewalk and I would periodically jump into the air, trying to get a peek at the little girl. After what felt like an eternity, we made it to the car. The little girl was still there. She looked down at me, "It's you. You're real and you kept your promise. What's your name?" Her eyes were large, she ignored Brian and just stared at me.

"My name is Dan, and we need to get out of here. Remember the dream and what happens next?" She nodded her head and slid off the car into my arms. As we turned to head back, I heard screams coming from behind us. I looked in that direction and saw something that did not make sense at first. The zombies had finally showed up, but they were moving way too fast. Not like their cousins we dealt with in the tower. Oh shit, here it comes. "Brian, we need to go now! Fast!" We took off running. The little girl was heavy in my arms, but I wasn't going to put her down. We passed a small side street and something went flying by the side of my head. "Engaging. We have things coming in off of Beale. Holy shit, there are a lot of them."

I reached down with my free hand and pulled one of my collapsible batons out of my belted holster. I flicked my wrist out and felt the baton lock into full size. "Hold onto my neck and wrap your legs around me, kiddo. I need one of my hands free." Angel wrapped her arms tight around my neck, snuggled her head against my left shoulder and squeezed her knees against my sides. I held the baton in my right hand and prepared to fight if need be. There was no spot free enough for us to run, so I tried Brian's tactic and screamed at people in my best authorative voice.

Chapter 25

"Move the fuck out of my way! Official police business! Move!" I yelled until my voice started to feel hoarse.

Brian looked over his shoulder and the look on his face almost scared me into freezing. "Keep going, do not stop, Boss. I got your back."

171

He slowed so I could pass him. I could hear his gun going off sporadically but as I ran, his tempo picked up. The crowd started screaming and moving in the same direction we were. We weren't going to make it. I could feel it. Two men turned on me, I could tell by their faces they were scared and about to try something stupid. The big one pointed at my gun on my back, "Give me the guns and we'll let you pass!"

I was done with this, and knew what I had to do. I gave him my best enraged look and swung my baton at his legs. His buddy stepped to the side and swung at Angel and I. Just as he was going to connect, he spun away in one direction as his arm went in another direction. At that point, my baton made contact with the big guy's left knee, cracking it and knocking him to the ground. He screamed out loud and grabbed for his knee. His buddy was lying in a pool of blood, unconscious from trauma and blood loss. The best I figured, was Apache had seen what was happening and had shot the guy in the shoulder. I looked around quickly, trying to find a clear path.

Brian came up on my side and pointed to the barricade coming up. He called over his radio, "We are going to need help getting through this crowd and the barricade."

"Roger that. The NG guys will make a path for you near the big brown UPS van," Kuppers called out.

In front of us, we could see NG troops concentrating fire on the rear of the crowd. A small team was moving forward, making room for us near the UPS van Kuppers had described to us.

Brian came up on my side with a smile on his face. "What the fuck are you smiling at?" I yelled at him.

172

"No swearing. That's bad," admonished the little girl.

"Just nice to finally have a little pay back. We are coming up on the barricade, head toward those three guard guys. They will get us behind the barricade. Move it!" he yelled.

I doubled my efforts and the guard moved around us, letting us through a small opening off of the UPS van's bumper. Vic came running over and pointed over my shoulder. I turned and saw the carnage. The zombies were slicing their way into the crowd, attacking anyone and everyone. Then, the zombies turned and started toward the barricade. I could see further back in the crowd and more zombies were coming up through the back of the crowd and off of other side streets. They were much faster than anything Brian and I had dealt with in the tower. God, that seemed like ages ago. I watched as people were taken down, ripped asunder and torn apart. The zombies seemed so fast and much more viscous. The crowd started pushing harder at the barricade, ignoring orders being shouted by the guard. The guard kept pouring on the fire over the heads of the crowd taking out zombies left and right, but they were not head shots and the zombies started getting back up. "In the head! Shoot them in the head!" I screamed as loud as I could. The guards' fire shifted and they started making more headshots. But I could tell that no matter what, we had lost this battle.

Apache with Doc at her side, peeled away from their positions at the barricade and ran to our side. Brian joined them by the UPS van and covered the NG who had gone forward to protect us as they retreated. Vic got behind me and pushed me in the back towards the ferry building. "Head toward the barge. Cupcake has the Beast loaded. Get on the barge, don't wait just go! Brian, protect those two!"

Brian peeled away from the barricade and joined us as we ran in the direction Vic had ordered us to. Just then, I heard a noise above us. I sneaked a look and saw four airliners flying close over the city.

"Oh no," the little girl said.

One of the planes, just like in my dream, tipped over and crashed into the Coit Tower. Other planes started falling from the sky. One hit the bay bridge, breaking up into pieces and taking away cars and parts of the deck into the bay below. Two others looked like they might make it to a higher elevation, but they both turned on their sides, then their backs and impacted into the city. I could feel the heat and pressure from their explosions. We kept running, ignoring the horrific scenes around us.

We made it to the Ferry building, I stopped and turned, to find the rest of the team fighting as they ran our way. Apache caught my eye and yelled the word 'GO'. Brian grabbed my arm and yanked hard, almost pulling me off my feet. We ran and ran, I could feel my legs turning to lead and my arms were on fire from holding the girl. Something inside me kept telling me to ignore the pain and just keep going.

We skidded around a corner and saw two of the ferries already backing out of their slips, overloaded with people. I looked around frantically and finally spotted Cupcake waving us on to his position. We came up on him and he pointed to the barge. I didn't wait and ran up the gang plank onto it. I slid the little girl into the Beast. "Sit down and buckle up. I'll be right back, honey."

She smiled and rubbed my arm, "Thank you for keeping your promise." I smiled back and turned to find Brian with his rifle up to his shoulder. He hadn't fired yet, but was scanning the area.

Cupcake came running around the corner with the rest of the team. "Get the barge going now!" I turned and ran to the front and found a pilot house. I scanned the instruments and saw the gauges were showing power. I hoped this meant the engines were already running. I grabbed the throttle and advanced them and I felt the little barge start to move. I stepped out and looked around the Beast. I could see us starting to move, then I saw the ropes were still securing us to the pier. I reached back in and advanced the throttle a little more, then ran for the ropes.

I pulled the Kabar that Doc had loaned me and attacked the first rope. It disintegrated under the Kabar, popping and whipping back towards the dock. I saw the team jumping onto the barge. Kuppers and Little Jonny were still on the pier laying down fire, so the others could board. Apache and Cupcake were now firing over Kuppers and Little Jonny as they hit zombies left and right. But they were only knocking them down. No head shots. I made it to the other rope and cut it quickly using the Kabar. I turned and yelled over the gun fire, "HEAD SHOTS!"

Apache nodded and slowed her firing while taking more accurate shots, Cupcake copied her shots and gave Kuppers time to get on the barge. As Little Jonny turned to jump on the barge, he was hit from behind and then piled upon by five other bodies. They tore into him and he screamed. The stocky little Irishman started punching the creatures in the heads and throwing them off the pier and into the water. Doc started taking measured shots at the creatures advancing on Jonny. From around the corner, a large herd of zombies flooded out and ran at him. Doc tried but couldn't get all of them as they piled back onto Jonny. He somehow got his side arm free and started shooting the zombies on him. He was barely on his feet now, blood flowing from too many bites to count. He looked over and caught Kuppers' eye, he snapped off a salute, placed the gun under his

175

chin and fired. I screamed till my voice was raw, "NO!!!"

Brian grabbed my arm and pushed me back toward the pilot house. "Get us out of here, move it. He did the right thing. You know he did. We got this, Boss."

I turned my attention away from the zombies and ran into the pilot house. I advanced the throttles to their stops and grabbed the wheel. I steered us around one of the ferries and looked back at the one still docked. It was a house of carnage. People being attacked everywhere. I could hear more firing and that's when I saw the NG firing on a pier across the way. About twenty was all that was left. I pointed the barge in their direction and yelled into my radio, "The NG need help, come to the front!"

Like magic, the team appeared and started taking measured head shots at the zombies converging on the NG. I reached up and grabbed the wire over my head pulling it hard, hoping it was the horn. A mighty bellow let loose across the bay and the NG stopped and looked in our direction. The Master Sergeant was with them, I'd noticed. He started pushing men into the bay and pointing at us. The men started swimming and Apache stopped firing to help the NG's climb aboard. The Master Sergeant locked eyes with me and nodded, then he started firing faster into the crowd. It was down to him and one other soldier.

I screamed when I noticed what was about to happen. The Master Sergeant grabbed the last soldier and launched him into the water. That one act gave two zombies enough time to tackle the Master Sergeant taking him to the ground and ripping into him and his gear. Just like Little Jonny, he pulled his side arm and started drilling holes into the heads of the zombies around him. He got to his feet shakily, waved at us, then ran into the crowd of zombies using his rifle to bash heads in. We heard his blood curdling screams, then a single gunshot.

I pointed us toward the bay and increased our speed. I dropped my head, feeling tears burning down my cheeks and blurring my vision. Then a big arm pulled me into an embrace. My stress level was so high I felt like I was out of control and my emotions were taking over. "Dude, for a man who was never a soldier, you've done a masterful job keeping it together. Just keep putting one foot in front of the other."

A little hand slid into mine, I looked over at Angel and she smiled, but with tears in her eyes, "We have further to go. I need you to come back to me." I stopped crying and looked into her soft little eyes. I was drawn back for a second, she had one pale blue eye and one brown. I wiped my eyes with my right hand and gave her a little smile.

"You're right, we do have farther to go. Thank you," I whispered the last part so just she could hear me. She winked, took Brian's massive hand and led him out of the pilot house, leaving me alone. I straightened up and scanned the waters.

Vic and Kuppers came in then, and they both looked out onto the bay. "So, where are we going, my pilot?" asked Kuppers.

"Not sure yet, but the traffic is really picking up. I don't think it's safe to be floating around. What do the NG guys say?" I sounded and felt a little more in control again.

"They said they called in for a helo to come and get them. So, where ever you think we should drop them safely, sounds good to me," Kuppers answered.

"I have an idea, but not sure what you guys are gonna think of it,"

I said.

"Well, son. Say what you gotta say. You've done good so far. Oh and later on, you'll need to explain that little girl to me," Kuppers said.

"I don't think I understand that little girl much either, but Vic knows as much as I do. He can fill you in. So, my idea is for us to head to Alcatraz. We can drop those boys off and from there, create a plan and figure out what we've got," I explained.

"That's not so crazy, I like that plan. It has a place they can lay a helo down on, and we should be able to secure it. You were right, Vic. This guy is smart, we'll keep him around a little longer. Alright, head on over," Kuppers instructed.

I gave him a thumbs up and pointed the bow to the west. I clicked on my radio, "I need eyes all around the barge. Call out traffic before it gets near us. This thing turns slowly, I can't see shit from the pilot house, and this is close to as fast as she goes. We are heading to Alcatraz." I took a moment and looked out at the city. The fires from the airplane crashes were out of control, burning through Telegraph Hill and out toward Pier 39. The whole city looked like a pyre; flames reaching into the sky from many neighborhoods.

"Left side, we have two sail boats coming our way pretty fast," Doc called out on the radio.

"Behind, in front, or bearing down? Can't react without knowing more," I called back out.

"Thirty yards off bow, if we cut back power to half, they should pass by," came Apache back on the radio.

I cut back the throttle and craned my neck over. Suddenly, there they were, two sailboats went rocketing by. Must've been running on the winds the fires were creating. Once they were half way across the bow, I hit the throttles to maximum again. "Close call. Keep calling it out, guys!"

"More traffic coming up on the bow eighty yards out. They are slow, looks like all kinds of pleasure craft. We can't go around, we are gonna have to slow down and stay behind them. I'm afraid if we try and pass, they may try boarding and that will swamp us. The Beast is heavy. Hell, we are just about overloaded now." This came from Kuppers, so I chopped the throttle down to a quarter, just enough for headway.

I could see the crafts coming up in front of us. At first I thought they were heading our way, but noticed we were coming up on them quickly. I chopped the throttle to stop and popped out of the pilot house. I had to see the big picture. I ran to the Beast and climbed on top. Everybody turned their attention to me. I stood up high and could see the bay spread out in front of me.

The boats in front of us started making headway from our barge. Like a flock of birds, they turned as one, eastward toward Oakland. I looked over towards the docks by Pier 39 and saw the blue and gold ships pulling out from their slips. I knew they were heading to Alcatraz and knew I had to beat them there, so we could dock. I'd need time since I had never done that, plus we had no rope to tie up with since I'd cut them so we could escape. I jumped to the hood and onto the deck running back to the pilot house. I got on the radio and called Kuppers to meet me there. I slid into the house and pushed the throttles to their maximum power settings and felt the barge start gaining speed way too slow. It felt like we were in syrup instead of water.

I looked to my left and saw Kuppers come running in, "Give me the skinny, kid."

"Those ships pulling from Pier 39 are headed to Alcatraz and if they beat us there, I won't be able to dock. And if I do beat them there, we have no way to tie up, I cut the ropes to get off the pier. I need you guys to figure something out, and let me know how close those ships are gaining on us. It's gonna be close," I yelled back.

"Got it, kid. Keep up the good work. I'll take care of this." He clicked on his radio and called out, "Apache and Brian, stay at the bow and call out when those big ships start getting close, we need to beat them to Alcatraz or we are screwed. The rest of you bastards, meet me at the Beast. We got some planning and improvising to do. Double time it."

We needed more speed. I felt like getting out and pushing the damn barge. I could see Alcatraz filling up my windscreen, and I knew I had to start turning to swing around to the east side of the island where the docks were situated. Brian came over the radio, "Looks like they are headed to the north west side of the island."

"They are going to slide into the docks first, since they won't have to make a U-turn like us." As if by magic, I felt the barge pick up speed, finally hitting her stride. And I cranked the wheel and slid around the tip of Alcatraz.

"Looks like two of the ships have collided and the third is having to slow down to get by them. We are going to make it," Apache reported over the radio.

Since we were on the short end closest to the docks, I could make the piers out. I could see that there was a newer dock on our side, so I wouldn't have to U-turn. I chopped the throttle to almost nothing, then started swerving right and left to bleed speed. There are no brakes on a boat and the last thing we needed was to crash into the dock. "There is a new dock on our end. I am trying to bleed speed so when I hit that dock, I'll need those ropes out and tied off or we are gonna just float away and lose our spot," I called over the radio.

I swerved back to the left and saw that my speed had been chopped back to a quarter of its original speed, but still too fast to dock. I smacked my head with my palm and groaned. The barge had reverse, I pulled the lever and the transmission shifted into reverse. The barge shuttered and a terrible metallic screeching came from the rear. The sound didn't die, so before the transmission could destroy itself, I shifted it back to its forward gear. I heard Kuppers yell on the radio, "Brian, we are going to need your retarded Sasquatch strength, get over here now!"

At about ten yards from the dock, I turned towards it and put the throttle to dead stop. We still had slightly too much speed, and I knew we were going to float on by the dock. To my shock, the barge came to a dead stop and then pulled closer to the dock. I reached over and switched off the engines, grabbed the key from the ignition and put it into one of the many pouches on my vest. I ran out and around the Beast to see Brian and Kuppers on the dock tying off black skinny ropes attached to the barge.

Chapter 26

I left the pilot house and found Vic standing on the side of the barge looking over to the dock. "Where the hell did they get ropes?"

181

"They are rappelling ropes that we had on the APC. Doc and Cupcake wove them into the ropes you cut and then Brian and Kuppers jumped onto the dock and used their own strength. They slowed us down."

I thanked him and went to the Beast to find the little girl. I found her sitting next to Apache, they seemed animated in discussion. I waved at her and the little girl blushed and waved back. I saw the guard guys running to the other dock.

"What's going on over there, Doc?"

Doc spit a big wad of gum over the side into the water and squinted at me. Damn, he really did look like an old west cowboy, except for the gum instead of chewing tobacco. "They're going to check every person on that ferry to make sure no one is infected or bitten. You did a good job, Dan. Where did you learn to pilot a boat?"

"Up to this point, I've never piloted one in my life. The engine was running when I climbed into the pilot house so I pushed the throttles forward and after cutting the ropes, I just tried to drive it like a car. It was kind of like one, except you have to think way ahead before doing anything," I shrugged my shoulders telling him the truth.

Doc started laughing and slapped me on the back. "Not too fucking shabby! Good job, buddy. I'm glad you decided to join us."

I stood there, kind of lost with nothing to do. I heard my name called out and looked up to see Brian waving me over. I trotted over and jumped to the dock. Vic, Kuppers, and Brian motioned for me to follow them. Over the radio, I could hear Kuppers relaying orders to the other parts of the team. "Apache, stay with the little one on the Beast. Cupcake, Doc, and Senshi, stay behind and secure the dock and barge. Back up the guard if they need you. Be right back."

We crested the hill and came up on a section that allowed us to see the city. I was blown away at the sight. A brown cloud hung over most of the city and we could see flames engulfing the docks. Brian handed me a pair of glasses and while looking through them, I could make out individual people running around looking for safety or help. Instead of safety, they were being dragged down and ravaged. "I just don't get how quickly people are changing over, and see how fast they are moving? This isn't what we witnessed in the tower."

"Has to be a mutation in the disease. For both issues," Brian answered.

I turned and scanned the bay out to Treasure Island and Berkley. They seemed tranquil, almost idyllic. I knew that wouldn't last long, once the refugees who were infected made it over the bay. I checked out the Bay Bridge and saw total bedlam. When the plane had hit, it'd made the bridge impassible. That was a good and bad thing, the way I saw it. The zombies could not make it over to the other side, but then again neither could anyone else. In fact, it trapped the ones who were on it, turning it into a buffet for the zombies. I handed the glasses back to Brian and shook my head.

"Well, your idea of staying away from the bridges was a good one. I've seen some bad shit overseas, but this looks very apocalyptic. So what's our next step, Dan?" Kuppers asked.

"We should probably stay here and wait for the boat traffic in the bay to thin out a little. Then we can head out of the bay, under the Golden Gate, head north and come up on Highway One at Stinson Beach. From there, decide where everyone is going," I answered truthfully.

"I can't find fault in Dan's plan," piped in Vic. "But what do we do for or to the people coming off of those ferries?"

"Let's make sure they can get into the buildings and secure them. Then, it's up to the NG to feed and protect them. We can spend the night here on the island and then head off at first light," Brian added his two cents to the plan.

"I can agree with that, but two people must stay with the Beast at all times. I suggest we keep Apache and Cupcake with the Barge along with that little girl. No safer place for her," Kuppers added.

We all nodded our agreement and Brian and I moved out toward the buildings to make sure they were accessible for the refugees. Vic and Kuppers headed back to the Beast to let the team in on our newly formed plan. At one of the closest entrances into the main cell block, Brian and I ran into a couple of park rangers as we were trying to figure out how to open the locked doors without damaging them too much.

One of them, a tall, blonde female, seemed to be in charge. I walked up and shook her hand, "Ma'am, we are with the SFPD Tenderloin SWAT. My name is Dan and this gorilla is Brian. I take it you're up to date on what is happening on the mainland?" The male guard eyed me suspiciously, but took my hand and shook it.

"I'm Charlotte and this is Douglas. We are the Rangers on duty right now. We don't have much info of what's going on over there, except for what came over the Coast Guard radio. Something about rioting and some sort of deadly flu."

"That is somewhat the truth. Most of San Fran is on fire and the rioting is actually, and I know you are not going to believe me, heck, I barely believe what I am about to say and I witnessed it, zombies," I informed them.

Douglas started laughing at me but stopped when Charlotte put her hand on his chest. "What do you mean zombies?" she asked.

I handed her Brian's glasses and point toward the pier, "Why don't you see for yourselves."

I watched as Charlotte's features screwed up and then grew into panic and fear. She handed the glasses to Douglas and stared at me for a beat or two. "So how can we help the SFPD, gentlemen?"

"A ferry of refugees has made it onto the dock. The National Guard has a small team going through them now, weeding out the sick and infected. We just need a place to house them till an evacuation can be worked out and implemented. This will be a National Guard mission and we are just helping before we move on," I informed her.

Douglas seems glued to the glasses and had a look of shock and amazement on his face. He slowly handed them to Brian and squeezed his eyes shut. "Whatever we can do to help, gentlemen. Consider all buildings open and us standing by to help," Charlotte answered. "Douglas, go unlock all doors and prop them open. I am going to go down to the docks and see if I can help get things moving."

Douglas mumbled an "okay" and took off into the building. Brian and I turned and started back to the docks with Charlotte in tow. We made our way to the main gate where we saw a crowd of people milling about. Charlotte unlocked the gates and put her hands up, quieting the crowd.

"Everyone, my name is Ranger Alvarez. Please be patient. When my partner comes down, we will start dividing you up and guiding you into the main cell building. Till then, just hold on and wait." She eyed a national guard soldier hurrying over to her.

"I'm Staff Sergeant Cooper, ma'am." He held his hand out to shake. Charlotte smiled and shook his hand warmly. "I have two hundred and twenty refugees, ma'am, that are not infected or sick. I also have twenty or so with bites and showing signs of infection. I made a call to my command and alerted them to our situation. They are sending reinforcements and supplies. I only have eighteen other guardsmen with me right now. There are also two damaged ferries in the water. The captain of this ferry is going to attempt a rescue of the others if he can. My question is, what do you want us to do with the infected?"

"Put a bullet in their head, Staff Sergeant. They will turn into one of those things and start spreading the infection again," Kuppers voice came in strong as he walked up adding his advice.

"I can't do that, sir. At least, not in front of their loved ones." He chewed on his bottom lip.

Charlotte reacted to Kuppers' suggestion with shock that hardened into anger. "You can't just murder these people."

"To protect these other people I would, could, and will." Kuppers cut a steely glare at Charlotte, causing her to back up a step. "But if you want infected roaming over this island, attacking and eating everyone then, that's your call, but make sure you're the first one to go down. It's not pretty to watch."

"Ok, I understand your point. Why don't we open the old Guard house here to hold them, and then we can do it once the people have moved on," she shook her head and pointed at the building next to us.

"Very well. I'll get my soldiers to take care of that, if you can show us a way in." Charlotte walked away with the soldier in tow.

"These people better get their shit together soon or this is going to turn into a buffet very quickly. Looks like you two have finished your jobs. Come with me back to the barge." With that Kuppers turned and walked away, expecting Brian and I to follow.

At the barge, Apache and Cupcake stood guard. They had their "don't fuck with me" looks on. Brian and I climbed on board and sat down, resting against the side of the Beast. The little girl came out of the Beast and stood in front of me. She looked uneasy and a little scared. I put my arms out to her and she came in quickly for a hug and then snuggled onto my lap.

"What is your full name, little one?" I asked.

"Angel Penelope Anwen," she answered with a tired little voice. Her head rested on my chest, warming my soul and giving me the chills at the same time.

"Angel, where is your family? How did we have the same dreams?" I asked trying to get answers before she fell asleep.

"I've been having those dreams for a couple of days. I don't know why, but my mother said you were my protector and that I needed to find you. They were attacked two days ago and dad was able to hide me in that car where you saved me. They were both taken," she held back a small sob and gripped me tighter.

"Well, I am here, Angel and I will do my best to protect you, I promise. Now go to sleep, have some happy dreams." I kissed the top of her head and felt her body relax and soon could hear her little breaths slip into a rhythm as she sank deeper into sleep.

"Wow, Boss, I guess someone else now believes in you, not just me anymore," Brian smiled and rested his head against the Beast's massive tire.

I held her close, feeling more at peace than ever in the last week. I rested my head on hers and let the world go black and slipped into darkness. I awoke with a start and looked around. Brian's deep rumbling snores shook the deck under us. "How long was I asleep?" I asked Vic who stood nearby, staring off into the bay.

"Fifteen minutes or so." He looked down at his watch.

"Feels like it's been hours." I felt slightly more refreshed. I looked down at Angel and saw no wrinkle or worry on her face.

Apache came over and took Angel from me, as I stood up to join the group. We could barely hear each other over Brian's snores. "Apache and Cupcake, I want you two glued to the barge at all times. We lose this, we lose everything. Doc, I want you to be our liaison with the NG unit. When they get some supplies, they owe us 5.56 from helping them out at the barricade. Try and be smooth and get some MREs while you're at it, and anything else you can cajole, beg, or steal. Senshi, you go up to the high ground and keep watch on incoming ships. Let us know when we have a safe enough lane in the bay to boogie. Vic and Dan, you two go work with the Rangers and the NG. Make sure they know what has to be done with the infected. If you have to, enforce it yourselves. I'll play radio operator, and I'm going to go play tourist. Our radios are strong enough for what we need them for, and we have our own emergency channel to use. Is there anything I am missing?" Kuppers dictated.

I raised my hand like an idiot and Kuppers just shook his head, rolled his eyes and said, "This isn't school, Dan. Just speak your mind."

I lowered my hand and blushed, then pointed at Brian, "What is an MRE and what about him?"

"It means Meals Ready to Eat. It's horrible tasting military food, but has all the calories one needs to survive. Let the Sasquatch sleep. If I need him, I'll have Apache wake and direct him. Maybe we can use him like a mule and get him to carry the supplies the NG brings in." He looked each one of us in the eye, then nodded as if he'd come to a decision and walked away.

Vic grabbed my arm and we walked away, back to the docking ferries and to meet up with the Rangers. Doc caught up and wrapped his arm around the NG guy's shoulders, steering him away from everyone.

Vic and I saw Douglas and headed in his direction. "Hey Douglas, this here is SFPD's head detective, Vic. Know where we can find Charlotte?"

"Charlotte is over there, helping the injured into the old guard house." He pointed up the walkway to another building.

"How many does she have with her? Oh and do me a favor, stay near one of these Guard guys. They are armed and just in case something happens, they will back you up."

"Last count was twenty. I know she has three soldiers with her. Yeah, I think I will go hang out with one of them." Douglas waved good bye and made his way over to three Guards directing civilians where to go.

Vic and I marched our way over to the guard house. I pushed my foot between the door and the frame before it could close all the way. We filed in together and Vic smiled at Charlotte as he closed the door. "Hi Charlotte, I never had the chance to meet you. My name is SFPD Detective Vic Reynolds. Douglas informed us you were taking the injured up here. Where are the Guard that are supposed to be with you?"

She looked back at us and moved her body, trying to block our view behind her. Before she could, I caught a glimpse of something moving behind her, but she moved quickly, cutting me off. I looked up and she locked eyes with me for a second before casting her eyes to the floor. 'Oh shit,' I thought, 'she is going to let the people go.' "You have no jurisdiction on my Island, detective Reynolds." She tried to stand her ground and take control of the situation.

"Ma'am, no one does at this moment, except for the ones with the guns. If you let these people go, you are putting everybody at risk. This infection can turn someone quickly and in turn, they will attack someone else and then we are fucked. So where are these people?" Vic removed his side arm from his leg holster holding it at his side. I saw his finger disengaging the safety, then it slid down to the trigger guard.

I removed my collapsible batons and flicked them out to their full length, they snapped audibly, locking in place. I turned away, ignoring the ongoing conversation with Vic and Charlotte. I decided to investigate what I'd seen, when she'd tried to block my view earlier. I slowly started making my way in that direction, trying not to not make too much sound. As I came around the corner, I saw three infected zombies kneeling over a couple of people. At first, it seemed like they were being intimate. Until I saw the blood and heard that awful slurping sound from the tower. I lost it, raised my batons and charged in. I crushed the head of the zombie nearest me and turned quickly in place, snapping out one of the batons onto another's head, cracking it open. By this point, the third was standing up and coming in my direction, a loud boom came from my left, almost blowing my ear drums out, and I felt something go speeding by my head. The zombie's head exploded like a watermelon after being on stage with Gallagher. All the fluids sprayed onto the wall behind it, coating it like red paint. I stood there out of breath, shaking my head trying to regain my senses.

Vic came up to my side and fired three shots into the victims' heads on the floor, turning them into red mist. He turned to Charlotte, grabbed her arm and pulled her over to witness the scene. "Where are the other sixteen?"

"I put them upstairs. There is no way out from up there," Charlotte whined.

Just then, I recognized one of the victims on the floor as a NG soldier. I pointed at it, making sure Vic saw it. He shook his head and groaned, kicking Charlotte in the back of one of her knees and sending her to the floor. He handcuffed her wrists, then pulled out two big black zip ties and tied her ankles up. "That man's death is on you, Charlotte. Now stay. I will deal with you when we are done cleaning up your mess." Vic looked over at me. "Got a little more in you?" I nodded yes and he clicked on his radio, "That female Ranger has fucked up bad. We have one dead guard, three reanimated, and three dead. There are fifteen more infected upstairs in the guard house. Dan and I are going to clean up this mess. Be prepared. I have put Charlotte under arrest, she is bound and down on the first floor of the guard house. Send someone to corral up Douglas, her partner. Also, send someone over here to back us up."

We headed over to the stairs, listening to the voice over our radio ear pieces. "Roger that, Vic. Apache, wake up Sasquatch and have him put Douglas under arrest. I'll back up Vic and Dan. Everyone else hold positions," Kuppers voice came over the radio.

I took lead since I needed room to swing my batons and we headed up the creaky stairs. I brought my head above the top level and stopped in place, looking into the eyes of another guard. This one was alive and stood there with his weapon shouldered. I waved him over, "Prepare your weapon, we had an incident down stairs and lost one of your guys to the infected. Are any of your infected unconscious?"

The young man pulled his gun off his shoulder and removed the safety. "Yes, ten are, the other six are sitting against the wall across the room."

"Where is the third Guard?" Vic asked as we finished coming up the stairs and faced the room.

"He is still outside. Only two of us came in to help the female Park Ranger. What should we do?" he asked with fear in his eyes.

Vic dropped the magazine from his gun and inserted a fresh one. "Remember what happened on the dock before we got you?" The young man nodded yes, and the fear notched higher in his eyes. "Exactly. We need to end this now. Any more come in from the other ferries and we need to do the same thing or the rest of the people coming here will not be safe. Now follow me. Dan, go down stairs and watch over that bitch." As I headed down, I saw Vic moving into the other room followed by the young

Guardsman.

Even though I'd expected the shots, they still surprised me when they broke the silence, jolting me almost to my knees. I was so upset and I made my way over to Charlotte, watching as she tried to make it over to the dead guard and his M4. I stepped on her hand, eliciting a hiss of pain from her, and picked up the gun before she could. I looked it over, looking for the safety, then engaged it and slid it onto my shoulder using its strap.

Charlotte rolled over onto her back and sneered up at me, "What you are doing is murder! You cannot just kill people who are sick and injured. You can also not detain me. I am a federal officer!" she screamed at me causing spittle to fly out from her mouth.

I focused on the dead Guard and pointed at him, "Your actions killed that young man. This is what happens when you show weakness, you kill the people who are looking to you for safety. I have been fighting these things for days now, trapped in the fucking Transamerica Tower. I've had to kill friends and coworkers. Now look around, you did this! Stop being stupid, open your eyes!" As I spoke my anger took over and I ended up shouting at her.

I almost jumped out of my skin when a hand rested on my shoulder. I looked up to find the hand belonged to Kuppers and his eyes were as hard as rocks and had no kindness in them. "People like her are sheep, son. They will never understand, or do what has to happen. Why don't you go outside and take a breather? I'll back up Vic and take care of her." I nodded in agreement and stepped outside.

I bent down and used the concrete to pop the locks on my batons and collapse them back to their normal size. As I was about to holster them, I noticed the blood on them. I headed to the dock with my head down, trying to not make eye contact with anyone. I sat down and washed the blood off of the batons, and holstered them. I raised my head after a moment and watched as Brian walked Douglas up towards the guard house. I sighed and cracked my back to release some of the tension, and jogged off to catch up to Brian as he took Douglas inside. I slid in and shadowed them over to Vic, Kuppers, the Guard from upstairs and the trussed up Charlotte on the floor.

"What is going on? Why is Charlotte being detained?" Douglas inquired, quietly since Brian's hand was resting on the nape of his neck, reminding him that he better be calm.

"This fine young man from the Guard here has requested she be detained till she can be tried in a military court for allowing a National Guardsmen to lose his life due to her negligence. She was trying to release these infected people, some of them re-animated into zombies, and killed the others along with the Guard." I examined Charlotte and noticed someone had stuck tape over her mouth. "Son, the question is, are you gonna hitch your cart to hers and go down with her? Or do you want to work with the fine men of the National Guard and help protect these poor people on your island?" Kuppers asked in a quiet yet demanding voice. Since meeting Kuppers, I'd finally figured out who he reminded me of. He looked and sounded a lot like Colonel Miles Quaritch, from the movie *Avatar*. He was able to scare and inspire people at the same time, so it was no surprise when Douglas opened his mouth.

He wiped the sweat from his forehead, looked down at Charlotte and then back up at Kuppers. "I had no idea what she was doing. I am more than happy to help the National Guard and protect these people."

Kuppers smiled and handed Charlotte's key chain to him. "You might want to give these to the Guard in charge, outside on the dock. Also, someone needs to get in the cell house and help people settled in."

"Yes, sir. I will." Brian removed his meaty paw off of the kid's shoulders freeing him. "Oh and by the way, until we are ready to deal with her, there is a cell I can lock her in."

"Excellent. I will follow your lead, sir." Kuppers reached down and lifted Charlotte to her feet. "You need to hop or I will throw you over my shoulder and carry you outta here, missy. Up to you." Charlotte screamed from behind the tape and shook her head. Kuppers rolled his eyes, picked her up and threw her over his left shoulder. "Have it your way, sweetie. Lead on, son." They left the guardhouse, leaving the rest of us standing around.

"I guess we should clean up these bodies. Should we toss them into the bay?" Brian asked.

I shrugged and asked the guard and Vic, "What do you guys suggest?"

"I'll get a detail once the traffic outside has thinned, and take care of these bodies. Thanks for your help, guys," the Guardsman answered. His name tag listed his name as Schillinger.

Brian, Vic and I turned to leave when suddenly, I remembered I had the dead Guard's M4. I took it off my shoulder and handed it over to Schillinger. "Here, this belongs to you guys. I took it from him," I indicated the dead man on the floor.

"Thank you, but I am sure we will have a lot more than we can use soon. Why don't you keep it?" He handed it back to me.

I nodded my thanks and slung it back on my shoulder, where it started banging into the shotgun that was already perched there. Brian, Vic and I made our way back to the barge and I secured the M4 onto a rack in the Beast. I realized that I was really going to have to learn how to use those damn things soon.

A whumping sound ripped through the air causing me to look up, just as my ear piece crackled to life with Senshi's voice. At least, I thought it was him, I'd only heard his voice twice before. "Three choppers coming in from the south. Two are carrying slung pallets under them. Looks like the one with nothing slung is heading to the north eastern side and the other two right up here to the exercise concrete pad." Then, his voice was gone.

Brian tapped my shoulder to gain my attention, pointed up the hill and took off at a jog. I on the other hand, had to sprint to catch up to his long legs. I finally caught up with him at the top of the hill and the flat concrete area, just as one of the helicopters released the pallet's canvas sling. I had to bend over to catch my breath. While doing that, I watched three Guardsmen struggle to move two pallets out of the open area to give a clear landing space for both helicopters to land.

Brian didn't waste a second. He ran over, dropped his shoulder and hit one of the pallets, grunting, pushing, and roaring out loud. Slowly, the pallet started moving faster as he gained his footing, and he moved it all by himself to the side of the hill. The other Guardsmen had stopped in their tracks, out of his way and had watched his massive feat of strength in awe. The guardsmen then looked to me for guidance. I shrugged and pointed to the other one. We ran over together and started shoving it away from the landing zone. Once the pallets were far enough away, the two helicopters

196

set down and the men within disembarked. Once everyone was out, the two helicopters took off, staggered so they wouldn't hit one another.

A man wearing what looked like some kind of officer rank on his collar walked over while examining my uniform and gear, "You don't look like you're in the Guard."

"Nope. I am with the SFPD SWAT, name is Dan Welko." I held my hand out to him and he stared at it for a minute, then shook it with a strong grip.

"Dan, that there is a Captain in the Air Guard, 129th out of Moffett, unless my guess is wrong," Brian said walking up to us.

"When did SWAT start hiring Bigfoot?" the Captain laughed. "I am Captain Phillips from the 129th. We brought some supplies and have more on the way. What the hell is the situation here?"

"My commander, John Kuppers is on his way down, sir. He will brief you in on the situation, sir," Brian answered. Just then, Doc, Kuppers, and another Guard came trotting down from a walkway that winded up to the cell house.

Kuppers walked right up to the Captain and punched him on the shoulder hard enough to make the Captain hiss in pain, "Well, if it ain't Captain Phillips! Gee, it's been what five years since we got to practice SAR up in the Sierras?" I found out later from Brian that SAR meant Search and Rescue.

The Captains eyes went wide, as his smile deepened and he punched Kuppers' shoulder back, "Ironman! Holy shit, good to see you alive. So give me a no shitter, what's going on here?"

Kuppers took the Captain's arm and moved him away, out of ear shot of the rest of us. Doc and the Guardsman; Franklin, his name tag said, started opening pallets. Doc's eyes grew in size, like a little girl getting a pony for Christmas, at what he'd discovered. A couple of 129th Air guys gave Doc a detailed inventory of their contents. I watched as Doc read through the inventory reports and his smile just kept growing and growing till I thought his face was going to split in half. He craned his neck looking around, then headed over when he'd located Kuppers. He waited for a short time before breaking in on their conversation. Doc showed Kuppers the inventory and babbled on a bit till Senshi's voice broke over our radio, "We got another three copters coming in. Same heading, same set up."

Doc's attention was torn away from his discussion with Kuppers as he looked up searching for the helicopters. As before, they dropped their pallets and we all worked at moving them over before they touched down to let their men disembark. I noticed that this group had more Army, instead of Air Guard guys. They disembarked with their rifles in hand and marched straight up to the guardsmen standing with Doc. They saluted and started in on the conversations going on. Brian and I looked at each other and shrugged. We both felt a little left out of the going ons.

As if reading our minds, Kuppers and the Captain, along with the new Army National Guard arrivals made their way to where Brian and I were waiting patiently. "More of the same coming," Senshi reported over the radio.

Kuppers stopped at a pathway nearby and motioned for Brian and I to meet up with them. The Captain spoke up first when we entered the group, "Kuppers just sang your praises, Dan. Good work on the Transamerica building, you too, Brian." He shook our hands again, but this time with more warmth.

One of the Army Guardsman introduced himself and his command group, "I am Captain Scott and this is First Sergeant Hinton and Banks. We are with the 49th MP Brigade that you already have here. Sounds like we owe you guys some ammo and supplies since we had to borrow from you earlier. By the way, before we go any further, I am in debt to you and your team for saving my men and getting this place under control. Your man Doc here, was just telling me what we owe and that shouldn't be a problem. We brought more than enough. I'll get a detail together and have them take it down to your barge. I take it you guys are not sticking around?"

"Thank you for the supplies. That young man, Dan is the one who rescued your men," Kuppers motioned to me.

The Army Captain turned and held his hand out to me, I took it and shook his hand, "No problem. We were at the right place at the right time to help. I'm just sorry that we couldn't save everyone."

"We can't be everywhere at once. They did their jobs."

"So Ironman, tell us why are you guys running out on us? Do you know something we don't?" inquired Captain Phillips.

"We have our own mission to complete. I won't bore you with the details. But give me your frequency and codes, so if we find any information to share I can call you. Or who knows? We may need an air taxi," Kuppers laughed out loud.

I took that moment and left the group, making my way out to the landing area and watched as more helicopters came in. 'How did they find this many supplies and get them out over here so quickly?' I thought. Suddenly, the sun was snuffed out and a large arm plummeted down on my shoulders, almost buckling me to my knees. I moved my head to the side and had to look up as Brian leaned a little on me and laughed at my discomfort.

"Hey Brian, what do you think about all of this?" I asked.

"It would've been nice to have had these resources when we were in the tower. A lot would be different right now," he sighed.

We trotted over to the side of the hill and stood out of the way, watching as Doc ran to each box and pointed to items within. The Guards followed him, reached in and removed the items he had indicated, then took them over to an empty pallet with a box on it.

Kuppers caught my eye and trotted over, "Ok, it's getting late. I suggest we bring everyone to the barge, except Senshi. We'll keep him on his high station as over watch. Doc has most of his supplies figured out and they are going to use the next chopper to transfer them to the barge." He started down the hill and we followed, as he probably expected we would.

He called over the radio informing everyone to get off the barge except Cupcake, so the NG could deliver our supply pallet. We arrived to find Apache, Angel, and Vic standing on the dock waiting for us. I wondered when Doc would show up to help.

I heard and felt the thumping from the helicopter blades as it approached. I scanned the sky looking for the helicopter and was taken back by the sight. Doc was standing on the pallet, waving and shaking his hips, dancing while holding on to the straps securing the pallet. He was laughing like a child, enjoying his ride.

"Damn idiot," Kuppers grumbled.

I watched as Cupcake climbed onto the top of his beloved beast. He used hand signals to direct the pilots to land the pallet on the barge as close to the beast as they could. Once down, Doc reached up and hit a lever, signaling to the pilot he was clear and to move on. The pilot waved back and gained altitude, then banked to the south and flew off. I was awed at the sight and the feats of the pilot. That man had to have nerves of steels to do what he did.

Kuppers jumped on the barge and pointed at Doc, "What kind of toys did you bring us?"

Doc sat on a big box beaming with pride, a giant grin that stretched from ear to ear was plastered on his face. "Well, we have twenty cans of 5.56 ammo. Each can carries about 800 rounds, so about 16,000 rounds. We also have fifty preloaded M4 magazines, so that is another 1,500. Twenty boxes with twelve MREs in each of them, so we have about 240. And twenty fifteen-gallon tanks of diesel. We also got in the deal five two-man tents along with sleeping bags and toilet paper. They also provided us with twenty-five gallons of water And I found some other toys that the Army didn't know they were carrying." Doc reached back, opened a box and took out two round items and tossed them to Kuppers.

"Why were they carrying frag and white phosphorous grenades on a rescue mission?" Kuppers asked.

"I have no idea, but somehow I became an owner of thirty of each. Did I do a good job, sir?"

"Very good, son. Now, get everything packed up and onto the Beast. We leave tomorrow at first light. We can take shifts sleeping inside the Beast tonight. Senshi will stay on over watch till we leave. Vic, figure it all out and get everyone fed and then it's bed. I got some shit to take care of with the Guard." With that, Kuppers headed back up the hill towards the supply helicopters.

"All right, everyone grab an MRE and eat up. Doc, I want you and Cupcake to pack up this gear and get it on top of the beast and secured. Brian, Dan, Angel and Apache, you will take first shift of sleep. Doc, Cupcake, Kuppers and I will take second shift for sleep. I'll run an MRE up to Senshi. I expect you four to have eaten and be prepared to sack out when I come back." He looked around one last time, grabbed an MRE and headed up the hill.

Doc threw some big plastic packages at us. Apache opened one for Angel, using her knife. I watched her closely, then pulled my Kabar and mimicked her ways of opening the MRE. Apache sat down with her back to the Beast and patted the ground next to her, motioning for Angel to sit down. Brian winked at me and patted the area near him. I threw him the bird and sat down Indian style in front of them. I dug out the contents of my MRE, putting them in order in front of me. I had never eaten one of these and had no idea what to expect. I stared at the bigger pouch, took out my Kabar and cut off the top. I stared at the contents and took a sniff. It smelled bland, so I dipped a finger in, scooping some of the sauce out. I sucked my finger and even though not impressed, I gave in to my stomach and looked around for a way to eat it.

"I got chili and beans. What did you guys get?"

"Looks like spaghetti, I think," I said while looking for a fork.

"Raviolis! Yummy, but do I need to eat it cold?" This came from

Angel.

"Give it to me, sweetie." Brian took her pouch and used the cardboard sleeve and some other thing and gave it back to her. "Give it a couple of seconds, but be careful. It will be hot." Angel sat down and stared at the cardboard, waiting for it to heat up.

I found a spork in one of the little packets from the main pack. I stared at it and the main food packet and tried to figure out how to eat it with the little spork cleanly. Finally, after getting pissed off and frustrated, I dropped the spork and slowly started squeezing out the contents directly into my mouth. I chewed the food and tried to enjoy the blandness.

Brian bent over laughing, "Wow, took me a month to start eating these things like that. Every meal, I ended up using half my water ration for the day to clean my arms." He also turned his food package upside down and squeezed the food into his mouth.

I watched as Apache magically pulled a plate out and dumped her warm food onto it. She then produced another one and dumped Angel's food onto it and handed it to her. She smiled at us and they started eating like civilized people. "Sure, if I had known we had plates I would've done that too." I stuck my tongue out at Apache.

The two girls ignored my childish humor and they sat there eating their food in silence, while Sasquatch and I worked on ours like the Neanderthals we were. When done, we volunteered to help Doc with the packing and securing. He was happy to put us to work. We took the boxes he handed us and tied them onto the roof of the Beast. Something came to me, so I vocalized it to my companions. "If we tie everything to the roof and we come under fire or something happens, won't we lose most of our supplies?"

Doc stuffed more gum into his mouth and twisted the ends of his mustache as he stared at me. "Good thinking, Dan, but I already thought about that." He reached down and picked up one of the big black backpacks at his feet and pointed at it, "Meet your new best friend. I loaded yours with ten MRE packs and since you are rucking around that shotgun, I added some ammo for it and just in case, five magazines for that M4 you got from your new NG buddy. You also have some toilet paper, some other little things I thought you might need, along with a sleeping bag, a small med kit, and even though I don't want you to touch them, I added a couple of the frag grenades in there. I call these our Zomgo bags. If everything goes tits up, you grab your pack and go, go, go." He threw my bag at me and I found out very quickly that it must've weighed close to fifty pounds when it almost pushed me back onto my ass.

He pointed to the boxes we were tying up, "Those boxes have some supplies it would be nice to have but not essential, like the rest of the food and stuff. The important things like ammo and some of the fuel are going inside the beast. Some of us, like Sasquatch there will be carrying double, if not triple the ammo load out everyone else is carrying in their packs."

I climbed up on the beast next to Cupcake and we made sure to tie down the boxes. Then, using the cradle net that the pallet was flown in on, we draped it over the supplies and secured it down. Afterwards, Doc ordered Brian and I to go to bed, or 'sack out' as he'd called it.

Brian and I climbed into the beast, took our seats, closed our eyes and were out in seconds. This time I didn't dream. Instead, I slept the sleep of gods. I felt someone shaking me and calling out my name. I opened my eyes to see Apache staring down at me, "Time to get up, buddy. We need you to pilot the barge."

"What? Don't you mean, it's time for me to take my turn on watch?" I undid my seat belt and followed her out of the Beast, knuckling my eyes and tried to clear my blurry vision.

"Nope, we let you and Angel sleep. It didn't look like we would need you last night on watch, so you got some beauty sleep. Now come on, let's go." She took my hand and walked me to the pilot house.

Chapter 27

"Great, but do you mind if I relieve myself first?" She pointed to the edge of the barge and gave me the go for it motion. I stepped up, unzipped and really enjoyed that release. I zipped back up and reached into my pocket, removing the hand sanitizer I'd picked up from the locker room back at the SFPD. I cleansed my hands and walked over to the pilot house with a big smile on my face. I reached into my pocket and took out the keys I'd removed the day before from the control panel. I slid it into the ignition and waited a second, looking over the board. I had no idea what to do next. I saw a light come on and then, I pushed the start button. The engines rumbled to a start. Engines must be diesel, so maybe I'd had to wait for the glow plugs to warm? I was just guessing.

I stepped out of the pilot house and caught Brian's attention, "Cast us off when you're ready." I popped my head back in and looked over the myriad of gauges. The engines seemed to have heated up and our fuel gauge showed close to full. I then noticed a small screen on the top of the control panel and reached up to hit the power button. The screen came on with a message welcoming me to the Furuno FCV30BB 4 Kw Commercial Sounder. It powered up and showed a graph of the depth of water beneath us. I had no idea what the particulars were, but I figured we had enough water under us.

"Dan, all aboard and we have been set free of our tie down. Do your stuff," Brian called out.

I got on my radio and requested Kuppers come over to the pilot house for a pow wow. He came over and had something in his hands. "First, give me your radio while you are pulling us out into the clear waters." I undid my radio and handed it over. He shut it off and connected a new one to my headset, turned it on and secured it back to my vest.

I engaged the throttles a quarter and moved us out, away from the island. I could see more ships anchored in close to Alcatraz, waiting for their turn to dock. "Kuppers, we never really discussed the details of our trip. I have an idea and wanted to run it by you."

"I know you said something about Stinson beach. That's good enough for me for now. Once we get there, we can flesh out the details and figure out how to get the beast off. I replaced your radio with a recharged one. Sasquatch is making some coffee and I'll have him bring some over to you. Need anything else?" he asked.

"Yeah waffles, boysenberry syrup and some bacon would be nice," I chuckled. Kuppers growled something, stuffed a cookie into my mouth and walked away.

'I think I am growing on him,' I thought. "All right team, just like yesterday. Everyone take a position and call out traffic, debris, and obstacles. Apache, can you get on top of the Beast, so we have a slightly higher eye out on the bay?"

"Roger, on my way," called out Apache as I looked over and saw her appear on top of the Beast, standing tall and craning her head in different directions. She looked over to me and gave me a thumbs up.

"We need to head to the Golden Gate and pass under it. Once there, we need to stick to the northern shore but not close enough to break up on the rocks. Once free of the bay, we need to head north to Stinson Beach. Just want to give you guys the full rundown of my intentions." I increased the throttles to half. I got a gaggle of rogers on the radio.

"Clear to the immediate bow, port and starboard. Although, I don't remember which is which," Doc radioed over.

"Port is left and starboard is right facing toward the bow, you dork," answered Cupcake.

"Wait. Whoa, how the fuck did you know that? I'm still amazed you know your right from your left," commented Apache, making fun of him.

"I grew up in Maine. My dad was a fisherman and that's just something I remembered. Also, I know how to bait lobster and crab pots," answered Cupcake.

"Wow, interesting stuff. Now shut the fuck up and direct Dan, so we can get back on shore," Kuppers growled over the radio.

"Apache, how are we looking with the bridge and traffic?" I asked on the radio.

"We are doing good. Free of flotsam and traffic. If you want to, we could advance our speed and be ok," she answered back.

"Roger that, keep your eyes open, boys and girls. I can't stop this thing on a dime," I alerted everyone. I reached over and advanced the throttles to three quarters and relatively soon, I got the bridge filling up my windshield. Having the pilot house at deck level in the middle of the barge, and to the right of the Beast made it very hard to see anything.

"This is Brian. Cut to starboard slightly. Flotsam in the way about fifty yards."

I turned the wheel to starboard, bringing us slightly over to that direction. "How's that, Brian?"

"Good, it will be going down our port side very soon," he answered back. "All looks clear. Stay on this heading."

I kept staring at the bridge as it became all that I could see in my windshield. 'Damn, that thing is big,' was all I could think. Suddenly, something fell down and hit the suicide net underneath it. Oh shit. I then saw more people jumping and landing in the net. The net started to become filled with bodies.

"Oh shit! Everyone, eyes up! Watch out for falling zombies. Call out if you see any get free of the net!" I yelled through the radio. I didn't want to wait for the inevitable to happen, so I pushed the throttles to their max. Again, the barge slowly picked up speed and headed towards the bridge.

"Off our starboard! Two bodies falling, should miss us," Doc radioed out.

"Off to the port, six bodies falling. Steer to starboard slightly," radioed in Cupcake.

I looked up and saw two bodies make it over the net and start falling down at us on a direct line. There was nothing I could do to maneuver. "Heads up! Center of deck off bow. We are going to get hit! Watch out!" I yelled over the radio.

I watched the two bodies collide with the deck. I didn't have time to look at them as I had my head back up, watching the net. Five more bodies fell. I glanced to starboard and port and cranked the wheel to port. "Five more, heads up! Steering port!"

That part of the net seemed less crowded than middle of the net. I tried to push the throttles higher, but they were already maxed out. I guess all I can do is grin and bare it. "More falling, too many to count, on our last position starboard, but not too far off" someone radioed out.

I looked further to port and saw the bridge legs coming up. I didn't have much more room to maneuver, but I should be under the bridge and protected by the deck above. I could hear the bodies colliding with the bay like a waterfall to starboard and slightly to the stern. "Are we clear and under the deck completely?" I asked over the radio.

"Yes, we are clear. I think we only got hit four times. We rolled the bodies into the bay," Vic's voice came over the radio.

"Everyone, we will be heading out from the other side soon. I'm hoping we can get clear fast, but keep your eyes open and eyes to heaven." Just for the hell of it, I cut the barge to starboard for a minute then back to port, straightening out.

We burst out on the other side. Bodies start falling into the ocean where we would've come out if I hadn't make the course correction. I wiped the sweat off my forehead and head. 'I really need to shave soon,' I thought. I cut back to the right and kept an eye on the depth sounder. I didn't want to slam into a hidden rock or sand bar, we'd never be able to get the Beast off.

"I can see ships at about twenty miles, look like they are anchored or free floating. Hey Vic, can you contact that Air Force Captain and tell him to send out copters to tell these people where it's safe?" Doc answered.

"On it."

Twenty minutes later, we came up to the south of the Point Bonita Lighthouse. I swung out further south knowing that the light house was there to warn ships of rocks and obstacles. We came out into open ocean and the barge started to rock more. I came around the Lighthouse and tried to skirt back towards the shore, but far enough away to not be grounded.

The radio crackled. "If you look to the east, we are gathering a pretty good group of people watching us from shore. These people are alive. I think we need to go west a little more so these people don't get the idea to come out to us and flood the barge." This came from Brian.

I cut west and we took on the bigger waves. After about fifteen minutes, I cut back north. The waves were coming at us from the west and rocked the barge back and forth. "We should be ok, but any bigger waves and we may flip. This thing is not made to be used in the open ocean," I broadcasted over the radio.

"What we need is a sea anchor. How much longer do you think we will be out here?" This came from Cupcake, our only person even close to being a sailor.

"I'm not sure, maybe about two and a half hours. I don't have a GPS in the place it should be, so I am fully guessing," I answered honestly.

"If the tide starts coming in, we may be screwed. I suggest we figure a way to create a sea anchor or find another place to run this thing up on a beach," Cupcake answered back.

"Muir Beach is coming up soon. It has a pretty big beach and we can drive through the rich houses and onto Highway 1 from there," Senshi replied. Wow, that was the most I had ever heard him say.

"How the fuck do you know that, Senshi?" Kuppers asked over the radio.

"I was dating a girl out there last year. Nice house," he answered back.

"Ok, let's go ahead and go for Muir Beach. But I'll have no idea where that is if we don't move closer to the shore," I radioed out.

"Senshi, get your ass to the pilot house and direct Dan in. Dan, cut east and come closer to shore, but no closer than a hundred yards," Kuppers ordered.

Within a minute, Senshi was standing next to the pilot house keeping his gaze on the shore. He pointed out to the north and starboard, "There it is. We should start angling in now to the beach or we could hit the rocks there at the point."

I cut in our barge angling toward the beach when we were about a hundred yards away. I felt that we were coming in too fast and I reached out to chop the throttles, but Cupcakes hand landed on mine, stopping me from moving them back. "I'm going to start my girl and move her to the stern so the bow will come up out of the water a little. That will allow us to slide in closer to the beach. We have no ramp, so I'll have to drive this damn thing off. Keep it steady." He ran away and jumped into the Beast and started it up. The rumbling easily droned out the sound of the barge's engines.

Within seconds, he backed the Beast up and I could feel the bite of the propellers as the bow came out of the water. I cut the wheel in as the beach came up on us. "Grab on to something people and stay away from the Beast!" I yelled over the radio.

I looked around as we came in closer and realized everyone was holding on to the pilot house. Brian and Apache were blocking Angel and keeping her safe from the force of the impact. Just as we hit the beach, I heard the Beast rev up, and then roared down the barge and off the end of the bow. As it went off the end, the barge's gravity shifted forward allowing the Beast to not get caught on the edge of the bow and throw its ass end up. The front tires hit the sand, gripping and pulling the Beast onto the beach. The bow then tilted back up after the Beast roared off and stayed there. I turned the key and shut down the engines.

I stood at the bow, watching Cupcake pull the Beast up the hill and onto the parking lot at the top. Once there, I saw him get out and stand at guard waiting for us. I watched as each team member left, jumping off the bow and landing on the beach seven feet below. I'm not that athletic so I waited. I then saw Angel standing there at the bow, looking over the top and out onto the sand down below.

"Brian, come over. I'm going to lower Angel down to you." Brian trotted over and raised his hands.

I picked up Angel and gave her a hug, "I'm going to hold your wrists and lower you down to Brian. Ok?"

She nodded at me and smiled, "I trust you, Dan." I took her wrists and held her over the edge and watched as Brian easily reached up and grabbed her by the waist, placing her onto the sand.

"Can you do that for me, too?" I said out loud and watched as everyone laughed.

"I betcha he won't jump," said Doc.

"He won't, but see he is smarter. He will find a way to get down without having to be too physical," Brian said.

I looked around and then dropped to my knees. I grabbed the edge of the bow, swung my body out and let it hang. Now, I only had like a foot and a half to drop. I let go and bent my knees to absorb the impact. I turned around and took a bow, smiling and laughing.

Apache, Vic and Angel clapped and laughed. The rest just shook their heads and headed towards the hill following in the deep ridges in the sand that the Beast had left. I took Angel's hand and we walked up the hill together. We gathered at the Beast and I knelt down to sit next to Angel, as Brian sat down on the other side of her.

"I think we need to have a talk, ladies and gentlemen. A talk which could change the fate of our team here. We need to decide where we all want to go and what we think is our main destination. And once there, what to do," I announced to the whole team. "I have someone who means a lot to me, living up in Fort Bragg just north of here. My focus is getting to her.

I want to make sure I am very clear of my intentions. I am not being an ingrate or anything like that, I appreciate each and every one of you. I would not be alive right now without your support, and kindness, and in Little Jonny's case, his ultimate sacrifice." I wiped a small tear before it could release down from my eye.

Brian lifted his hand, "I have been fighting by Dan's side since the beginning, I have nothing else out there. So, I will be staying by his side for the duration. Good or bad, I've got his back. Like he said though, thank you for all of you guys and what you've done for us." He made sure to look into everyone eyes while delivering his little speech.

"As you all know, my ex-wife lives in Portland. I spoke to her yesterday and told her I was coming. So, I will be traveling with Brian and Dan," Vic walked over and stood by us.

The team got quiet. As one, they turned to Kuppers. He stared back at them, putting his hands on his hips and then sighed, "Guys, as of right now, you no longer work for me. I cannot and will not make this decision for you. I, as of right now, owe Vic for a lot in our time together. So I will be following him to Portland. From there, I have no idea. But before any of you make your decisions, I need to ask Dan and Brian some questions." He turned towards me and fixed me with a gaze that could've either been a death glare or something close to it. "What are your future plans? After you pick up your friend in Fort Bragg? What's your ultimate goal? Give me a reason to follow you."

I looked to Brian for advice or I guess comfort. But it was Angel who reached out and touched my face, smiling. "Guys, I cannot ask you to follow me. My father lives near Spokane, Washington on two-hundred acres of land with forests and a small lake. I received an email from him before we left the SFPD that said he was going to fortify it and stock up for anyone I could bring with me. He was in the Navy most of his life, but is one of those back country guys that will be able to weather anything that is thrown at him. So my full plan is to go for Julie, that's my friend's name, then accompany Vic to rescue his wife. Then, from there to my dad's place. Any or all of you are welcome to follow for all or part of the trip." As I was speaking, Angel had taken my hand and given me the strength to speak.

Kuppers stared at me for a while, then nodded his head as if coming to a difficult decision. He then walked over to our side. "Alright, I never got married or have kids, so this plan is good enough for me, I'm in. The rest of you need to make your own decisions based on your families and responsibilities."

Apache was the first to pipe up. "I was born on a reservation and lived with my people till I was old enough to find my place in this world. The Army, I thought could be my new tribe, but I was wrong. I found my tribe when I joined with you guys. You are my family, my tribe of warriors. But I believe that my path is clear. I will stay by Dan's side." She walked over to our side and patted my head, standing behind Brian.

"My family is in Texas, living on one of the biggest privately owned cattle ranches. I think they can do without me for a while. Anyway, what good is an Indian without a Cowboy? I'm in till this shit calms down, then I am going home to check on ma and pa." Doc spit out his gum, stroked his mustache and walked over to stand next to Apache.

All that was left was Senshi and Cupcake standing next to the Beast. "I am not married, and have been between girlfriends for a while, so I have nothing here to live for. My parents are old and they are far away. I must come to grips that I would never be able to get to them in time to do anything. When Doc leaves, I will follow him south. Till then, I will continue to fight next to my fellow warriors." Senshi walked over and stood behind me. As he walked by, he muttered quietly enough for only me to hear, "If you are lying, I will kill you myself."

Cupcake threw his hands into the air and shook his head theatrically, staring up into the sky. "Well, I'm not letting anyone drive my girl, so I guess I will continue to be your taxi driver. That and something has come clear to me just now. Kuppers here made sure to build his team with warriors who are unattached and have no kids, but I have a secret. I have children, three boys, but they live in Poland with their mom. I have no way to reach them, so until I can get home, I will stay with the team." He slapped the Beast's side, "Mount up! We go north."

Kuppers stared daggers at Cupcake. "You are right, Anthony. I made sure all of you were unattached. If I had known about your boys, I would've kicked you to Tufo's team. I do not like making phone calls to loved ones about how someone on my team died and won't be coming home to their family. Wrote too many of those letters while serving in the military. Now get your ass in there and get us to Fort Bragg. I'll kick your ass later."

"Hey everyone, we have one more person who needs to make their decision." I looked to Angel and she stiffened, staring back at me. The team halts and all heads turned towards the little girl. Her dress is smudged and her hair's once pretty curls have gone flat. Her eyes though, have not lost their shine and hope.

She looked to everyone and then turned towards me, "I have nothing left. I lost my mommy and daddy and have nowhere to go. But I feel like I have a new family, I have all of you. I feel protected and loved.

There is nowhere else I would rather be then with all of you." She'd turned and looked me in the eyes when she'd said that last word. She then hugged me tight and then walked around to everyone in turn and gave them each a hug.

I climbed back into the Beast and took my spot, buckling up and securing my weapons. Brian reached out and patted my knee and banged his helmet against mine. "Good speech, Boss. Good job keeping us altogether."

"That was pure luck, buddy. I feel like we were all meant to stay together though," I answered back. I leaned my head against the wall and passed out.

Waking a short time later, I look over at Vic who has a worried look on his face. He taps Cupcake on the shoulder and points outside the windshield. Cupcake nods and pulls the Beast onto the shoulder. Vic raises his voice to be heard by everyone, "Everyone, up and out. We need to talk."

Chapter 28

Kuppers opens his eyes instantly coming awake. He hits the button by his head and pops the doors open. He steps out, raising his gun and flicking on the light mounted on a rail on the top of his weapon, illuminating the immediate area. He sweeps an arch around our position and then waves everyone out. I take Angel and pop her onto Kuppers vacated seat. "Stay here, sweetie. You can see us from here, ok?"

The team gathers around the back of the Beast and look toward Vic. "We've only gone four and a half miles since we landed at two this afternoon. We are at a spot on the map called Webb Creek just outside of the community of Stinson Beach. The highway has been a mess with broken cars and we have been stopped twice by CHP. I explained we were on our way to a call in Point Reyes Station, about seventeen miles from our current position. They have warned me that they have had break outs on this highway and that they think they have dealt with it. They were also in a hurry to go south. I have a feeling they are being called back toward San Fran to handle those traffic issues on the bridges. I really feel like we should hold up right here tonight, instead of chancing it by entering Stinson Beach when we can't see much. I suggest we pull further off the road and set up guard shifts to protect the area. We need to let Cupcake sleep and refuel the Beast."

"What did I tell you about calling my baby a beast?" Cupcake says with mock irritation.

"To call it a Sexy Beast?" Apache says with humor.

"Yes, well as long as you say the 'Sexy' part in your head, I can handle you calling her a Beast," he says flipping Apache off.

"Doc, Senshi, and Apache, walk down that road. According to the map, it's called Rocky Point Road. Recon and radio back when you find a place for us to hide this thing and make camp for tonight," Vic orders.

All three grab new radios from the back of the Beast and head out down the road. I reach out and grab a new radio and attach it to my vest, connecting the earpiece. I put both guns in the Beast and turn to Vic, "I need to walk, so I am going with them. I would refuel now if you can, just in case we need to go quickly." He gives me a mock salute and dismisses me with a wave. I pull out my batons and flick them out to their full length. I then jog to catch up with Apache and her team.

"Decided to come along? Tired of being cooped up in that thing?" Apache asks as she walks next to me.

"It's starting to smell bad, plus I need to feel like I am helping. Hopefully, I won't be a nuisance."

Apache punches my shoulder and points at my batons, "We really need to teach you how to use your guns. I kind of wish we had silencers, it would make life so much easier. That or we are all going to need to learn to fight like you. Quiet is sometimes better than our loud ruckus."

The punch kind of hurt, but I was not going to complain. I didn't want to give them any more reasons to think less of me. We moved in silence. With the sun going down, it was getting harder to see into the bush. Suddenly, Apache grabs me and throws me to the ground, covering me with her body. I see that Doc and Senshi have also thrown themselves to the ground. All of my air explodes out of me in a rush and I am having problems getting more into my starving lungs. Panic starts to well up into my chest.

"Relax, Dan. I can tell you had the air knocked out of you. I am going to move off of you. I want you to try and breath slowly trying not to make much noise. Up ahead there are some guards, but they haven't seen us yet. So when you can breathe, I want you to crawl over to the rocks and stay hidden. Keep your ass down and use your arms and feet to move forward," Apache whispers into my ear so softly that I barely hear every word.

She shifts her body's weight off of me and I pull in a small amount of air. I can feel myself wanting to cough but I bite it back, covering my mouth with my sleeve. My lungs finally inflate and I look towards the rocks Apache had indicated. I pull my hands forward and shift my hips, pushing my ass down as I pull myself forward. I keep repeating this maneuver till I make it to the rocks. I hear over the radio. "Four incoming, MP5s on slings. They haven't seen us. Dan, stay where you are. Doc, come up on their right, I got left. Senshi make contact." I hear what sounds like clicks and static come across the radios.

I watch from behind a small boulder as the men have their flashlights out sweeping the ground in front of them. I watch as their lights shine on something in the dirt that gets their attention. One of the guys in the middle steps out and kneels down to pick up whatever he has seen. So quick that I almost miss it, I watch as the other three men are knocked down and disarmed. The man kneeling stands and starts to turn when his feet fly over his head and he lands on his back. I can hear the thwack as his head bounces on the dirt road. In seconds all four guards are down, disarmed and secured by Apache and her unflinching M4. I hear over the radio, Doc reporting back to the team and calling up Kuppers.

A minute goes by and Kuppers comes walking out of the dark and into the midst of Apache and the men on the ground. "You know, you can probably hear more Dan, if you get up and go over there." I flinch from the voice and roll onto my back. Senshi is standing there, relaxed with his weapon hanging down in front of him and resting his hands on the buttstock. He offers a hand and I take it.

"Holy crap! I almost pissed myself. What are you a ghost or something?" I ask Senshi.

He shakes his head and steps back, melting away into the dark. He has to show me that trick someday. I walk over to Kuppers and Apache slowly, taking my time. I had no idea if there were others out there. I came within ten yards, stopped and listened to the conversation.

"Who the hell are you guys, and what are you doing patrolling this road?" Kuppers asked in a conversational tone.

"Fuck you! We're just out taking a walk when your thugs hit us and knocked us down. I want someone to come look over our friend. I think you hurt him." The man speaking was wearing black BDUs similar to ours, but his vest was festooned with what I took as magazines and all that, was sitting over some pretty cool armor. The man seemed defiant and had longer hair instead of a military cut and to me, looking like anything but military.

"Sir, if you are just out for a walk, where did you find the H&K MP5s and that nifty armor you are wearing? Your friend will be fine, he will have a headache when he wakes up, but that should be it. Now, want to tell me another story?" Kuppers seemed totally at ease like he was used to doing this very thing. I realized he probably had done things like this. He was a SWAT commander for the SFPD and had been in the military.

"I'm not answering any more of your questions, old man. You don't scare us," the guy spat out.

Kuppers walked over to me and took one of my batons and Kabar, then walked back. He made sure the men could see his hands and the weapons he held. "Son, you may not say anything, but once your friends here see what I do to you, I'm sure that will get them talking. Anyone want to take me up on this?" He said everything calmly and with no anger in his voice. Just a matter of fact, like he was talking about something in a manual. That man scared me. "No one wants to speak up? No problem. I mean, I haven't done this in a while, but I am sure I'll remember after a couple of minutes."

Kuppers whipped out my baton, catching the guy on his ankle and cracking the delicate bone, then very quickly chopped a hand across the man's throat. The man's eyes bulged and he started wheezing, trying to pull in a breath or make a sound. Kuppers took his former position looking down at the rest of the men. "Anyone want to speak up? Or do I need to start cutting things?" he asked again, making sure to keep his voice calm and emotionless.

The two men still conscious had murder in their eyes instead of fear. Kuppers' shoulders slumped and he sighed. "Ok. I tried the nice way, guys. I guess I need to do this the not so nice way." He handed the baton back to me and I took it, stepping back. I'm not sure I really want to see this.

"I spent a lot of time overseas, boys, places that I can't officially name, you see. But I met some really interesting people by being in these places. People who, let's say have some very special talents at getting information from people. Sometimes, they left the person a shell of themselves and begging to be killed at the end, instead of living like that. Well, these nice guys taught me some of their art, for an art it is. You see, we start with nice things like pulling off nails. You know, some hardy men can handle that, so we then move onto the next step, which is to remove fingers. Oh, we don't remove all of them, usually they left the pinkies. I asked why the pinkies once, but they never answered me. After the fingers, they like to cut the Achilles tendon down at the back of the foot by the ankle. You see, once that is cut, you can't ever walk right again. So of course, they usually leave the rest of the legs alone. Instead, they move to the eyes. More to the point, they cut off the eye lids, then goes the nose. At this point, ninety percent of the people being asked questions, cave and answer them all. Heck they'll sell out their own grandma. Now for the real tough ones, well, I'll need a blow torch to cauterize all the blood and keep you alive. Just believe me when I say it's a mess and most of the time, it kills the person before they can give away their secrets."

He takes the Kabar and grabs the guy's hands and moves the edge towards the man's nail on his left ring finger. The man's eyes grow huge and he squeaks something out looking at the other two, I can tell he is pleading them for help or to talk. The other two men finally break. Kuppers stands, comes back, hands me the Kabar and winks at me. I keep my face emotionless and slide the Kabar back into its holster.

"Ok, so one at a time, boys." He takes a small notepad from his breast pocket and starts writing their story down.

I slink away back towards where Doc is holding position.

"What are those lights shining over there?" I ask him. The lights are strong and come up from down below us.

"There's a little compound-like looking place down there. I wouldn't worry about it yet. I'm sure Kuppers will let us know soon." Doc spits a big wad of gum out of his mouth and into the darkness.

Just then, Kuppers comes over. "Apache and Senshi are going to take care of those guys. Why don't we move back to the Beast, so we can inform them on the nice story those boys just gave me?" He looks at me and smiles.

Chapter 29

Doc and I follow Kuppers back up the road and to the Beast. I can see they closed the rear hatch, I just hope Angel is in there safe. Kuppers make a motion and the rest of the team waiting at the Beast come and form a ring around him.

"So, we have four guards back there armed with some pretty nice H&K MP5s and some other nice toys. I had to ask nicely, but they finally told me their story. Seems they work for a private security group called the Ridder Group. They have contracts with worldwide corporations and with some of the foreign governments out there also."

Brian interrupts, "I remember running into those guys in Afghanistan. They are pricks, worse than Blackwater. Rumors over there are that if you interrupted one of their ops, they would light you up without even alerting you."

"Yeah, they are bad news. They hire only the worse, and the best part is they hire from any country. They don't care if you're Russian, Iranian, French, American or whatever. If you are good at killing and marauding, they'd hire you. Well, it seems they are working for a private firm. Which one? They didn't know, and trust me I asked real nice, but honestly I think these guys are the lowest on the rung of soldiers, pretty much glorified security guards. The tier one teams must be somewhere else. They have a base that they moved into about the same time that the flu took over the East Coast. According to these guys, they are not allowed in the buildings. They work out of an office in the cafeteria building. They did say that they send patrols out and round up healthy, unaffected people, as well as the infected. They bring them back here and hand them over to the people in the labs. The guards never see the infected or other people ever again, but they did say that big Blackhawks show up twice a week and deliver supplies. The trash, in the form of big black plastic bags, is just tossed over the cliff into the ocean below. Another helicopter is scheduled to come in tomorrow, and the guards were notified that they didn't need any more people rounded up tonight, so they had some down time. They figure there must be about fifty personnel down there in that makeshift base, that includes about eleven more guards," Kuppers informed us.

"So what do we do? Should we find another place to move to?" Cupcake asks.

"What worries me is that they are taking in infected and non-infected, and yet no one comes out of there. My suggestion is that we send in Apache and Senshi to do a little sneak and peak. Information is key here, before we make any other decisions," Vic points out.

"Do we all agree?" Kuppers asks.

We all nod yes and Kuppers clicks on his radio, "Bravo, have you taken care of that little problem?"

"Alpha, we took care of the problem." Apache answers back.

"Bravo, listen, we need some more information on what's going on down there. I want you two to do some sneak and peak. Doc, provide over watch and back them up," Kuppers orders.

"Alpha, roger that. We will keep it low and slow. Be back with some gossip," Apache radios back.

Cupcake looks around and then gets our attention, "We need to get the my girl under wraps or at least off the road. I feel naked out here."

"No one wants to see you naked, Cupcake. Ok, let's move down the road there and park where we found the guards," Vic suggests.

"No good. That road is narrow and I don't think I could turn my baby around very easily down there. There is a hill to our left and a pretty big drop off on the other side," Cupcake counters.

I stop and think for a bit, "Why don't you back up the Beast and park her around the first bend? No one from the road will be able to see us and we will be able to boogie if we need to. Plus, we can support Bravo."

"I can do that." He climbs into the Beast as we move away to give him some room. He fires up the powerful diesel and turns her around. He slowly backs her up as though he does this a thousand times a day. Soon, he is around the bend and we cannot see him anymore. 'Well, that has been taken care of,' I think to myself.

We make our way to the Beast and I give Cupcake a thumbs up, "That is some awesome driving, my man." He smiles, does a little exaggerated bow and shuts down the engines.

"Brian, set up guard at the head of the bend just off the road. Alert us if anyone comes looking. You will also be our first level in defense, so be prepared," Vic orders. Brian grabs his Zomgo bag, gives me a mock salute and disappears around the bend.

I climb into the back with Angel and we open some MREs and warm up our food. I knew she must be hungry, last time we ate felt like yesterday. She has raviolis again and I chow down on some chili. But this time, I find the plates that Apache had secured under her seat and we eat cleanly and happily. Afterwards, I take out my dessert and give it over to her. She giggles and thanks me. While she devours that, I use some water to wash our plates and stow them back, so Apache wouldn't kill me.

"We need to find you some real clothes, kiddo. That dress doesn't seem to be holding up too well. And if we have to run, those shoes which are very pretty, will fall apart within minutes," I point to her wardrobe as I talk.

"Yeah, some pants and some running shoes would be nice." She runs her hand down her dress trying to smooth the wrinkles out of it. "Uhm, I need to use the restroom," she asks with a red face full of embarrassment.

"Oh yeah, hold on." I open my Zomgo pack and root around till I find some toilet paper. I pull it out and hand it to her. I open the back of the Beast and she jumps out. We walk over to an area surrounded by boulders. I turn my back to her to give her some privacy.

A couple of minutes later, I hear her come up on me. I reach into my pocket and take out some hand sanitizer. I turn to her and she hands me the leftover toilet paper. I take it and put it in one of my vest pockets and squirt some sanitizer on her hands, allowing her to clean them. We walk back together to the Beast and climb inside to relax and wait.

I look through some of the hatches and drawers in the Beast and find a pack of cards and a small sweater that has the words SWAT emblazoned on the front. I give the sweater to Angel and she slips it on over her dress and rolls up the sleeves to gain access to her hands. We end up playing fish, crazy eights and my favorite from when I was a kid, war.

Two hours go by and we wait for Bravo to return or report in.

The back door of the beast opens and Vic motions me to come out and follow him. "I'll be right back, Angel. I want you to stay here, got it?"

She sticks her tongue out at me and giggles, "Ok, I'll wait for you to come back, so I can beat you some more at war." I stick out my tongue back at her and secure the Beast's door.

I jog to catch up to Vic. We walk up to the full team, minus Brian and Doc. Kuppers looks at me and nods at my presence, "Team, we have some decisions to make. I have Brian and Doc on the radio so they can hear us and chime in." Kuppers looks to Apache and hands off the discussion to her.

"Senshi and I made it down to the facility unseen. We discovered thirteen permanent buildings, mostly small looking cabins, but two others are much bigger. We gained access to one of the cabins and found it to be a bunk room holding enough beds to sleep eight. We checked them and found half occupied by what we think are scientists. We came to that conclusion after listening to a couple of conversations and reading through some notebooks. Unfortunately, we have no idea what it said. It seemed to be outlining some kind of bacteria or biological condition, we can't be sure though, since neither of us have ever been exposed to that subject. We then made our way to the two larger buildings and gained access. These are being used as locker rooms and showers in the smaller of the two, and the biggest is a cafeteria. We kept the big prefab tent in the middle for last."

Apache pulled out her smart phone and passed it around to show pictures she had taken on her mission. "That place is scary. Seems like they are experimenting on the infected. On one picture, you will see that they are doing dissections on them while they are still alive. You will also see that they are experimenting on the healthy. From what I saw, I have to say it looks like they are infecting the healthy ones in different ways. I actually saw them force feed dead flesh to a healthy young woman and inject fluid from an infected into a middle aged man. Senshi counted twenty healthy prisoners being held for their turn in the experimentation rooms. I gotta say, it took a lot out of me to not just go in killing everyone. I know Senshi feels the same."

"Thanks for the briefing. So now we need to decide what we should do. We could just pack up and move on, since this isn't our problem anymore. We are no longer police officers," Vic explains.

"Bullshit. We took an oath to protect those who couldn't protect themselves. All of us, whether we are paid or not, we have a duty. I say we go in there and kill everyone and release those poor people," Apache answers him.

Kuppers looks at everyone and each person nods affirmative. Over the radio, Brian and Doc throw in their agreements. "Ok, let's start working on a plan. The first problem I see, is what to do with the healthy people once we liberate them. We have a new mission and destination. We also have very tight resources and none to share."

"I have a great answer to all those questions. Call Captain Phillips from the 129th. Advise him of what we've found and what we are planning to do. See if he can send some helicopters over to pick these people up. His job is to protect California citizens and he did offer to help," I lay out.

"You know I keep saying it, but I'm really happy we kept you around. So far you have done a good job pulling your own weight. Does everyone agree on Dan's plan?" Kuppers looks around and sees everyone agreeing. "Alright, I'll make the call." The team gathers around the Beast going through their equipment and making sure they have what they need to do the job. Apache removes her M4 and lays it in the Beast along with the ammo in her pouches. She catches my inquisitive looks, "I've already been down there. All I need is a pistol one of your batons, and lots of zip ties." I hand her one of my batons and she opens a small door on the side of the Beast, reaches in and removes a bag of zip ties, handing them out to everyone.

Kuppers comes walking back up with a smile on his face, "The Captain is pissed over what we've found. He says he will fly in a small force of MPs to hold the area after we have liberated the captives. He will be on his way in thirty minutes with a flight time of fifteen. Listen close, this is what I want to happen." He opens another hatch on the Beast and removes a small white board and dry erase marker. He draws a section of small cabins, the two bigger buildings and the prefab tent. "Our first objective needs to be the individual cabins, showers, and cafeteria, then we can move onto the prefab tent. Do not fire unless fired upon. I want these people trussed up and waiting for the MPs when they get here. After we have secured the captives, just leave them where they are. You know how to handle the infected."

"Brian, at first I was going to leave you here, but I need someone on over watch. This place is way too big to handle without everyone on the team down there." He reaches out and takes Senshi's M14 and hands it to Brian. "You are also going to take Angel with you, so make sure you pick a defendable position. Dan will be coming with us. I need an extra person to even out the Team. But you will be there as a mule only. Apache, show him how to use his sidearm, just in case all hell breaks loose while we are down there."

Apache breaks off from the group, takes my arm and walks me down the road a little. She pulls my handgun from my leg holster, "Guns are easy to use, but dangerous as hell if you are not paying attention to them. What you need to know first, is where the safety is." She turns it over in her hand and shows me a little thumb switch near the trigger. "When you are ready to use it, thumb off the safety. Then, just point and pull the trigger. It's that easy, but remember you only have eight shots. One in the barrel and seven in the magazine. If you run dry, the slide here on top slides back and does not go forward. Then you'll need to hit this button on the side which will eject the magazine, take a new magazine and slam it home. Then take the slide, pull it back and let go and you are ready to fire again. Got it? Any questions?"

"No, I think I got it, but I am pretty sure I won't need to use it. I'm going to be with you guys," I say enthusiastically.

Apache shakes her head in disbelief, grabs my lapels and pulls me in closer to her. "If you are coming with us, you'd better be prepared to pull that thing and get our backs. We need to be able to trust you and know you won't let us down. Now be prepared, don't panic, and shoot straight." She releases me and walks back toward the team.

I stand there, watching her as she inserts herself back into the team conversation. I look at the gun in my hand and really feel unsure. I have never been a gun person, but let me explain what I mean. I live in San Francisco, where cops and bad guys are the only people allowed to have guns. So I'd never felt like I needed one, or really ever formed an opinion about them. I have never shot one. Hell, I have never even held one before now. So I am uncomfortable with them. I carry that shotgun on my back, but to be honest, except for moving it when I sit down, I never even think of it. The gun on my leg holster has also never entered my mind, till Apache took it out and showed me how to use it. Not sure if I've explained myself or not, but the short story is that I don't think of guns as I have never wanted one or needed one. Till now that is, I guess I do need it now. I hope I never have to use these things, but if my friends are threatened, I guess I will find out if I can. I holster the gun and drop my head in resignation.

I slowly make my way back to the team and listen in on the rest of the planning, Kuppers is leading. "Brian, go ahead and take Angel and go get settled in on the rocks above the camp." Brian takes Angel's hand and they walk away down the street towards a rock formation just above the camp. "Dan, you are with me, Vic and Apache, Senshi and Cupcake, and Doc, you will be our back up. If someone runs into a problem, you will foot it over to their position and back them up. Load up and be prepared to move out in five minutes." Kuppers looks me over as the rest of the team disappears to do what they need to do to prepare.

"You ok? You look a little green," Kuppers asks.

"I am a middle manager. I have never done anything like this before and I am finding it hard to relax. I feel out of my league." I remove my helmet and wipe my head. Holy shit, it's only been a week or so since I have shaven, but I feel really fuzzy now. The most I've been in years.

"Stay by my side, listen to what I say, and you will be fine. Be prepared to move and remember the most important thing, we need to stay as silent as can be." Kuppers is trying to get me to calm down and does his best to deliver a pep talk of sorts.

Chapter 30

The rest of the team forms up, Apache and Vic take point leading the rest of us off the road and down a hill, quiet as ghosts. Each smaller team of two, spread apart, away from the rest, staying in a close formation, but far enough away so as not to be clumped up, in case we come under attack. We come to a crease in the mountain side and each team proceeds slowly, waiting for the team in front to make it halfway before the next team follows. It comes to our turn. Kuppers turns and shows me how to climb down the crease safely. He crabwalks by shoving his feet onto the crease's side and using his hands to slow him down, tightening or loosening his grip on the rocks to each side. He moves pretty quickly and is half way down before I can even start. I slowly make my way over to the crease and try to mimic his moves. It's much harder than I realize, but I do much better than I thought I'd be able to. Hiking is about the only exercise I ever really do, and I don't do much off trail stuff like this. I make it to the bottom in one piece, although my hands are cramped beyond belief. Kuppers pats me on the back and then trots off toward the team's position. I jog after him and rub my hands together, trying to get them to loosen up.

He whips around as silent as if he was a ghost. I on the other hand, sound like a herd of elephants compared to him. He puts his finger to his lips and motions for me to hunch down. I bend my knees, hunch my body over, and follow him around to the far end of the camp and we hug the cliff, making our way to the last cabins in the group. I can tell Kuppers is going slow for me because the rest of the team is nowhere to be seen. We make it around the last cabin and everyone can be seen down on one knee in a group, waiting for us.

Kuppers takes lead and he clicks on his radio, "Brian, you and Angel in position? Do you have a visual on us over?"

"Roger, we are in position. I have a visual on you and the team. Can't see anyone else out there. You are clear," Brian reports in on the radio.

"Let's do this quickly and quietly. Have you already checked these last four? Are any of them occupied?" Kuppers inquires.

Senshi answers back, "The first one here and the last one in the line are occupied. Two in the next line. We left the first line alone, so we could keep our presence hidden."

"Good job, Senshi. You and Cupcake take Doc with you and hit the last one in line. Remember, no killing unless they draw on you. I want them trussed up and tied to their bunks. Meet us back here." They take off on their way to the cabin. "Vic and Apache, take lead on the door take down, I will be back up. Dan, you watch our backs. Get your gun out, turn off the safety, keep your finger off the trigger." He shows me how he wants my finger along the trigger guard so I can move it in quickly to fire. I feel uncomfortable, but I do as I'm told, remembering Apache's words earlier.

Vic and Apache take each side of the door. Vic reaches in and turns the door knob slowly, then slides the door open quietly, allowing Apache to enter. She steps to her left allowing Vic to enter to the right. Kuppers steps in and stays at the door. I put my back against the door jamb with my gun resting in my hand at my side and watch the walkways around us. I don't hear much from inside the cabin. I keep all my senses concentrated on my surroundings, but soon Kuppers' gloved hand rests on my shoulder. He whispers in my ear, "We have three down, gagged, and secured. You take lead. Walk our same steps back to our meeting place. We will follow. You got this."

I take a deep breath, paying attention to my surroundings again, and then slowly walk back the way we had come to our previous meeting spot. The rest follow me in single file. We arrive and the other team is waiting for us. Doc winks at me and throws me a thumbs up. "Everything went well I figure?" Kuppers asks. Senshi, Cupcake, and Doc nod positively. "Great, so there are three cabins on your side clumped together and same on our side. When you complete your objectives, head to between the cafeteria and showers. Radio if you need help. Any questions, concerns, or gripes?"

No one speaks up, Doc and his team rise and move on to their next objectives. "Brian, all covered above? Anything we need to worry about?" Kuppers radios out.

"All clear, Kuppers. Not a soul except you guys are down there. Angel is using glasses and is acting spotter," He announces with pride in his voice.

We rise and Vic takes lead, Apache follows, and I come up next with Kuppers covering our rear. I notice everyone is walking heel to toe, so I try and mimic their steps. I still sound like an elephant compared to these guys. My eyes continue to scan all around us and I listen as closely as possible to my surroundings. We come to the next cabin in our line and Vic comes around the corner to the door and we repeat our same entry steps as the cabin before. We catch three sleeping and within minutes, Vic and Apache have zip tied them to their beds and gagged them. They were so quick, that the people inside had not had a chance to wake up before they were gagged. We rolled out of the cabin and shut the door.

I took lead and moved us to the cabin to our left. When I reached the door, I fell out of line and took a knee on the path in front. As Kuppers went past, he rested his hand on my shoulder. I stood up and stepped back, waiting for the door to be breached. I then heard a scream that was cut off as fast as it had been raised. Kuppers came up to my side and we both took a knee watching and listening for any alarms. "Brian, report. We had someone let off an alarm, but we were able to stop it quick. Anything moving or making noise out there?" Kuppers asked on the radio.

"Wait one." A full minute passed and Brian came back on the radio, "Someone just stepped out of the cafeteria. He looks like he wants to start walking in your direction. Finish up your cabin and I will continue to watch him. If he starts in your direction, I'll pop him. Out."

"Roger, only if you have to." Kuppers looks at me and points to his eyes and then points at the corner of the next cabin.

I read that as he was saying for me to watch that corner closely. I moved my eyes in that direction and paid close attention. I sense the door behind us closing and the others come up on us. Apache's breath flows across my neck as she whispers. "Move to the corner and stay very low. I am going to move around the other side of the cabin and deal with that interloper." I nod my head yes and raise myself to my feet and slowly make my way to the point she'd stated for me to go to.

I looked to my left and see that Apache has already disappeared, Vic and Kuppers made their way over to the other corner taking up position. I drop back to my knees and slowly move my head around the corner. I can now make out the guy. He is slowly sneaking his way in my direction. I keep my head low, thinking he can't see me. He raises his rifle and I can see a smile spread across his face as he looks through his scope at me. I start pulling my head back when I lose my balance and fall onto the ground. The guy starts to redirect his aim when he stops short, drops his gun onto its sling and tries to turn. I see Apache appear behind him. She's hit his knees with the baton she'd taken from me and shoved her knife into the man's throat. I can hear him gurgling as his throat fills with blood, choking him and drowning him. Apache catches my eye and winks at me as she lowers the man's body to the ground.

I get back onto my knees and make my way crouching over to Apache. Together, we drag the body to the rear of the cabin and dump him onto the ground. Kuppers comes up and checks on the guy and then looks at us. He gives us a thumbs up and then points, indicating the front of the cabin. We join back up into our line and I take lead. We creep to the front door and I take a knee again. I keep my 1911 pointed to the cafeteria's front doors as the team takes down this cabin. I keep my eyes sweeping across the windows and then over to my left, watching Doc and his team working their way over to the showers. Doc gives me a thumbs up and I shoot one back at him. Vic comes up to my side and indicates I should take rear as we move on. Apache passes and Vic takes his place behind her. Kuppers steps in front of me and walks away. I come off my knee and follow, making sure to keep checking behind us.

We make it to the rendezvous site and both teams take knees with their guns pointing out around them. "How did you guys do?" Kuppers inquires.

"Seven down, trussed up like turkeys. No issues, no roadblocks," Senshi informs him.

"Great. Clear the showers, then work your way to the cafeteria and protect our rear as we take down the chow line," Kuppers orders.

Senshi pounds his fist with Kuppers and his team detaches and makes their way to the showers, bathrooms, and locker room combos. Apache rises, takes the lead again, followed by Vic. Kuppers points for me to take the next in line and he will cover the rear. I put my hand on Vic's shoulder and squeeze it, so he knows who is behind him. He nods his head ok without ever looking back at me. We continue to the front doors and Apache enters first, but stays low and we continue our way in, following her. The hallway is long with four doors to our right and a single entrance off to our left halfway down the hall. I figure that the doors to the right were at least two bathrooms and maybe two offices. The entrance to the left must lead into the main dining room and access to the kitchens.

When we arrive at the first doors to our right, Apache and Vic disappear into it. I stop and Kuppers passes me and makes his way to the next door, then motions for me to follow. I push open the door and we enter the female's bathroom. I drop to my knee and drop my head to the floor to look under the stalls. I notice a pair of feet in the last stall and point to Kuppers, then point at the last stall raising my index finger into the air. Kuppers motions for me to wait as he makes his way down the stall doors to the last. He stops and waits, making sure his feet are aligned with one of the posts holding the door. He waits till he hears the toilet flush, then drops his gun onto its sling and pulls his handgun. The door opens and his hand swings up fast, slamming the gun butt into the woman's head. She starts to fall, but he catches her and lays her on the ground. He quickly zip ties her hands and ankles, then cuts off pieces of her shirt, balling it up and shoving it into her mouth. Next, he removes a roll of duct tape from one of his many vest pockets and rips off a large piece and wraps it around her head, securing her mouth and creating a gag.

We secure the rest of the bathroom and make our way to the

hallway where Apache and Vic are waiting for us. Kuppers motions that we took one down, Vic motions they found nothing in theirs. We continue down the hall and stop before the entry to the left and the last two doors to the right. Kuppers points to the two offices, then to him and I. He points to the dining room and then to Apache and Vic. They nod their approval. Before we move off, Vic takes my handgun and puts it back into my thigh holster and hands me his which has something attached to the barrel making it look longer. He whispers into my ear, "It's a silencer. Makes the gun a little quieter, but not silent." I nod my understanding.

They head out to the left, I turn and follow Kuppers toward the first office door. It is closed. I reached out and turned the knob, then push the door open and step back, giving Kuppers room to move in quickly. He returns fast and shakes his head no. I follow him to the next one and I repeat the door entry. Kuppers moves fast, I hear a quick struggle and have to fight with myself to not look in, to protect our exit. I have to trust that Kuppers can take care of himself. A couple of minutes pass and my curiosity gets to me. I turn my head after checking the hallway one last time. I see Kuppers standing there with his hand on his hips and a body was lying on the floor in a pool of blood. He looks over at me, shakes his head and makes his way over to me. He advances toward the cafeteria and I follow him. We enter and stand against the far wall, scanning the room looking for Vic and Apache. "They must've cleared this room and moved on to the kitchen. Let's move up and see if we can help them clear it." I nod my agreement and follow Kuppers towards the kitchen doors.

Kuppers opens them slowly and enters and I follow him in. The kitchen is a bright white with stainless steel, gleaming under the strong florescent lights. No shadows could exist under this glare, so we make our way to the rear and come upon Apache securing the wrists of a woman, two men had already been put down. Vic is guarding the back door keeping his eyes open scanning the room. He waves at us as he continues his scanning. A door is offset next to him and to me, looks like a broom closet. For some reason, my gaze stays glued to the door. I think I see it move a fraction and I raise my gun, pointing it at the door. The door opens fast and I see a knife appear, heading towards Vic. Without thinking, I start pulling the trigger, putting three shots into the door. Vic moves quickly away and shoots a glare in my direction. He then looks down at the bloody knife lying on the ground next to his feet.

Vic moves fast by kicking the knife away and then opening the door to reveal a small broom closet with a bleeding man lying on the floor holding his arm and shoulder. Vic covers the man while Kuppers goes over and pats the man down, looking for weapons. Once done, he drags the man out of the closet and next to his friends. Apache removes a medic pack from her vest and tries her best to stop the bleeding on the man's arm. Once done, she secures him with zip ties.

Vic comes over to me and reaches out and removes the gun from my hands. I notice my hands are shaking slightly. He put his hand on my back and pats me. "Good job, Dan. Thank you for the assist." He removes a cigarette from his vest, lights it and hands it to me. I take it without thinking and take a puff off of it, feeling the nicotine wash over my body, relaxing me. I stand there and finish the cigarette, and then look at the team. They are standing around watching me smoke my cigarette. Apache makes her way to me and gives me a small hug, "I knew you could do it. Now just breathe and relax, the adrenaline needs to bleed itself out of your system." I remove my own gun from its holster and motion for the team to move on.

I was fighting the normal guy inside of me that was telling me that I'd probably just murdered a man. I told it to go fuck itself, that if I hadn't shot the man then Vic would be the one on the ground watching his life force bleed out. I know I wasn't the same guy from last week, but I wasn't sure who I had become or was becoming. I followed the team, staying behind Vic again and watching the area around me. The gun was in my hands and raised in the air following my eyesight. Anytime my vision came across Vic's body, I would lower the gun barrel toward the ground and raise it again to point in its new direction. We made our way to the big white tent at the end of the camp and rendezvoused with Doc and his team again.

"Apache and Senshi, give us a rundown of what we are going to find inside, and how to get in without using the front door," Kuppers ordered.

Senshi took the lead, "We entered near the rear where there is an unguarded entrance. They guard the front door while leaving the rear wide open. Once inside, we will come up on the zombie pens. To the left are the infected, to the right uninfected, but they are bound to gurneys and medicated, probably tranquilized. Further in the middle it is wide open, broken up with work stations where the personnel are conducting their experiments. Near the front is another pen where they put the newly infected, waiting for them to turn."

Apache took over the briefing, "I counted twenty technicians, with six guards. Two guards watching the front entrance, the other four patrol the pens and check on the newly infected. They also move the dead bodies after they destroy them, out to the rear and throw them into the ocean."

"Usually, I would have one team at each entrance and work our way to the middle taking people down, but that isn't going to work this time. We will work as one team. Doc and Cupcake, you will take rear guard Next, Senshi, Vic and Dan, will follow behind Apache, I will take lead on this one. Let's try and take some prisoners, but if someone points a gun at you, don't hesitate to take them out," Kuppers finishes, then points toward the rear of the tent.

We get into formation and make our way down the side of the tent. I make sure to continue to do my best to stay quiet and walk the same way they are. The radio clicks on and Brian's voice comes on. "Hold!" Everyone comes to a quick stop and drops to their knees. I follow their moves and drop to my knees, pointing my gun up and out of formation. "We have movement from the rear of the tent. I count three, wait one, new count is five. They are all armed and making their way to the side of the tent you are on. If they continue on, I will take out the lead and then work my way down the line. But it's gonna get loud since I don't have a silencer."

"Brian, Kuppers. We are going to fan out so we can put more barrels on the corner of the tent. When they reach the corner, fire one and let us know how they react. We may be able to get to the corner fast and stop them if they try to retreat back into the tent. We can't let them do that or we will have a hell of a time gaining access. Senshi, Apache, be prepared to boogie fast to take them if they attempt the retreat."

"Roger, looks like they are slowing down and taking their time. They stopped and look like they are taking time to talk it out. If I was you, I'd send Apache and Senshi now. I can alert them to drop if I need to open up," Brian calls out.

Apache and Senshi don't wait for orders but instead, take off running. Brian's voice comes over the radio just as Apache and Senshi are about ten yards from the corner. "Drop. Guns up. Taking shot." They throw themselves to the ground and raise their weapons, prepared to defend themselves. Since Brian is not that far away, you can hear the shot shortly after he pulls the trigger. Two shots ring out in short succession. "Up. Two down. The rest are taking cover. Their eyes are on the surrounding mountains, so they won't see you if you hurry. They are against the tent wall and look like they are thinking about running back inside."

Apache and Senshi disappear around the corner and we hear four quick shots. "Team, move up quickly," Senshi orders over the radio.

We get to our feet and run quickly around the corner seeing Apache and Senshi already entering the tent. We enter behind them and are immediately shocked upon seeing the pens. I hold my gun up looking left and right, looking for danger. Doc breaks off and moves up to Apache and Senshi. They take the left of the tent while the rest of us go to our right. We come across a work station where Vic and Cupcake take down the two technicians hiding by their computers. Kuppers and I continue on and come across another work station. This one drives me crazy with what I see. A young girl is tied down on a gurney as two technicians are standing there, one holding a needle and attempting to inject black liquid that looks like it came from an infected. They continue their motions as we come around the corner. I don't wait and take two aimed shots, hitting the first technician in the chest knocking him back, blowing blood, bone, and pieces of lung out of his back and onto the coworker standing behind him. Kuppers moves in quickly, knocking the still standing, confused looking technician down onto the ground and zip ties him quickly.

Kuppers looks up at me and nods. He regains his feet and we continue down our walkway, Vic and Cupcake catch up to us. As we come around a corner, we see the last couple of guards with their guns raised and pointed in our direction as six other technicians run for the entrance. Suddenly, two shots ring out and the guards fall to the ground screaming out in pain. I look to my left and catch Senshi lowering his M4. We finish clearing our side and move towards the entrance quickly, trying to catch the fleeing technicians.

I follow the rest of the team as we run outside. The scene ahead mesmerizes us all. There are three helicopters coming in from the ocean turning sideways and the soldiers inside aim their guns at the technicians. Our radios click open, "Oh yeah, hey guys, the cavalry is here," Brian calls out.

"Apache, Senshi, and Cupcake, go secure those maggots," Kuppers calls out. He turns to me and puts his hand on top of my gun hand. He pushes it down slowly, "You can safety that thing and holster it. I think this is all but over." He clicks back on his radio, "Brian, keep an eye open for any more of those Ridder guys. I have a feeling they know what just happened and I don't believe they will just sit idly by."

Chapter 31

The helicopters land and Captain Phillips and his men disembark. They make their way over to Kuppers. The Captain and Kuppers shake hands and smile like old friends. "You need to see what they were doing inside. Hopefully, you have many more men and copters coming in. This situation is pretty bad."

I follow them inside and walk over to the pens in the rear of the tent. One of the soldiers following closely behind, turns and starts vomiting on the floor. I guess the scene and smell don't quite sit well with him. "We need to interview those technicians out there and get the skinny on what they were doing, although to tell you the truth, I think we figured it out. We just need to know who told them to do it, how many other places are they doing it in, and find out the real reason behind why they are doing it. I think we should let the detective on my team run the interviews," Kuppers commented.

"I concur. My medics are on their way and will help with the survivors. I'll have my guys take care of the infected. You guys have done enough," agreed the Captain.

"Dan, can you start collecting any papers or files, so we can go through them? There has to be some kind of intel in them to help us figure out this mess."

"Anything I can do to help." I walk toward the stations and start rifling through paperwork and files that I find. I scan through them, looking for memos or something to shout out to me about what's going on. Most of what I find has medical jargon on it. I start piles of the documents, clumping together the medical papers that I don't understand, piles of hand written notes, and when I finally find it, memos or printed emails with orders on them.

Three long hours and five stations fly by and I have become the owner of some pretty big piles. Mostly medical documents. I'm starting to feel a little discouraged when I come across a file with a tag that says *Zed Project*. I adjust the shotgun on my back and sit down on a leather office chair. I open the file and start reading. "Holy Shit!" I say aloud. I click on my radio, "Kuppers, any way I can get you, Vic, and that Captain to come into the tent and meet with me?"

"Roger, be there in five mikes," Kuppers radios gruffly over the radio. "That means minutes by the way."

I sit back and keep reading through the file, amazed, discouraged, and upset at what I find printed inside. I look up to find all three men looking down on me.

"You look pretty pissed. Is that file there the reason?" Vic asks.

"This is sick and twisted, guys," I answer back. "According to what's in this file, it outlines most of this little encampment and to a limited part, about what's going on with the zombies." I hand the file over to Vic, close my eyes and start to outline what I had read already. "Seems that the Ridder Group is working for a group called the Culling Initiative. This Initiative for some yet unknown reason has unleashed the flu that started all this. Now I am paraphrasing what I've read, but you will get the gist. So, Ridder was hired to run four main mission components. One, disperse the flu into five airports on the east coast. Two, disrupt national responses and FEMA. Three, act as a security force for the main group of the Initiative, which it doesn't identify. Four, to run experiments on the infected and uninfected, in order to find ways of transmitting the disease and monitoring mutations. So to summarize, some group calling themselves the Culling Initiative hired a group of mercenaries to destroy civilization and stop us and the Government from helping and protecting the populace." I opened my eyes to find all three men in different acts of emotions. The Captain has a look of astonishment, Vic seems engrossed in what he heard and what he is reading, And Kuppers has a look of intense anger and coldness on his face.

"Guys, this follows pretty close to what I am getting from my interviews with the prisoners. They said they are identifying alternate ways to spread the infection, instead of just transmission through saliva. I also found that many of the technicians are actually from overseas. Some are from Germany, Italy and Iran. They all spoke broken English, they say they were hired by Ridder to do research on a highly infectious disease. The weird part was they were hired three weeks ago, before the outbreak. So it seems that this has been planned out meticulously by someone out there. We need to find out more information." Vic hands over the file to the Captain. "I suggest you summarize this through your command structure in the Guard. I would keep it out of federal hands until you can identify who is part of this 'Culling Initiative'."

"I can agree with all of that. I also think I need to share this with the MP group attached to us." The Captain looks like he is about to start asking questions when his radio goes off. The Captain puts his hand over his ear and has an intense look on his face as he listens, "Roger that, we are coming out." He looks over at us, "Gentlemen, we were just overflown by a Blackhawk that isn't one of ours. One of my pilots said it circled the camp then headed out towards Stinson Beach. I wonder if we are about to get a visitor." The Captain turned to walk away and we gathered our documents and followed.

The sun was starting to make an appearance over the mountains to our east, painting the sky in red. "Red skies in morning, sailors take warning," I whisper. While we had been inside discussing the issues we'd found, more helicopters had dropped off troops and supplies. We walk over to one of the big helicopters and the Captain reaches in and takes out a radio handset. I didn't understand the language or military lingo he used, but figured out he was passing along some of the information we have and asking for air support and more troops.

I pulled Kuppers aside and asked a question on my mind. "If that Ridder helicopter flew towards Stinson, how do we know if they have other troops there or what their intentions are?"

"I have those same questions on my mind, Dan. Hold on, I have an idea." Kuppers clicks on his radio, "Senshi and Apache, I have a mission for you. Get over here and let me lay it out for you. Brian, cease your over watch and bring Angel down here. Cupcake, retrieve the Beast and get it down here. Doc, scare up some more ammo from the Guard guys and bring all you can over here." He looks over to me and points to the ground, "You, stay here and have everyone rally around the Beast when it gets here. Not a word to anyone. I'll explain it all out when I get back." I nod my agreement and he walks away to the Captain's command helicopter.

I look north toward Stinson and wonder what is going on over there. I think about our team and what we are about to go through. I think about the people we've lost already. I think about how there is a group of people out there calling themselves the Culling Initiative and how they are the source for the pain we have gone through and the death of millions. I think about their name, the Culling Initiative. It seems that their name has come to fruition, a Culling is exactly what is going on here. But to what end? How many must be culled? What is their final plan? And finally, if they know that we know, will they send Ridder to try and destroy us?

"Hey, what are you doing, Boss man? Studying the sky?" I was pulled from my deep thoughts by Brian and Angel walking up to me.

I hunched down and picked Angel up, giving her a hug. "Hey kiddo, you having fun hanging out with Brian?"

She hugged me back, "He let me eat some candy and a cookie he had, but he said to keep it a secret, so don't tell anyone." She looked quickly over to Brian and winked at him. He smiled back and winked at her conspiratorially.

The Beast rumbled up and stopped in front of us. Cupcake turned off the engine, popped open his hatch and walked to the rear. We came around and saw he had opened up the back and was leaning against the door. I carried Angel over and put her in, so she could sit down on one of the chairs. Apache and Senshi walked over and sat down on the ground around the rear hatch. "So what's going on, Dan?" Apache inquires.

"I was ordered to keep my mouth shut and let Kuppers tell you all," I answer back.

Doc comes over, pushing a small pallet of ammo and weapon parts. "I think we should start cleaning our weapons and loading extra magazines." He started handing out cleaning kits to everyone but me. Instead, he sits me and Angel down with a crate of loose ammo and a crate of magazines. "Dan, if you and Angel can fill those magazines for us, that would be very helpful."

Doc shows us how to fill them and explains that yes, the magazine can hold thirty but only to load twenty-nine, so the springs wouldn't fail. Angel and I start a game of it, to see who can load more magazines in a ten-minute period. She wins by one magazine because she has smaller hands and can load faster. I just lost my next three desserts to her and her little hands. While we are working, Kuppers comes marching up with Vic hot on his heels. Our entire team is finally present.

Kuppers stands there and takes in each member. "So far, our

journey has had many trials and tribulations, I am sure you would all agree with that. For it being just a couple hours past two days, we have lost a lot and gained a lot. We lost our brother Jonny, but we've added to the family Brian, Dan, and Angel. We have connected with the NG to help save civilian lives and now we have won a battle with the Ridder Group. Information gained by Dan and Vic has also answered and yet asked many more questions. We now know of a group calling themselves the Culling Initiative. This group is responsible for creating this seeming apocalypse. They are responsible for the murder of millions of innocent people. Through their dealings with the Ridder Group, they have released this plague and they have set up these camps to research more ways to murder even more innocents. They have also ordered the Ridder group to slow down, if not stop the Government and FEMA from helping save as many as they can." He stops and looks around at the team again. I see the same horror and pain in his expression that he now sees in the rest of his team's expressions. "We were over flown a little while ago by what we believe was a Ridder Blackhawk, gathering intelligence on what we're doing here. The Blackhawk we believe landed in Stinson, the small town to the north of us. The Captain of the NG force agrees with me that Ridder must be acquiring more troops to face us and take back their camp, but we have no solid intel on this. I volunteered Apache and Doc to gather the intel we desperately need to prepare a welcoming committee for them, if and when they decide to come after us. We cannot board the Beast and avoid this fight, since they stand squarely in our way. That and our family are not cowards who run away from oppression. We will stand and we will fight if necessary. The Captain is trying to find more air and ground assets to bring to bear on this upcoming fight. But as of right now, we are on our own. Any questions?"

I think for a while, looking at the Beast and the helicopters.

"Couldn't we just evacuate the scientists and civilians, destroy the camp and retreat?"

"Parts of that plan are already underway. The civilians were loaded up and as of right now are flying out to relative safety. But we believe that time is not on our side. We do not have the resources to get everyone out before we believe Ridder will attack," Kuppers answers.

"When do Doc and I leave? We are wasting time sitting here debating," Apache stands and starts to replenish her ammo and weapons for the upcoming mission. Doc joins her in the process.

"Go ahead and get moving. We will keep planning and let you know the details when we have them hammered out," Vic orders.

Apache and Doc check on each other's supplies and gear, making sure they have what they are going to need. Then, they take off up the hill and back out towards the road, disappearing into the rocks and scrub brush. Kuppers puts his hands on hips and points at Senshi. "I want you to go find First Sergeant Hinton. Work with him on planning some defensive positions and a good place to stock supplies for the upcoming battle. Also, see if he has any ground to air weapons. We may need them if Ridder decides to support their troops from that direction." Senshi grabs some more loaded magazines and heads towards the temporary command post. "Cupcake, you and Brian, take the beast and park her up against the tent there on the hill side. Keep Angel with you, buttoned up in that thing. See if you can find her some body armor to wear and a helmet. She needs to stay in there at all times." Cupcake and Brian climb inside the Beast, firing her up and moving her back to the appointed position.

Kuppers and Vic turn their combined attention on me. "You've done good to this point, but we need to get you up to date on those weapons. I can't spare you anymore or treat you with fragility. It's time for you to start pulling more of your own weight. Vic, you got this?" Vic nods yes and Kuppers pats me on the back and heads off to the command post.

Vic wraps his arm around me and we walk to the rear of the tent, facing some hills and more importantly, away from people and machines. "Get that scatter gun off your back and place it on the ground along with your side arm." I loosen the shotgun strap and remove it from behind my back and place it on the ground with the barrel pointing away from us. I also remove my handgun from its holster and place it the same way next to the shotgun.

Vic hands me his M4 and shows me how to hold it against my shoulder and points out where the safety, select fire switch, and magazine release button is. He walks me through removing the magazine and ejecting the round in the chamber. Then, he shows me the process of inserting the new one and how to use the charging handle to chamber a round. He has me practice snapping the weapon to my shoulder and using the front sights to acquire a target. Once I have practiced that more times then I think are necessary, he has me practice clicking on and off the safety. Never once do I place my finger into the trigger guard or onto the trigger itself. I feel very uncomfortable. This is not natural for me. Of course I have seen guns used on T.V. and movies. But for me, this just feels wrong. If it wasn't for my new family needing to rely on me to carry my own weight, I would be putting this gun down and relying on my batons. Instead, I listen and pay close attention to every word and action Vic demonstrates. "Ok, I think you are ready to shoot. I can explain all about the rifle and give you some pointers on aiming and using the sights, but the rest is up to you and how well you learn to adjust. You will not be perfect on these weapons after today, but I want to make sure you know at least how to handle them." Vic hands me some yellow ear plugs and I stick them in. He brings his hands up as if he is holding the gun and I mimic his motions, but with the M4. I flip the safety off and bring my finger onto the trigger. I start to squeeze the trigger and surprise myself when the gun fires and then rocks into my shoulder.

"Not bad for a first shot. At least you didn't blow your toes off and didn't overreact when it fired. I want you to slightly lean forward when you fire and when the barrel starts to rise, I want you to correct and pull it back down." Vic reaches over and changes the selector to a different point and gives me the go ahead motion. I snap the gun back to my shoulder and slightly lean forward into the gun and again squeeze the trigger. This time, the gun bucks in my hands and the rifle raises. When I feel this, I pull it back down and continue till the gun clicks and fires no more. I hit the release button on the side and the magazine falls to the ground. I reach into my vest, pull a fresh one out and push it into place, pulling the charging handle back to load a round into the chamber. I work my way through two more magazines when Vic motions for me to safe the gun and lay it on the ground.

"No new holes, so you've proven to me you can aim, shoot and reload. Good enough for now. When we have more time, I will show you how to clear a jam and how to clean and lubricate it. Let's move on to the shotgun next. Pick it up and I'll explain it to you. We will learn to load it, aim it, and fire it." He walks me through how to load from in front of the trigger. We load the first round into the chamber and hit the release. Next, we feed seven rounds into the magazine tube. He shows me that the safety is a pin behind the trigger and to push on it to take the safety off. Next, he has me work on bringing it to my shoulder and aiming it. When I feel comfortable with it, Vic has me load rounds in. "Alright, I think you are ready to fire this thing. But let me warn you, it's gonna beat up your shoulder more than the M4 rifle did. As fast as you pull that trigger, it will fire. So I suggest one at a time, slowly. This is the kind of gun that works when you are surrounded by the undead. Instead of aiming at heads, you should aim this bad boy at their legs and force them to the ground. Let them create a log jam with the zombies behind them."

Vic motions for me to go ahead and fire the gun. I raise it to my shoulder, acquire my target and pull the trigger. I feel like my shoulder has been kicked by a horse. I look over at Vic who has a smirk on his face as he tries to not outright laugh at me. "You should be happy that it's not one of the older pump shotguns. Those kick harder. Just be ready for it and after a while you'll get used to it. Go ahead and empty the magazine, reload and do it again. Then, I want you to show me your skill with the 1911."

I roll my shoulders and stretch my neck, then slowly bring the gun up and trigger off the last seven in the magazine, taking a little bit of time between rounds to prepare for the next mule kick. I reload quickly from the side carrier and bring the gun back to my shoulder. I decide to see how bad it can be and continuously keep pulling the trigger after brief moments of correcting the muzzle climb. I start breathing harder and place the gun on the ground. It takes a while for me to catch my breath and get myself back under control, "Holy crap, that thing takes it out of you."

Vic laughs at me, "That's the reason Doc had you carry it. It's an easy gun to use and if you point it in the right direction, you are more often than not going to hit what you need to, but it will beat you up. Rest up, then pick up the 1911 and show me what you know." I walk in a little circle and stretch my back and shoulders out. I wanted to check for a bruise, but didn't want to give Vic any more reasons to laugh at me. I pick up the 1911 handgun and release the magazine to check that it is full. Then, I pull back the slide and eject the round that was in the chamber. After clearing it, I slide the magazine home and pull back the slide to load one into the chamber. I then do as Apache showed me and drop the magazine and slide the loose round in my hand back in topping it off, and slide the magazine home again. I check that the safety is on and hand it to Vic who shakes his head no. "You did the right things I was looking for, now take off the safety, point it at the targets and empty the magazine, reload, then empty that magazine."

At the beginning of this little lesson, I felt uncomfortable and really didn't want to do this. But now that Vic has taught me the basics, I am feeling a little more confident. I flick off the safety and using two hands, aim the 1911 out toward the little bottle targets that Vic had set up. I slide my finger over the trigger and slowly squeeze it. The gun goes off rocking the barrel up, but I have fired this gun before and know that I need to force it down and acquire my target again before firing. I quickly empty the eight rounds and reload with a new magazine. I fire off those eight rounds and find that I came close to the targets and on at least three, hit them. I feel good knowing that I don't have to be so afraid of these weapons.

Vic looks slightly impressed, "Not bad for a middle manager, Dan. So later when we have time, I will show you how to keep them clean and ready for use. I'll also teach you how to solve jams. For now, though, I feel competent you will not hurt yourself or your teammates if and when you need to use them. Load them back up, safe them, and holster them. Then, let's go eat and see if Apache and Doc are back or if we have any updates on the NG." I collect the weapons, reload them and holster the 1911, strap on the shotgun and swing it onto my back. I hand Vic his M4 and we make our way to the Beast.

Brian winks at me and throws one of those awful MREs at me. I catch it one handed and tear it open using the Kabar strapped on my hip. I open the rear hatch, finding Angel sitting there wearing a small set of armor someone had scrounged up. No matter how small it was though, it covered her from shoulders to feet. She wore a helmet on her head that just about covered her entire head. I laughed out loud and she ran up to me and gave a big hug.

"I'm a soldier now just like Apache!" she says with a big smile painted on her face.

I shake my head, laugh, and pat her on the helmet, "Have you eaten yet, sweetie?"

"Yup, Brian gave me some spaghetti and some more dessert." Her eyes light up as she tells me this.

"Good! Want to hand me one of those plates so I can eat?" She reaches under Apache's seat and hands me a plate. I warm up my beef stew. At least that is what it said on the package, but it looks a lot like Alpo Dog Food. 'Oh well,' I think, 'it'll keep my stomach full and keep me going.' I sit back, not really enjoying my meal but getting it down the old gullet without it coming back up, so I take that as a mark in the old win category.

I wash my plate off and down two bottles of water and start feeling a little more like a human again. I hug Angel and get her settled down for a nap in the back of the Beast using a blanket and pillow that Cupcake had scrounged up for her from the camp. "Good night, little miss. I'll be here when you wake up." She kisses my cheek and promptly passes out. Brian closes the hatch and secures it.

I walk around the camp looking for Kuppers or Vic and find them at the command post with the First Sergeant and Captain Phillips, along with Senshi. "First Sergeant here says that he has forty-five troops on the ground and we've worked out defensive positions by trenching in away from the cabins and some over near the foot of the hill. We also have three marksmen that are holed up on top of the hill facing towards the direction of Stinson. They will act as forward positions to alert us of any movement and as a trip wire force. We have no anti-aircraft missiles, but we do have a machine gun nest with a .50 Cal in it pointing towards the ocean. We can at least put up a curtain of deadly lead which may keep them from firing on us. I think we should put our team around the tent here to act as a backup or relief force. But if they bring more than a hundred troops or armor, we could end up being screwed quickly."

"Anybody got an issue with those plans?" No one spoke up. "Approved. Get going on your plans. Just make sure that we have enough ammo at each defensive line."

I stand there quietly reflecting on everything that has happened to me since the day I showed up to work and was forced into this nightmare. I think about Brian and what we lived through. I think about Matt and what he must've gone through when we left on our little mission. I reflect on the zombies that Brian and I had to kill in order to survive. Finally, I think about Maggie, her strength, her humor, and the pain I'd felt when we'd lost her. I go into that little place in my head that allows for me to work on problems without really using too much energy. The place I can just let go and allow answers to come to me. I feel something creeping in on the edges and try to focus on it. A hand lands on my shoulder, bringing me to the here and now in a flash. I look at the hand and then up to Vic's worried face. "You ok, Dan? You look like you were just tuning out."

"I was just chasing some elusive thought. Has anybody even approached the idea that Ridder might use the zombies as a feint or as a weapon to soften us up with?" I ask without even knowing what was going to come out of my mouth. I even shock myself sometimes when my mouth opens and spews forth its ideas and thoughts.

Kuppers stops talking to the Captain and focuses on what I was saying. "Say that again, Dan."

"What if the reason Ridder chose Stinson as a starting point was that they are going to flush the infected at us, to either use as a distraction or to soften us up before they come in and mop up?" I answer finally understanding what my subconscious had been trying to tell me.

Kuppers looks stunned as he turns in a circle, slowly looking over the camp. "We can't defend from down here. If they use the infected, they will charge down this hill into our camp like a wave crashing down on a shoreline. Vic, go get Senshi and Brian quickly." Vic takes off at a jog, while Kuppers grabs me by my straps and pulls me over to the command post. "Stand here and listen. Pay close attention and be a devil's advocate. If you can punch a hole into something, then speak your mind." I nod my head yes and lean in to hear the conversations.

"Gentlemen, we can't stay down here. Dan brought up a very important point, one with dire consequences. If Ridder pushes the infected at us they will come flooding in our little valley and kill us all. We have to move our merry little band of marauders out of here and into the hills above. I need a detailed map of the area," he announces. A Private standing nearby pulls a map out of a messenger bag and hands it over, along with a red marking pen. Kuppers opens it wide and starts studying the map in earnest, making marks on it, then scribbling some out and making new ones. "Look here, the only spot we would have to defend is at the top of the entrance road from Highway 1. To the south is an elevated position, with boulders to provide some security along with vegetation. We also end up with a choke point, to funnel the infected into. Any suggestions?" He shows the map to everyone and I look over his shoulder and study his markings.

"What about the camp, the prisoners, and the helicopters?" I ask trying to remind him of the reason we are fighting.

"All good points. Gentlemen, suggestions?" Kuppers looks over at the Captain and First Sergeant.

"I say we secure the prisoners and stash them in the locker and shower rooms. Then, lay explosives throughout the lab tent and cabins. We can also scatter some debris around the areas a chopper could easily land in," the First Sergeant points out.

"Our copters can land further south and up on that other shelf above Highway 1. That way, we have access to them for an air platform to feed us a bird's eye view," he points to places on the map.

"Captain, can you get a bird up and have them scope out those areas? Tell them to stay far away from Stinson. I don't want to expose them to enemy fire or to tip off Ridder." The Captain nods and turns to a pilot standing by to give him orders.

"First Sergeant, start moving the prisoners and prepare the explosives." The Sergeant turns and starts yelling orders to his squad leaders standing nearby. They all scatter to pass on their orders.

"Dan, go load up our supplies and ammo into the Beast and ride with Cupcake up to the top of the hill and find a good spot for her. Good job, yet again. Keep this up and I'll give you a rank." He shakes my hand and punches me in the shoulder, leaving a tender spot and a bruise, I am sure.

I take off running just as I hear a helicopter come to life behind me. Its blades start to turn and the wind created almost throws me off balance and onto the ground on my ass. But I gain my balance and continue to run toward the Beast. "Cupcake!" I yell out getting his attention. He looks up from doing something under the hood of the Beast. I slide to a stop beside him grabbing onto the front of the Beast to stop my momentum. "We need to load all the ammo and supplies into the Beast and drive to the top of the road and find cover to park the Beast up there. Orders from Kuppers."

Chapter 32

Cupcake looks back under the hood, finishes tightening something up, wipes his hands on a rag and slams the hood down, latching it tightly. He looks at me and arches his eyebrow, "Then what are we waiting for? Wake up little Angel and get her belted up. Lets load this thing up and get in front." He turns and walks away to the rear to start packing up the supplies.

I open the rear hatch to see Angel already sitting in my spot and buckling in. She has her pillow and blankets on her lap. "I heard you two talking, so I decided to help." She gives me a thumbs up. I return it and turn to help Cupcake.

We load up the ammo and magazines that Angel and I had finished loading, along with the MREs and Zomgo packs. I secure the rear hatch and jump in the front seat strapping in. Cupcake climbs in behind the wheel and starts flipping switches and sits back waiting. "It's a diesel engine, so I need to wait for the glow plugs to warm up before starting her," he explains. An amber light turns on and Cupcake reaches under the dash and suddenly the engine rumbles to life. He drops the transmission into drive and we slowly roll forward, threading our way around running soldiers and supply crates, making our way to the road and then twisting to climb out of the camp. We come to a point that has a small ditch before it climbs out into the fields above the road. Cupcake turns his head so he can see Angel, "Hold on tight, honey. We are gonna do some off roading and it's going to get bumpy." Angel whoops and cheers from the back.

Cupcake throws a lever near the transmission which engages the four-wheel drive system. He revs the engine and we roll forward and bounce in and out the other side of the ditch easily. Cupcake speeds up as we roll through small bushes and over little rock formations, rocking the Beast on its massive suspension system. We roll to the top where the vegetation is thick enough to hide us from the highway and anyone traveling down it. We come to a stop and Cupcake and I climb out and walk around the field, looking for a good place to hide the Beast, but would also be easy to mount up and escape if we needed to. I spot a section that looks wide enough to back into and hide the Beast from prying eyes and also, with an area where the vegetation is light enough about two-hundred-feet away, to drive through and onto the highway in a hurry. While Cupcake moves the Beast into its new home for the time being, I walk around the field looking over the boulder formations and thick vegetation. I am looking for places to station troops at and keep them hidden from the possible oncoming zombies and Ridder troops.

I click on my radio and call down to the camp. "Kuppers, we found a home for the Beast and I have been looking over the field. Can you send Vic and Senshi up, so I can show them what I've found?"

"Roger. They are on their way, along with two dozen guards and supplies. We have one of the choppers loading up the rest of the ammo and supplies. It should be showing up soon, so be prepared. Over," Kuppers radios back.

"Roger, thank you. Over?" I try and use his same military slang. I know I sound stupid, but I am determined to become one of them so they don't need to change things on my behalf.

Cupcake comes over and stands by my side looking over the same things I was studying. "Little Angel is back to relaxing on her make-shift bed. I pulled the ammo and some of the supplies out of her way. I also gave her a little drawing pad and some pens. We need to find her some toys or something later, poor thing has to be bored. By the way, are you thinking what I am thinking? We can use these boulders to conceal some of the NG and our team too?" I nod at his observations.

"Something like that." I point across the highway. "Over across the highway is a heavily vegetated area with a creek. I'm no strategist, nor do I understand military doctrine, but If we station troops there and here we can cover more area. If the infected or Ridder come through here, we can hit them from two different positions and if we need to retreat, we have a way to cover it. Does that make sense? Do you think you can explain what I am trying to say to Kuppers?"

"No worries. I understand what you are suggesting and I'll brief him on your idea." Cupcake keeps scanning the area.

I hear a loud sound and look up to see a big helicopter coming to a clearing to land. It hovers for a moment, gauging the terrain and then slowly descends and lands. Four men jump from the interior and start to pull boxes of ammo, MREs, and heavy weapons. They stock everything nearby and then jump back on as the helicopter raises back into the sky and points toward the camp, moving slowly in that direction. I look over and see Kuppers jogging up from the camp leading a group of forty men. They come up to the supplies, then fan out toward the boulder field and take cover, waiting for new orders. The same helicopter appears over the trees and comes down to land in the same spot, unloads its supplies, gains altitude and flies towards the camp again. As it moves away, another helicopter that had been hovering behind it, comes in for a landing and disgorges the Captain, First Sergeant, and support staff with their communications gear.

Kuppers meets up with them and guides them to our position. "So boys, any suggestions? You were the first ones up here."

Cupcakes points out the boulders and positions across the highway. "Dan here was suggesting we break our force in two. One digs in here by the boulders, another one across the highway in the vegetation. We can support fire missions, suppressive fire, and a retreat if the need arrives. I would also suggest we put our snipers farther up the highway before that big bend. That way, they can act as a forward operating position and alert us to incoming, but also support in sniping when we need them."

Kuppers nods his head yes to all ideas, then turns and drops orders to Senshi and the First Sergeant who had been listening in. I hadn't even seen or heard Senshi enter our little group. That man was scary quiet, I hope he can teach me some of that stuff, it would come in handy someday. They break off and start issuing new orders and help with digging the troops in and setting up lanes of fire.

My radio comes alive and we hear Apache calling in, "Come in, Alpha. This is Bravo. Over."

Kuppers grabs his radio and answers, "Bravo, Alpha. Go ahead. Over."

"Alpha, we got a whole crap of trouble heading your way. Infected, best guess three hundred, I repeat three hundred being led by a hundred count Ridder forces. Ridder has three armored APCs, two loaded with M240s, one with a .50 cal M2 Browning. No count on ammo, but I would assume full load outs. Ridder also has two Blackhawks with M60Ds. I give you twenty mikes before contact. We are beating feet to get back ahead of convoy. We are ten mikes out. Over," Apache alerts us over the radio.

"Shit!" Kuppers swears and spits on the deck. He yells toward the Captain, "We have twenty mikes before contact with three hundred infected, one hundred troops, 3 APCs and 2 Blackhawks. Double time this operation quickly. No time to fuck around!" He clicks on his radio, "Senshi, you hear last from Bravo?"

"Roger that. I'm relaying to First Sergeant and he will cross the highway with his contingent and hunker down. I have these dogs digging in quick and having ammo spread out to each team. We should be ready in ten mikes. Over." Senshi clicks off his radio and I can see him moving faster and screaming at the men around him to hurry and get their butts moving. I see the three snipers picked for forward duty load up and start sprinting to their assigned positions ahead.

Brian and Cupcake come up and lead me, along with Vic back toward the Beast. "We need to get our positions prepared. We will be the backup force if need be. Cupcake, prepare the Beast to boogie in a hurry when needed. You will be the lone guard, so be prepared to move. Dan, you will stick to Brian's side and do as he does or as he orders. I'm putting you at the back of the front line. I am going to be acting as spotter for the command post as Kuppers quarterbacks the operation from the front." Vic gives us his orders, grabs his Zomgo pack and extra ammunition and takes off at a dead run to the command post. Brian hands me my Zomgo pack and a messenger bag full of magazines along with a small amount of loads for my shotgun. He grabs his supplies and then fist bumps Cupcake, and we are out of there, making our way to the trenched in soldiers.

We find a boulder and go to our knees, taking positions to each side facing out to the highway and the side road to the camp. I hear the helicopters take off and head south towards their designated waiting area. I feel like puking and am fighting to keep it down and not to panic. This is so different than anything I have ever been a part of or witness to. Brian looks over to me and gives me a big toothy grin and thumbs up, "Here, I brought your M4 that you got from the NG. I cleaned it and loaded it for you. You'll be ok, Boss. Just breath and calm down. When the shooting starts, just hold off till you see me start using mine. Ok?" I nod yes, not trusting myself to talk, in case I barf all over the ground. Talk about being out of your element. Shouldn't I be in a meeting discussing projects and running reports? That was what I was trained to do. Not fight the undead or professional mercenaries. But when you are thrown into something like this, I guess your best is all you can give.

Apache and Doc come running in out of breath and slide in next to us. "Hey guys, mind if we hang with you?" Doc asks, chewing his ever present wad of bubblegum.

"They should be here in the next five minutes. Saw the forward force hunkered down. I think they should go unseen. I don't think they know that we moved out of the camp," Apache informs us.

A sound like no other rips from north of us. At first, you can hear the APC engines, but then a loud growl growing in volume vibrates the air around us. My bladder feels like it's about to release, along with my bowels. They feel watery, and I fight to hold them from escaping. "Breathe, Dan. You can't fight if you don't breathe, sweetie." Apache rubs my back and I blow out the breath I had been holding. I hadn't noticed till my eyesight felt like it was starting to darken and Apache alerted me. I take in slow small breaths and start to feel a little calmer.

"APCs coming around the bend. Keep weapons tight and your heads down. If anybody falters now, I will kill you myself," Kuppers informs us over the radio.

I look at Apache and she shakes her head, "He is tied into the NG net also. That little message was for them, not us. Just do as we say, you'll be ok."

Brian brings his gun to his shoulder and Apache and Doc copy his move. I bring my M4 to my shoulder and stare over the iron sight and watch as the infected come into view. Some are running to keep up with the APCs, the ones coming in behind them are much slower. I feel my breathing start to speed up, but I will myself to breathe slower and deeper and to calm. I watch as our team clicks off their safeties. I reach up, find mine and flick it to single shot and bring my messenger bag full of magazines to my front, so I get to them when the need arises.

The infected follow the APCs down the entrance road to the camp and everything looks like it is going to plan. Of course, a certain entity known as Mr. Murphy raises his head and says, "Oh, you think things are going well? Well we can't have that can we? How about we whip up a wind that carries your scent to the infected?" The rear hundred infected or so stop and turn their faces into the wind. Oh my god, did they all turn like a flock of birds? They lift their heads into the air and start moving slowly towards our little hill hideout. I feel a burning rising in my chest, like my heart is about to explode. Apache shoulders me again and gives me a "really again?" look. I let out the breath I had been holding and try again, to calm and breathe normally. The infected can't seem to figure out how to climb the little cliff in front of them instead, they push against each other causing a small ramp to be created by the infected in front being squeezed and pushed down. The infected in the rear start to make their way onto the hill by climbing over the ones in front.

"Stay calm. Do not fire yet. The main Ridder force has not appeared. I'd like to bring them in closer before we start making noise. Over," Kuppers orders over the radio.

The infected stop after they reach the hill and just stand there. They haven't seen anything to attract them yet and the wind has died down, taking our scent away from them. The radio comes alive again. "Ridder is coming around the bend, but they have stopped in their tracks when they saw the infected horde on the hill. Let's wait and see what they do. First Sergeant, let me know when your team has Ridder in your fire lane. We will do this on a two front attack. Then, when the infected are done, we will back you up. Over," Kuppers reports.

I reach up and wipe my head and face. Gee, the sun is up but with the wind you'd think I wouldn't be sweating buckets. Could it be from nerves? I take my eyes away from the infected and look back toward the Beast thinking of little Angel. "What are you doing?" I whisper to myself. "Get back to paying attention. You are gonna kill yourself if you keep this shit up," I say to myself. Apache slowly turns her head to me giving me a bewildered look. I shake my head no to her and bring my attention back to the infected.

The whole hill force stays quiet and doesn't move an inch, all heads are kept low and hidden. The infected look like they are losing interest and some of the ones in the rear turn and walk off the cliff back towards the main force. Till they see Ridders group ahead. They then start shuffling in that direction, growling and moaning, hands held out in front of them, clawing at the air as though they can reach the intoxicating flesh. The rest of the infected on the hill turn and follow their horde. They fall onto their faces and don't seem to care. They just stand back up and move on. We stay silent, mesmerized at the zombies' actions. The radio clicks on. "Kuppers, this is First Sergeant. Seems like the infected are shuffling back toward Ridder and they don't seem to know what to do. Is it possible they don't want to give themselves away, thinking we are still down in the camp? Over."

The zombies start getting unsettling close to the Ridder troops and they look nervous. Someone on their line opens fire and starts shooting his gun at the horde. He is taking body shots not head shots, though. More and more people on their line open up on the shuffling infected. They now start making head shots and taking down the horde, but not fast enough. The horde reaches their line and it's now hand to hand as the Ridder group tries to retreat. "Forward snipers, open up. Do not let Ridder retreat from the herd. Maybe the infected can take some out for us. Over," Kuppers orders over the radio.

Far away shots can be heard and Ridder seems to be confused on what to do. To their left is a cliff they cannot climb, to the right is a cliff falling to the ocean. Behind them they are taking fire, before them are the infected. Panic seems to set in and they scatter. Some push back on the unseen force, firing on them blindly, while the others open up with all their weapons on the infected. Kuppers lets them take out half the herd before he has his forces start taking shots, but telling them to wound the soldiers not kill them. Thus leaving them to fight more of the dead.

I wonder where the APCs are and if they have been radioed to get into the fight and are alerted to our positions. My questions are answered as one of the APCs with the M240 comes roaring up the road and starts firing into the horde. First Sergeant's troops start pouring fire into the APC, trying to stop it or destroy it. Kuppers orders over the radio, "I wish we would've had time to name teams. Force on the hill to the ocean side, disengage and keep cover, but find those other APCs and report. Over."

Doc raises and takes off in the direction of the soldiers called out by Kuppers to lead them on their mission. The APC on the street turns its fire onto the First Sergeant's team keeping them pinned down and out of the fight. The hill force shifts fire and starts taking shots at the APC. Ridders foot soldiers start to reorganize and sharpen their fire on our forward forces trying to keep them pinned down. Loud explosions rip the day and I watch as someone in the Ridder force triggers some kind of rocket and it races out to the forward positions, exploding, maiming, and killing men. With the forward forces taken out, Ridder soldiers concentrate their fire back on the horde attacking them. They take aimed shots now, quickly eliminating the danger. They advance using the APC as cover. "Everyone open up on the APC or the troops, if you have a shot," Kuppers orders.

Apache raises slightly and starts firing towards the troops she can see. Brian raises the M14 he got from Senshi and had never given back. He is taking shots at the APC, trying to find a weak point. I raise my M4 and start pulling the trigger towards the soldiers I can see. I try breathing naturally and calm, but I feel like I'm panting, my shots start going wide and wild. Someone's shot, probably Brian's, takes out the M240 on top of the APC, disabling it and halting the murderous fire.

Just as soon as we make a step forward, another APC comes rocketing out onto the highway, using its body to protect the Ridder soldiers, allowing them to bring their rifles into the fight. NG troops start to fall from well-aimed shots from Ridder. I watch as men fall screaming and holding onto various body parts. I watch as one man grabs his belly and tries to hold onto his insides to keep them from falling out. I drop my M4 onto its sling and take off running through the gunfire. I can hear Apache and Kuppers yelling over the radio for me to get down, but I ignore them. I slide up to the downed soldier and meet his eyes. They are filled with pain and panic. I grab his shoulder straps and start pulling him back towards our position. The man is screaming for me to leave him and to save myself, but I can't quiet the voice inside me telling me to save this man. I keep low, bent over and pull the man back closer. Apache appears next to me and grabs one of the straps I'm holding and together, we pull him back to a quieter safer area. A medic comes running up and drops to his knees looking over the damage and starts pulling these giant bandages out of his pack and gets to work trying to save the young man. Apache grabs me and pulls me back and towards our shooting position. She grabs my rifle and shoves it into my hands and out towards the battle raging on. I look into her eyes, pleading with her to let me do what I can to help. She raises her rifle and starts firing quick shots toward the APCs and Ridder soldiers. She stops and looks down at me and motions me to copy her moves. I replace the magazine as fast as I have ever done so and raise it, taking aim and firing shot after shot towards the battle.

I drop my eyesight and look over our soldiers. I see another fall, grabbing his arm off the ground and looking around as gunfire erupts around him. I stand a little taller, replace my magazine again, and pour out rounds after rounds toward the Ridder troops who are firing on the soldier. I crouch lower but keep up my firing, replacing magazines as needed and duck walk towards the hurt soldier. I make it to him and kneel over him, keeping up my rifle fire. Suddenly, another rifle is firing on my targets and allowing me to help the fallen soldier. I grab him and pull him back, stopping every couple of feet to fire, trying to keep the murderous gunfire away from us. The other rifle starts up again and gives me the breathing space I need. I grab the man's straps again and pull with all I have. I drag him back and two medics come up to take over the dragging. I bring my rifle back onto the targets and start firing again. I make it back and find Apache had been covering me. I know we had only been in the gunfight for less than five minutes but already I feel like it had been hours. Suddenly, the .50 cal APC shows up and starts unloading in our direction. Boulders are being pulverized and the ground around us is being ripped up.

Our forces start to collapse backward, looking for cover from the deadly .50 firing at us. The Ridder soldiers seem to be recovering quickly and now they start moving out of their cover, coming up on the hill and taking better shots at us. The other team being led by the First Sergeant hasn't fired any shots for what seems like forever. I pray they are still alive and just finding a better position. Suddenly, a very loud gun opens up from across the highway hitting the APC with the M240 on it. Holes magically appear in the armor. The APC with the .50 on it shifts its fire to the same position the big gun was firing from and rains death down on it. I hear a sound from above and look up seeing two Blackhawks that aren't ours, show up and pour their metal hell down on us from their door gunners. We are being pounded on and eliminated fast from the air and the APCs out in front. I feel hopelessness and dread pouring out of me. I watch as Senshi is hit in the chest and knocked down to the ground. I scream and start firing again from my M4. I have no idea when I had stopped firing. I look around me and see that everyone is down, covering themselves from the fire. I watch as the Ridder force moves forward on our hill.

A hatred I had never felt before blows through my mind and body. I start taking shots at the Ridder troops and slowly work my way to Senshi. He is family, I must help him, that is what we do. We take care of each other even in the face of certain death. I make it halfway when my rifle runs dry and I have no more magazines or ammo. I drop it to the ground and bring my shotgun around to my front. I take aim and let off two quick shots taking a man down. I make it to Senshi and fire off the rest of my ammo. I reach down into my bag and frantically search for more shells. I find six more and load the gun as fast as I can. I drop one, but my hands have gone on automatic. I kneel over Senshi and kept firing until the gun runs dry. I reach into my messenger bag but don't find anymore shells. I drop the gun onto its sling and pull out my side arm and blow through the magazine as fast as I can pull the trigger. I drop the mag, pull another from my vest pouches, reload and start firing again. Suddenly, the entire air is hot and the ground rocks and rolls and I am thrown into the air. I collapse on top of Senshi and something flies through the air and slams into my head. As my vision slowly starts to dim, I think of Angel and how I am breaking my promise to protect her. I hear someone screaming, not sure who, could it be me? I try to fight back, but the darkness covers my eyes and something hits my arm and back. I feel intense heat and pain flooding through me. I try again to fight back against this darkness and climb out of it bit by bit, only to be thrown into the air again and landing hard on Senshi. This time, the darkness grabs me and pulls on me harder dragging me down into a hole, then I felt nothing.

ABOUT THE AUTHOR

James, resides in northern California, but has lived in other western states and spent six wondrous years in Edmonton Alberta, Canada. He has two great kids who keep his life interesting and on his toes. He has worked for numerous companies in a plethora of positions. From project management to customer service and an install tech for AT&T to name a couple. He has enjoyed Zombies since he first saw George Romero's original Night of the Living Dead! When not writing you can find James listening to books on tape, reading and doing research for his next voyage in the literal world. He loves meeting fans in person or on Facebook.

61507554R00165

Made in the USA
Charleston, SC
22 September 2016